2

3

This is a work of fiction. Names, characters, businesses, locations, events, locales and incidents are either the products of the author's imagination or used in a fictitious manner. Any resemblance to actual persons, living or dead, or actual events is purely coincidental.

Some people or owners of original locations in Maui have graciously given me permission to use their names.
This edition has been updated with the original name "Coconut Glen" instead of "Pineapple Peter". Thank you, Coconut Glen!

1st Edition, November 12, 2019

4

5

Many thanks to my friend Jane Harm Barr and my husband Paul for all their long hours of proofreading and brainstorming with me and to my mother-in-law Lucille who is always the first to read everything and encourages me to keep going.

6

Chapter 1

Inside the arrival terminal of Kahului airport, Lani shook Margaret Rosner's hand. Margaret was a veterinarian for the Maui Humane Society and had assisted her with getting her two Basset Hounds Lilly and Lucy through the Direct Airport Release to enter Maui. Lani had just flown in from Poughkeepsie in the Hudson Valley with a short layover in San Francisco.

She stepped out of the baggage claim area, pushing a luggage cart ahead of her, with two big suitcases, a carry-on and the two dog crates in front of everything. The sun was so bright that she was blinded for a second and dug through her purse for her sunglasses. Lani loved the warm balmy air and looked around at the familiar sight of swaying palm trees and tropical flowers everywhere with the West Maui Mountains and the beautiful dome of the dormant volcano Haleakala in the distance. She took a deep breath as if she could smell Maui. It was so nice to be back!

Lani was a bit irritated that she couldn't see Max anywhere. She knew the dogs probably really had to pee after the five-hour flight from San Francisco. But there he was: He came speeding up in a seven passenger van that he had borrowed from the "Hana Hotel" (written on its side) to have space for all of Lani's luggage and the dogs. After coming to a screeching halt right in front of her, he jumped out with his distinctive, always charming smile on his face. He rushed toward her with a quick "Aloha", placed a beautiful lei made with fresh plumerias around her neck and gave her a big hug that quickly turned into a romantic, tender kiss. They forgot the world around them until one of Lani's Basset Hounds, Lilly, started howling as if to say: "Hey, pay attention to me!"

Max and Lani ended their kiss and looked around at the crates that were about to fall off of the luggage cart. The Basset Hounds inside were going crazy with excitement, wagging their tails, craving to be in the center of attention and wanting to see who this guy was, who was getting a bit too close to their master for comfort.

"Well, well… who do we have here?" asked Max as he lifted one crate down after the other while peering inside. "Wow, they're heavy!" He hesitated and looked at Lani, a bit shocked.

"Can they wait or do they have to pee immediately?"

"It's probably better if we drive to some nearby area like a park or something. They might be able to wait until Paia. If we let them out here, they'll probably pee right here in the airport which might not be a good idea…" she replied as she looked around for some patches of grass in the parking lot that was basically only concrete with no green areas.

Lani pushed the cart up to the van and they lifted the crates and the luggage inside. Max exclaimed: "Wow, you're traveling quite light, considering you're moving here!"

"Well, I don't need much," she replied. "The house is fully equipped and I left all of my winter clothes and some personal things at my parents' house. Plus, I had a giant garage sale a few weeks ago and left all the big furniture for Anna and Mike. It actually feels quite liberating to have rid myself of all my old clutter! I'd never ship it over here anyhow."

She looked at him and caressed his hair as they drove out of Kahului.

"It's so good to see you! It's been too long…"

He glanced at her from the side. "Yeah, I've missed you terribly. I'm glad you're finally back."

There was no time for romance, but Max wished he could just stop the car on the side of the road, take Lani in his arms and kiss her again.

After coming to Maui for the very first time six months ago and deciding to accept the surprise inheritance from her great aunt Malani, Koki Beach House, Lani had to go back to the Hudson Valley and not only sell her nursery with all the plants, but also her house. Luckily, her assistant Anna and her friend Bill Vandern, who had now become a couple, bought the nursery "as is", which made things so much easier.

The worst chore had been to keep her two Bassett hounds, Lilly and Lucy, in quarantine for 120 days to be able to take them to Maui with her. She was glad that she had checked into the issue almost right away after returning to the Hudson Valley, since she could have easily missed that deadline.

Another very time consuming chore had been trying to get her orchids cleared by the agricultural department. She only had a few valuable specimen Cattleya species that she would have loved to bring with her to Maui, but it seemed so complicated that she had given up and asked her assistant Anne to take care of them until she might be able to figure it out. She would start a new collection in Maui with the help of her friend Phillip, the owner of Maui Exotics. It would be so much easier to grow them in Maui anyhow.

All other belongings – material things - that she had left behind, she didn't really care about. She was madly in love and ready for her new life in Maui with Max.

Lani was exhausted after the 12 hour flight, but they still had the two hour strenuous drive to Hana ahead of them, that was not going to be a quick one, as they had to stop at a few places to say hello to some friends that Lani hadn't seen for such a long time.

First, they headed toward Paia, the beautiful artsy little town outside of Kahului, full of galleries and gift shops, that everyone going to Hana had to pass through and most people stopped in to have lunch or buy some groceries. Therefore, Paia was quite a bustling little town that always seemed to have stop and go traffic on the main road.

On the left, Lani could already see the beautiful Pacific Ocean with the powerful waves crashing into the sand. The first place suitable for the dogs to get some exercise was Lower Paia Park. Max parked the van and they quickly jumped out and let the Bassets out of their crates. It was about time… There was a leash law in Maui, so they walked them under the trees and let them go potty in the shade where it wouldn't bother anybody and picked up after them.

The dogs had so much built-up energy from sitting in the crates for about twelve hours now, that both Max and Lani couldn't help feeling sorry for them. The beach was quite empty this late and they unsnapped the hooks of the leashes and let the dogs run down to the ocean. The dogs went crazy. They raced down toward the waves that were still powerful but much calmer than Lani remembered them from February, barking and chasing each other happily. Lilly, who loved water, ran right in, but had to quickly retreat as the first wave crashed right over her. It took her a second to regain her orientation, but she was quite indifferent, continued her swim and then walked back to shore. Lucy hated water and stopped right before the shoreline, running alongside the ocean, barking at the water.

Lani and Max had to laugh, watching them frolic.

"What do you think of those girls?" Lani asked Max.

"I don't know if I've ever seen Basset Hounds on Maui before. They're quite funny with their short stumpy legs," replied Max.

"They're certainly the clowns of the dog world," said Lani with a smile.

They looked deeply into each other's eyes again and wrapped their arms around each other, while their lips met for another kiss. They couldn't get enough of each other after being separated for such a long time. They just stood there, in the sunset in front of the ocean. Time seemed to be standing still. Until the dogs, after powering themselves out, ran back up and jumped up Max and Lani's legs, barking for attention, while almost knocking them over since they were so heavy…

"Uh oh," said Lani. "Look how sandy Lilly is after being in the water…"

Max laughed. "Oh boy… but, guess what, I actually brought a couple of beach towels, in case you wanted to refresh yourself and jump into a waterfall somewhere. So we can shower her off here and use one of those towels to dry her off …"

"You're a genius!" replied Lani. "That's why I love you so much!" She smiled at him and he smiled back. They were both so happy to have each other again and it seemed like they had never been apart.

Lilly was showered and dried off, thoroughly enjoying the extra attention, but they needed to get back into the van and on their way. The girls were both unhappy when Lani squeezed them back into their crates, but it was definitely safer on the Road to Hana than letting them sit on the backseats like Lani usually did.

After getting the Bassets some exercise, they stopped to see their friends Aaron and Mats at their beautiful art gallery, *"Ho'Onani",* on Baldwin Avenue. Aaron was Coconut Glen's younger brother. Coconut Glen had been one of Lani's mother Luana's best friends when they were in High School. Aaron had been a friend of Paul Kent's, Lani's father, and took painting lessons from him more than twenty years ago. Aaron, his longtime partner Mats and their friend William, an art expert and art dealer, had talked Lani into letting them organize a traveling exhibition with a collection of beautiful photos that the renowned artist Paul Kent had taken of Luana thirty years ago, along with some smaller paintings Lani had found in a crawlspace in Koki Beach House six months ago.

Aaron and Mats were very busy getting ready for the opening reception of the traveling exhibition. The exhibition would be going to various cities on all major Hawaiian Islands, along with some cities in California. The opening reception was going to take place at *"Ho'Onani"* in just a few days. They were currently having assistants hang framed photos and the paintings, while simultaneously a lighting director was working on the lighting to best showcase the photos. Most of the photos were blown up and framed, a few were still in their original size. They looked very impressive with the professional spotlights illuminating them.

"Ahhhhh! There she is!" exclaimed Aaron happily, as Lani and Max walked through the door, with Lilly and Lucy on their leashes.

Aaron and Mats both dropped what they were doing and rushed toward them. "It's so good to finally see you again, Lani! We missed you!" said Aaron while he air kissed her on both cheeks and then did the same with Max, "Hey, Max, my friend," and then went down on his knees to say hello to Lilly and Lucy, who were going crazy over him and the attention, their stumpy bodies wiggling happily.

Mats came up right behind him and gave Lani and Max both a big hug, then also pet the dogs. "Hey, guys! We'll have to go to Mama's and celebrate that you're back!"

"Definitely!" said Max. "Just not today." He looked at Lani who nodded.

"Yeah, I'm exhausted from the flight and the girls need to get home and settled after the long trip." She pointed first at Lilly and then at Lucy. "This is Lilly and this is Lucy."

"They are adorable," replied Aaron and Mats almost simultaneously and Mats added: "Yeah, that must have been a tough trip for them…"

Lani looked around the gallery. "Everything looks great, guys!"

They both smiled and nodded while Aaron answered: "Yeah, we're excited. Have you been in touch with William? He's been wanting to ask you to join him in some of the other cities when the exhibit moves on, especially Honolulu and Kona…"

"Yes, he's been in touch with me." Lani replied. "I want to get to Hana first and see what's going on with the house and then we can go from there. First let's get the opening reception over with next week."

They all nodded.

"So, what did you do with your nursery in the Hudson Valley?" asked Mats.

"I got lucky and sold it to my assistant and an old friend who ended up getting together while I was here in February. They fell in love while they were both working on the broken sprinkler system in my orchid greenhouse. Quite romantic…" she said and grinned.

"That's great," replied Mats, "although I hope you didn't have to give them a friendship price."

"No, they were quite fair. Bill does okay. He's also a landscape designer and sometimes he has clients in New York City."

They all smiled and nodded.

"Can we offer you guys anything to drink?" asked Aaron.

"No, thanks," replied Lani. "We should get going."

"Yeah," chimed Max in. "It's getting dark soon and we still want to stop and say hello to Glen."

They all hugged each other again, said goodbye and Max and Lani walked back up the street with the two Bassets and got into the van.

They drove back down to the main road, took a right and were on their way to Hana. Lani looked out at Ho'okipa Beach and the ocean while Max had to concentrate on the road that was still quite busy with tourists returning from their Road to Hana excursions. The pink sky above the horizon was quite spectacular with the sun slowly setting in the west.

****

Chapter 2

Dusk had already set in, especially with the thick rainforest canopy above the hilly winding road that didn't let much sunlight through. Lani could still make out the stand of beautiful rainbow eucalyptus trees on the ocean side and some of her other favorite spots on the Road to Hana. The views out onto the ocean were gorgeous and the sky looked beautiful with its pastel colors, while the ocean was unusually calm and eerie.

"I hope there's no bad weather coming up," said Max. "It looks a bit like the calm before the storm. I wish I had checked my weather app. Of course, now we have no reception…"

Lani looked around and out at the ocean nervously. She knew the weather in Maui could change very suddenly and that the Road to Hana could become quite dangerous in rainy conditions. It reminded her that her biological father Paul Kent had supposedly had a fatal accident here on the very same road 30 years ago during a bad storm.

She thought about that briefly, but tried to not let it ruin her excitement of being back in Maui with Max.

"Let's think positive," she said. "You're a good driver and maybe we'll leave the bad weather behind us."

The good news was that the road was completely empty because barely anyone ever drove in the dark except locals. The bad news was that it indeed started raining steadily, making the road more slippery and Max had to slow down quite a bit. He continued driving safely and steadily, his eyes riveted on the road.

"Maybe we should postpone our stop at Glen's house," he proposed. "We're really behind schedule already…"

"Yeah, I have to admit that I'm quite beat. Maybe we can just do a quick pitstop and visit him another time. The girls might have to pee again by then…"

Max glanced into the rearview mirror, but he couldn't see the crates all the way in the back.

"They seem fine right now. Are they always this quiet?"

"They like riding in cars," replied Lani, "probably because I usually take them to the dog park that way," she grinned.

Suddenly, there was a lightning flash, immediately followed by a loud clap of thunder. They both jumped in their seats. Max had to slow down even more as it began to pour. A very tight hairpin curve and then a tight, one lane bridge came up quickly and Max had to stop the van, yielding for someone else in an expensive sports car who was crossing the bridge. That person was driving way too fast and just as he was leaving the bridge in the curve, passing Max and Lani on the other side of the road, his back wheel slid down the muddy edge of the road just an inch or two, forcing him to stop as his vehicle was stuck. The driver, an older heavyset gentleman, with a younger blonde woman in the passenger seat, started panicking and pressed his foot down on the gas pedal too hard. The back wheel just spun into the mud deeper and deeper, while the engine roared. The wheel remained stuck in the mud, making the car's body scrape the road and rock helplessly.

Max and Lani sat there in their van just a few yards away, watching everything speechlessly. Max jumped out into the rain, ran over to the car and made circular motions for the older gentleman to roll down his window.

"Take your foot off of the gas," he said, trying to stay calm and not to yell, because the gentleman was obviously panicking. "My name's Max Palakiko. I'm a firefighter. You'll be okay."

Then he recognized who it was and rolled his eyes, turning around to see if Lani recognized the man. She had a disgusted look on her face, so he could tell she knew who it was. It was Joseph McAllen, the investor who wanted to build condos all along the coast of Hana. He had tried to buy Koki Beach House and had accosted Lani a few times during her last stay six months ago. He was the last person Max wanted to help, but did he have a choice now?

Max walked around the car, trying to assess the situation, while Joseph's girlfriend in the passenger seat on the ocean side was panicking and trying to get out of the car. She couldn't get out on her side since that would have been a step down of several feet, so she basically crawled onto Joseph's lap and over him, which looked rather funny in the tight little sports car, but she actually managed to open his door and climb out.

"Why don't you get out, too," said Max to Joseph McAllen. "Just in case. And you can help me try to push the car to see if we can get it up or whether I have to tow it out with a rope. It's probably too heavy for us though."

The remaining three wheels were all on the road. Max walked behind the car, followed by Joseph, and they checked whether they'd be able to push the wheel up back onto the road without getting too close to the cliff themselves.

"I think we can push it back up, but someone has to sit in the car and steer it to the left. Otherwise we'll just push it straight and the right front wheel might slide down too," said Max.

Lani, who had gotten out of the van to offer the woman the chance to get out of the rain, that had at least slowed down to a drizzle, heard the conversation and looked at the woman who turned pale and said "I'm not getting in there again!"

Lani said: "I'll do it," without even thinking about whether she'd be in danger or not and got into the driver's seat.

"Hit the gas pedal very gently and try to get some traction," yelled Max.

Lani stepped on the gas pedal very carefully, while Max and Joseph McAllen got in back of the car and both pushed the back bumper of the vehicle. The one tire of the rear wheel drive sports car that was still on the pavement gained traction, while the other one spun in the air, but then the fourth tire was back on the road too and Lani gently stepped on the brakes.

They all sighed a big sigh of relief. Joseph said: "I owe you guys, thank you very much!" He took a closer look at Max and Lani who had gotten back out of the car. "You guys look familiar, have we met before?"

"I don't think so," said Lani and Max shook his head.

"Well, I owe you guys, call me if you ever need anything. My name's Joseph McAllen and this is my girlfriend, Dolly. I work in real estate and we're on Maui quite a bit," said Joseph and pulled out a business card, which he handed to Max.

"Yeah, unfortunately," mumbled Lani while they both walked back to the van and Joseph and his girlfriend got back into their sports car and drove off, slowly and carefully. Joseph McAllen had learned his lesson to not speed on the Hana Highway anymore.

Max couldn't help it, but had to grin about Lani's comment.

"Wow, they were pretty lucky. But to have to run into them, of all people…"

They both rolled their eyes and laughed.

They started the van back up, and since it had stopped raining and they were making good time, they drove all the way to Glen's stand on the dark winding road. Of course, Glen's famous ice cream stand was closed now in the evening. They parked the van, got the girls out, let them pee and sniff a little and walked up the hilly driveway to Glen's house.

Lani enjoyed the eerie feeling of being in the middle of a rain forest in the dark, but it was also quite spooky. Since it had just rained heavily, it had cooled off a bit. They had a bit of a hard time finding their way on the cracked, overgrown driveway. The bamboo and other large tropical plants were hanging down into the driveway and still dripping quite a bit. All sorts of creatures were calling through the night: cicadas, maybe owls, but the noises sounded quite creepy and the shadows, illuminated by Max's phone's flashlight shining ahead of them to not stumble and fall, were moving around in the wind. Lani looked at Max and intertwined her elbow with his. It felt good to be so close to him and feel his muscular body. In the light of the full moon, every shadow looked like a monster about to jump out of the bushes. Lani shuddered, but had to laugh about her own vivid imagination. Max, who was quite a bit taller than her, looked down at her and smiled.

"It's quite scary here, isn't it?" he said.

"Yes, kind of cool, but I wouldn't want to be here by myself," she replied and smiled back at him as she nuzzled closer to Max.

They arrived in front of Glen's house and knocked at the door. After half a minute, Glen peeked through the curtain in front of the glass door and swung the door open energetically.

"Hey, guys!" he said, happy to see them. Lilly and Lucy immediately jumped up on his legs, trying to get as much attention as they could. They could tell that he was an animal lover as he kneeled down to pet them lovingly.

"Hi, Glen," said our two heroes simultaneously. Max continued: "It's good to see you, but we can't stay long. We just wanted to drop in and say hi. We got really delayed due to the storm and a bad driver almost drove off the road, so we had to help him out of the mud."

"Yeah, sorry, Glen, I just want to get home. It's been an awfully long day," added Lani.

"Yeah, I get that. It's good to see you, but we'll have another chance to visit," replied Glen. "I'll have to come to Hana and see these girls again, they're beautiful! They're going to be a hoot at Hamoa Beach!"

"It looks like I'll be driving back and forth quite a bit with the exhibition opening coming up." said Lani. "We stopped at Aaron and Mats' gallery on the way here. It looks great."

"Yeah, I was there the other day. It's really coming along," replied Glen.

"Any news on Luana?" asked Lani. Glen had been a very good friend of Luana, Lani's biological mother and was also very interested to find out whether she was still alive or not. He had tried doing some more research on his own, since Lani had found possible evidence of Luana living in Honolulu and owning an orchid nursery there.

"No, it seems that everyone who answers the phone at that nursery has been instructed not to give out any information about her. Alex, who seems to work in the office and usually answers the phone, is very tight-lipped."

Lani nodded. "Yeah, that's how he acted when I met him too. He immediately clammed up when I started talking about Luana and when he saw how much I look like the woman in the painting."

"I'd say you have to go there again without announcing your visit."

"The problem is, every time I go, she could be on a business trip or gone for some other reason. But I agree. I think I have to surprise her. She obviously doesn't want to see me, either because she's so embarrassed that she gave me up for adoption or because she really didn't want me."

"Well… I'm sure it's the first option," said Max as he took Lani in his arms to make her feel better. "She's probably horrified that she abandoned you and doesn't know how to deal with confrontation."

Glen nodded. "I agree. She's just super embarrassed and doesn't know how to face you. Enough of that subject. Can I offer you guys something to drink?"

"Thanks, I'm fine, but could I please use the bathroom?" asked Lani.

"Of course," replied Glen. "Do you remember where it is?"

"Yes," said Lani. She walked down the hallway and passed a collection of photos hanging on the wall. She remembered that one of the photos was an old photo of Glen, Luana and their good friend Alana, so she stopped and looked at it. Her heart hurt as she saw the girl in the photo that looked exactly like her. She really wished she could find and meet her. Even though her adoptive parents Lynn and Mark had been the best parents in the world and she had had a happy childhood, there would always be a void, knowing that she had biological parents whom she had never met and who had obviously experienced a tragic love story.

They left Glen's house and only had a few more miles to go until they arrived in Hana, passed through the small center of the village, drove past Henderson Ranch and took a left toward Koki Beach.

"Too bad the Huli Huli chicken stand is closed. I could go for some of that right now," said Lani.

"Well, what do you think I got for dinner?" grinned Max and looked at her from the side.

"Ohhh... yummy!" she replied and squeezed his arm happily. "That's awesome. Great minds think alike."

He turned into the driveway and they were home. Lani was excited to see Koki Beach House. She just stood there and became all teary-eyed. She felt so lucky that she had inherited this house from her great aunt Malani and that she was able to take on the task of renovating it.

"I want to go to the cemetery tomorrow to see Aunt Malani's grave. Do you have any plans?" she asked Max.

"No, I took the day off to be able to spend some time with you," he said with a smile.

The dogs in their crates started going crazy. They needed attention.

"Oh, I totally forgot about Lilly and Lucy," said Lani. "I don't think we should let them run free, they might run away in the dark, not knowing the area. What do you think?" she asked Max, while she walked to the back of the van.

"Yeah, I agree, especially since they're hounds. They might catch a scent and run off. People on the road here really speed at night, not expecting any pedestrians."

Lani got the leashes. As tired and hungry as she was, the dogs needed to stretch their legs for a bit.

"What do you think about me walking them around a little and you taking the luggage inside?" she proposed.

"Okay," he replied and started unloading the van, while Lani let the dogs sniff their way through the yard, down to the ocean. It was quite dark, but the full moon illuminated the beautiful backyard with the fruit trees, the overgrown veggie garden and the lava rock leading down to the dark ocean. The swing was swaying slightly in the wind and Lani wished she could sit down and just enjoy the peaceful atmosphere for a moment, but the dogs were quite curious, following various scents, so Lani just let them go wherever they pleased. It had been a tough trip for them. Thank goodness they were tired too, so soon they had enough and followed Lani up to the back porch door, where Lani looked inside and tried to open the door, but found it was still locked. She knocked against the glass to get Max' attention. He was in the kitchen, already warming up the Huli Huli chicken and let them all in. It smelled delicious. Lani fed the dogs, set the table and soon they were both sitting outside on the porch, enjoying their Huli Huli chicken dinner that brought back fond memories for both of them. It had quickly

become their favorite easy take-out meal six months ago when she had
first come here.

The full moon coming out between the clouds created a romantic
atmosphere, as they sat in the breeze and listened to the surf. As soon as
Lani finished eating, she took her wine glass, walked over to the railing
and Max followed her. The Bassets were drifting off to sleep on the
couch.

She lifted her face up and he gave her a gentle kiss. Lani loved being
in his strong arms and Max had not forgotten how much her skin felt
like satin. He swept her up and cradled her in his arms as she laughed
and sighed quietly. He carried her into the bedroom as the ocean breeze
and the sound of the waves carried Lilly and Lucy away, to the sleep of
the angels …

****

Chapter 3

The next morning, Lani had jet lag and was wide awake by 5:30 am. She let Max sleep, rolled quietly out of bed and took the dogs down to Hamoa Beach, which was so secluded, except for the stairs leading up to the road, that she let them off of their leashes.

It was so fun to watch them frolic around on the empty beach while the sun was rising above the roaring ocean, promising a beautiful day. Lani walked along the water, regretting that she hadn't brought her bathing suit, but then she remembered her very first experience here and the undertow that had almost carried her far out. Max had been here to rescue her. She had to smile as she thought of him. It seemed that they had been meant for each other since the first second they laid eyes on each other.

Even though it would be quite the challenge to restore Koki Beach House, Lani thought that she had never been happier before. She would miss her adoptive parents, but they had promised to come and visit soon.

Lilly was swimming a bit too far out for Lani's comfort and suddenly brought her back to reality. Lani had adopted Lilly as an eight-week old puppy. She had never had a bad experience in her entire life and was therefore fearless. While she kept swimming straight out deeper and deeper into the ocean, she didn't realize that she was almost past the first small wave break and needed to turn around. Lani shouted: "Lilly! Lilly! Come here!" but stubborn Lilly didn't care. She loved swimming. She wasn't even that far out, but Lani panicked. She pulled her t-shirt dress off, rushed into the hip deep waves in only her underwear and pulled Lilly back to shore by her harness.

Meanwhile, Lucy was trotting along the other end of the beach, not caring about anything, just sniffing some other dog "pee mail". Lani, who felt a bit uncomfortable in her wet underwear, quickly removed it and pulled her t-shirt dress back on. She was upset and wanted to go back home, but then she spotted Max coming down the stairs.

He came up with a happy "Good morning, I knew you'd be here," and gave her a gentle kiss.

"Hi, Babe," she replied.

"Didn't I tell you you're not supposed to go swimming when you're here all by yourself?" he looked at her wet underwear in her hand and grinned. "Did you go swimming on purpose or did you fall in?"

"Lilly was swimming out too far! I started panicking that she wouldn't be able to get back and went and pulled her out!" replied Lani upset. "She is such a water dog! She needs to learn some boundaries!"

Now Lilly was rolling on her back in the sand, getting all muddy, and they both burst out in laughter.

A bit later, after a nice Hawaiian breakfast on the porch with home made coconut syrup pancakes, fresh fruit and coffee from Maui upcountry, Max had to run a few errands and Lani wanted to drive to Honokalani Cemetery, also known as Waianapanapa Cemetery in Waianapanapa State Park, to visit her great aunt Malani's grave.

While they were clearing off the table, Max said "Instead of getting a rental car which would be quite expensive over time, I have a surprise for you. My friend Danny, one of the musicians you've met at Hana Hotel before, is touring for the next few weeks and offered to lend you his Mustang convertible until you have the chance to buy your own car. It's an older car, but it's fun to drive around the area." He handed her the key with a kiss.

Lani smiled and kissed him back. "That's awesome! How nice of him. Tell him I said thank you – I promise to be super careful with it."

They got in Max's old banged up truck and drove to his friend Danny's house which was on the way to "downtown" Hana, as they called it for fun, even though Hana was so tiny that the center couldn't really be called "downtown". Max punched in the garage code and the garage door opened. A few minutes later, Lani was driving the Mustang following Max in the truck, but he continued straight ahead to the fire station while she took a left into a driveway heading to Maui Exotics, the beautiful orchid nursery in Hana, to pick up some nice flowers. She also wanted to say hi to Phillip Bancroft, the owner who had also become a good friend of hers, not only because he had been a friend of her mom's, but also because of their mutual love of orchids and other plants.

"Hey, Lani!" called Phillip, full of excitement, as he saw Lani walking into the nursery.

"Hi, Phillip! It's so great to finally see you again!" They gave each other a hug. "How are you?" Lani asked.

"I'm great and now even better that you're back!" he replied. "I've seriously thought more about expanding the nursery and might really need your help. That is – if you're looking for a job…"

"I will eventually," she replied. "But right now, Aaron, Mats and their friend William are organizing that traveling Paul Kent exhibit. I think I told you about it. It might take me out of town for a few weeks…"

He nodded. "Well, just let me know when you're ready."

"I wanted to get a few flowers, I'm going to Malani's grave and afterwards to see my grandparents."

"Sure," he walked back to the front of the nursery, while Lani had a hard time tearing herself away from the orchids that she had been admiring. "Boy, I have to come back pretty soon to get started on my new orchid collection, Phillip," she said. "I gave up trying to bring my orchids through agriculture. It didn't seem possible unless you purchased them from a vendor with a stamp."

"That's the trick," said Phillip. "You have to sell them to one of your vendor friends and then buy them back for the same price. And then, of course after a certain quarantine time, they could give you the stamp without even doing anything illegal. It's a little insider trick."

"Wow, I wish I had called you. Now I have to have either someone else ship them to me or I have to wait until I'm in New York next time."

They had reached the front of the nursery where Phillip had an entire selection of beautiful tropical cut flowers and leaves, various types of ginger, anthurium, bird of paradise, heliconia and many others. He put together two big bouquets and handed them to her. "On the house," he said with a smile. "Your welcome gift."

"Thank you, Phillip," she smiled and gave him a big hug. "I'll be back soon to satisfy my orchid obsession," she said, ran down the stairs and jumped back into the car.

The cemetery, where Malani was buried, was not far from Maui Exotics. Lani took a left back onto the main road and looked for the sign for Waianapanapa State Park, which was just about half a mile down the road from Maui Exotics.

The beautiful little fenced in cemetery was right in the middle of Waianapanapa State Park with a view onto Black Sand Beach, the beautiful wild ocean and the big blowhole that had formed thousands of years ago in the volcanic rock. Lani parked the car and grabbed one of the bouquets of flowers.

As she walked from the parking lot toward the cemetery, a few funny looking long brownish animals, similar to squirrels or ferrets, crossed her way. She had to laugh. She had heard about these animals but had forgotten their name. Looking it up on her phone she found they were called mongoose. Mongoose were intentionally first brought to the Big Island in 1883. Sugar cane farmers took their cue from Jamaican plantation owners who imported mongoose to control rat populations. On Big Island sugar planters bred the mongoose to send them to the other islands. Rats turned out to be nocturnal and mongoose more active during the day, so it was a big fail. Nowadays, there was an overpopulation of mongoose and they were predators to birds, small mammals, reptiles, insects, fruits and plants. They even endangered sea turtles like the hawksbill sea turtle and caused millions of dollars worth of damage.

"Wow, you are little varmints and not that cute, I guess," thought Lani.

She opened the little gate and stepped inside the small cemetery, which was part of an ancient burial ground and only consisted of approximately 50 graves. They were all full of flowers. One grave looked fresher and was overflowing with fresh flowers and candles. A lot of the gravestones had leis draped across them and some had sentimental items placed on them such as photos and statuettes. One, sadly, also had an old weathered teddy bear and some other plastic toys on it, probably a child's grave.

Lani looked at the inscriptions, finally found Malani Kahale's grave and stepped up to it full of respect. This grave was also loaded with flowers, since Malani had been very popular. Lani carefully set her bouquet next to the others. Hawaiian gravestones had longer inscriptions that might talk about love, loss or beliefs. The inscription on Malani's gravestone read: "Beloved wife of Charles and beloved Auntie of all of the children of Hana". Wow, thought Lani, she must have really done a lot for the children and loved them, despite having none of her own.

Lani spoke out loud to Malani: "Hi, Aunt Malani… I really wish I had been able to meet you. Thanks for changing my life and bringing me here to this magical place."

From where Lani was standing, she could overlook almost the entire park, Black Sand Beach and the black lava cliffs surrounding the bay with a hiking trail leading along the ocean. She looked up into the clear blue sky as if she hoped Malani might appear there, looking down at her. The constant breeze of the trade winds blew through her long dark hair and, standing there straight and tall on the highest point, with the sun shining down on her, she looked like a Hawaiian princess talking to the Gods.

A little teardrop rolled out of her eye, as she thought about her biological mother and father's tragic story. She made a promise to Malani and to herself: "I promise I will find out what happened to Luana."

****

Chapter 4
Flashback (30 years ago – 1988) – Lanai and Honolulu

It was a beautiful morning, the sun was just burning away the last clouds, but it would turn out to be the hardest day in Malani Kahele's life. She stepped off of the first ferry of the day arriving in Manele Harbor, on the island of Lanai, just 38 miles west of Lahaina, Maui.

Her old friend and classmate Elizabeth Smith was already waiting in her pickup truck for her. A small group of people disembarked the ferry, while another group was already waiting to get onto the ferry and go back to Lahaina.

Elizabeth got out of the truck. The two friends hugged each other and both climbed into the vehicle. While Elizabeth turned on the engine, she looked at Malani empathetically and let the car run without driving. "I don't have very good news for you," she started.

Malani looked at her from the side and asked anxiously "Is everything okay with Luana and the baby?"

"Luana is gone."

Malani looked at her, speechless. All blood seemed to rush out of her head and she became lightheaded for a moment.

"Nobody in the hospital saw her leave. It must have happened while the nurses were switching shifts this morning."

"What about the baby? Did she take it with her?"

"No, she left the baby. It's a beautiful tiny baby girl."

Malani started panicking. "I have to look for Luana! Gosh, I wasn't even paying attention at the ferry! She could have been among the people who just got on the ferry! Then I'll never find her! She made me promise her to take her and the baby to Honolulu. She wanted to give the baby up for adoption and start a new life."

"Let's go to the hospital first," answered Elizabeth and started driving. "You should get the baby before they call Child Protective Services. If you don't, she might be given to the grandparents. I can look for Luana if she's still on Lanai."

"Yeah, let's hurry," replied Malani. "But what if I take the baby and Luana comes back? What if she changes her mind about everything? Oh God, what do I do?" Malani was quite desperate. Where had Luana gone? She really wished she had waited and spoken with her.

Elizabeth explained: "Even though Luana was always quite happy and upbeat while staying with us, she suddenly seemed quite depressed after the baby was born. She cried and cried and was inconsolable. She kept asking for someone named Paul."

"That's the father," replied Malani. "But she hasn't been in touch with him for months, as far as I know…"

After driving a few miles uphill through what seemed like a moonscape of red lava rock with bushes or sugar cane fields on both sides, they arrived in Lanai City, soon stopped in front of the hospital, jumped out of the truck and walked into the building. The receptionist of the little hospital nodded at Elizabeth, who had been here so many times in the past few days that she recognized her. Malani followed her to the elevator where Elizabeth pressed "2" for the maternity ward on the second floor. They went to the nurse's station and looked for the ward nurse, Rose, an older lady in her 60s.

"I don't know how she could have gotten past the receptionist downstairs," Rose defended herself.

"It's nobody's fault and I'm sure the receptionist couldn't tell whether she was a patient or a visitor," replied Malani.

Nurse Rose led them to the newborn nursery, to where she had moved the little baby girl after she had found out her mother was gone, so the nurses would take care of her. There weren't many babies in the nursery since it was a very small hospital. Malani held her breath for a few moments as she laid eyes on the precious tiny infant. Her eyes filled up with tears. The little girl was a perfect tiny human being with a big tuft of black hair.

"May I pick her up?" Malani asked Nurse Rose.

"Of course. The more body contact she has, the better. If you'd like, you can give her a bottle. She should be hungry again."

Malani picked up the newborn, sat down with her in a rocker and Nurse Rose went to prepare a bottle.

"We have to get her out of here, before someone informs Kumu and Leila," said Elizabeth to Malani. "They are the closest relatives and CPS might get in touch with them now that Luana is gone."

Malani had a big lump in her throat. Her heart was broken. She wanted to take this little girl home with her so badly. What if Luana came back and changed her mind? Malani would have helped her raise the baby. She wanted her own child so badly. She had just gotten married and she and her husband had found out they couldn't have any children of their own. But she had promised Luana to take the baby to an orphanage in Honolulu and give her up for adoption. And, she had to stick to her promise. She had actually already contacted a good friend who worked at the adoption agency that cooperated with the orphanage, run by a big church in Honolulu. They were waiting for this baby and had already found parents on the mainland who wanted to adopt her.

Nurse Rose returned with a bottle, a blanket, a diaper bag with some initial accessories and a baby carrier. She and Elizabeth were good friends. They had already spoken and had a plan.

"You," she said and pointed at Elizabeth, "take over feeding the baby," then she pointed at Malani, "and you go to Luana's room and check if there are any of her belongings that you'd like to take. I'll meet you here in 10 minutes and take you to the back exit. Luana's departure hasn't officially been reported yet, but when I report it and I have to do that soon, security will be getting really tight, and I'm not sure if Luana's parents will be contacted or not. By the time I file the report, nobody will know whether Luana took the baby with her or not. The only nurse besides me who saw the baby since Luana left is my niece Christel and she can keep her mouth shut. The next ferry to Lahaina leaves in 45 minutes. I think you'll still make it."

Malani handed the baby to Elizabeth who stayed and fed her while Malani went to Luana's room. There were only some clothes and toiletries, and Malani couldn't really see anything that she found important and worth taking with her. But when she opened the nightstand's drawer, she found a thick manila envelope with the name Luana written on it in big letters. She opened it and found an entire collection of beautiful photos of Luana and a young man inside, who was obviously Paul Kent, the baby's father. Malani was speechless, but she had to make herself stop looking at the photos. Now was not the right time. She closed the envelope back up. It was the only thing she took with her out of Luana's room. She rushed back down the hallway and met Elizabeth in the newborn nursery. Elizabeth had already wrapped the baby up in the blanket and put her in the baby carrier. They rushed down the hallway opposite the entrance and elevators. Nurse Rose handed the diaper bag and baby carrier to Elizabeth and Malani, giving them both a hug.

"Good luck, ladies," she said and opened a door for them, leading to a back staircase.

Elizabeth and Malani rushed down a flight of stairs and, while Malani waited, Elizabeth ran to the front of the building, got the truck and drove to the back where Malani climbed in with the baby.

While they drove down to the harbor, Malani, who was horrified about this entire action because she had no idea what to do with a baby or how to care for it, was able to catch her breath for the first time since she had set foot in the hospital.

She looked down at the baby girl, took a deep breath and said: "I will name you Lani, which means "Sky, Royalty, Heaven". Welcome to this crazy world, Lani. You are precious. I wish I could keep you."

Elizabeth looked at her and said: "I wonder if you should wait at least a few days. What if Luana comes back and changes her mind?"

"I had to promise on my mother's grave. And I have to follow through with this," Malani replied, even though her heart was heavy and she wasn't sure if she would regret it for the rest of her life. This might have been her one chance to have a baby of her own, but she had to fulfill Luana's one wish.

After the ferry arrived in Lahaina, Malani picked up the car she had parked there just a few hours ago and headed straight to the airport in

Kahului. Elizabeth had already booked a flight for her to Honolulu. The baby was unbelievably cooperative, just a quiet, easy baby. Even during the flight, Malani had no problems with her. She gave her another one of the bottles that Nurse Rose had prepared for her and after that Lani slept the entire flight.

From Honolulu airport, Malani took a taxi to a small orphanage that belonged to the famous Kawaiaha'o Church, a beautiful old historical church in the middle of downtown Honolulu. The church was built in 1842 out of coral brick and contained many royal portraits. It was known as the "People's Church" or the "Westminster Abbey of the Pacific" and had been the chapel of the Royal Family of the Hawaiian Kingdom. Some of the Hawaiian monarchs were crowned and some were laid to rest here. It was one of the oldest Christian places in Hawaii. Adjacent to the church were several mission houses. One of them was the small orphanage that worked closely with the adoption agency "Keiki Palekana".

A nun, Sister Melia, was already waiting for Malani when she walked up to the beautiful old church on Punchbowl Street, which had a row of King Palms on the left side and was surrounded by other beautiful, lush tropical shrubs and trees. Sister Melia greeted Malani warmly and led her to the smallest mission house in back of the church, which was the orphanage. They passed a baseball field, where some kids were practicing baseball with two coaches. Then they stepped inside the cozy, beautifully furnished building that had a comfortable reception/living room area with a library where several boys and girls were hanging out. They all said "Aloha!" when they saw Sister Melia and Malani, some of them ran up to see the baby and either shake Malani's hand or give her a hug. Malani, who couldn't stop crying anyway, had to cry even harder when she realized that all of these kind happy children were orphans or had to live here for other reasons.

They continued walking to a small nursery with a few cribs where Sister Melia took the baby carrier from Malani and handed it to another nun who took Lani out of the carrier. She placed her in a crib after

giving her a hug. Malani leaned over the crib and gave the baby a
gentle kiss. Then she turned toward Sister Melia and said: "Let's handle
the formalities later, okay? I'll stay in Honolulu for a couple of days,
just in case Luana happens to contact me." She gave Sister Melia a hug
and left without turning around. She couldn't handle all this any longer.

Blinded by the tears in her eyes, Malani stopped a taxi and threw her
dufflebag and purse inside. The taxi took her to Waikiki where
Elizabeth had booked a room in a hotel for her. She let the taxi driver
drop her off at the front of Kalakaua Avenue because she felt she
needed to get some exercise. She walked down to the water but had no
eyes for the beauty of golden hour. The sun was already standing very
low in the sky and everything was draped in a beautiful light. Just like
her niece Luana, she was a gorgeous Polynesian woman with long dark
hair. People turned around to stare at the woman, wondering what
heartache she was going through as she walked along the water,
carrying a dufflebag and a purse, sobbing uncontrollably, not caring
what people thought about her. She didn't know whether she was
crying more about Luana, who was missing, wishing she had been able
to take better care of her, or about the baby that she had just dropped
off at an orphanage while she couldn't have children of her own…

Malani rummaged through her purse and found some tissues. She
blew her nose and stood there, staring out at the calm ocean. "I hope
you're okay, Luana," she whispered.
She had reached her hotel, which was right on the beach, and walked
inside to check in. She needed to make some phone calls. Up in her
room, she grabbed the phone and called Elizabeth.
"Hey, it's me," Malani said.
"Hey, how did it go at the orphanage?" asked Elizabeth.
"Everything's okay. Sister Melia was waiting for me. The baby is
awesome. Didn't make a peep in the plane. Any news about Luana?"
"No, sorry, nothing. We drove around the island today, but couldn't
find any trace of her. It's basically like looking for a needle in a
haystack, but I'll keep asking people if they've seen her. All of our

friends are looking out for her. I also asked Mary from the ferry ticket booth and the Captain to keep an eye out for her. But they both said it was busy this morning and they couldn't remember seeing her on the ferry." She paused for a second, because she didn't know whether she should tell Malani or not. "There is a young couple that said they saw her up at Puu Pehe and she was very close to the edge, but I really can't imagine that she would have jumped, can you?"

Malani had to sit down, but she really also couldn't imagine that Luana had jumped either.

"No. I can't." But she couldn't let go of the thought and said: "Okay, well, thanks for everything. I'm going to call Charles now. I'll stay in touch."

"Bye, my friend. Chin up. You can't be responsible for everything that's going on and you're doing what Luana asked you to do. Please say hello to Charles from us."

"Bye, Liz. And thanks."

Malani hung up and sighed. She looked out at the ocean where the sun was going down now, into the ocean, like a big fiery ball and the sky and the ocean were lit up in all shades of red, orange and purple. The ocean was smooth and looked like a mirror image of the sky.

A giant lump was in her throat. What a twist of fate, to be in one of the most beautiful places in the world but to be miserable like this. Malani closed her eyes. She wasn't really so sure whether Luana could have jumped or not. She wished she could immediately go back to Lanai and look for her. She also wished she could go back to the orphanage, grab that tiny girl, inhale the baby smell again, run away and keep her…

She picked up the receiver again and dialed her home phone number. Her husband Charles answered the phone right away.

"Hey, darling, is it you? I've been waiting for your call."

"Hey," her voice cracked and she started crying again.

"Honey, listen, there's nothing else you can do right now. Maybe we can go to Lanai and look for Luana, but you know if Elizabeth can't find her, we won't either. And, as far as the baby is concerned, I'll support whatever you want to do. If you feel that you have to keep your promise to Luana, we'll just try to arrange for the baby to get the best home she can. But if you want us to adopt her, let me know and I'll support you. But you know that your brother might find out who the baby is and he would be the next of kin…"

"I know, but now there are people who say Luana might have jumped off of Puu Pehe…" Malani started sobbing again.

Charles swallowed. He was speechless for a second. But then he caught himself quickly and did everything he could to calm Malani down. "You don't think Luana would do that, do you? Seriously, Malani. She's not the type to commit suicide."

Malani pulled herself together and stopped crying. Her husband was probably right.

"I'll see you tomorrow. I'll come to the hotel, we'll have a late breakfast, go to the orphanage and adoption agency and take care of the paperwork, okay? We can arrange for the baby to receive a monthly stipend or a trust fund until she's done with college."

"Thank you for your unconditional support, Charles. That's why I love you so much."

"Love you too, my princess."

Malani hung up. It was almost dark now and the view down onto the beach was amazing. But Malani didn't feel like going out…

In the morning, Charles joined Malani at the hotel and, after brunch on the oceanfront terrace of the hotel, where she could barely eat anything, they drove to the orphanage in his rental car. After going to see Lani one more time, they were led to a small room in the back, almost like a broom closet, where an employee of the adoption agency, Petra, was waiting for them with a pile of paperwork.

"Is this the regular room where adoptions are handled?" asked Malani, a bit naïve.

"No, you must understand that we can't do this in an official manner," replied Petra. "We have to handle this case differently. Otherwise Child Protective Services will start looking for the mother and/or the next of kin immediately. We don't want that, do we?"

Malani and Charles looked at each other and shook their heads. "No," answered Malani. They felt like criminals. They signed some paperwork that Malani couldn't even concentrate on, but she trusted Charles.

They volunteered to send a monthly check for the baby's trust fund and were given the address of a lawyer in Kahului, Mr. Pike Kahananui.

"Okay, everything is taken care of," said Petra, as she took the pile of paperwork that they had just gone through and signed, straightened it by gently knocking the bottom against the table and smiled. She nodded at Sister Melia and shook Malani and Charles' hands.

"And the good news is that we already have a perfect couple in California waiting for her. They are elementary school teachers and scheduled to arrive in three days to pick her up. That way, you don't have to worry and she'll be off the islands."

Malani's eyes filled up with tears again. The whole procedure was going so fast and in three days Lani would be gone forever. It was what Luana had wanted, but a bit too final for Malani.

Sister Melia nodded and added: "Luana has three days to come back and change her mind. After that it's final."

Malani looked at Charles. "Okay, let's go to Lanai and look for her." They left the church, got in their rental car and drove off, toward the airport.

Malani never got over the fact that she gave the baby away, especially since she never had children of her own.

****

Chapter 5
Back to present time

Lani tore herself away from Malani's grave and walked back to the car. She left the state park, turned right onto the main road and drove a few miles further out of town until she arrived at the Island Grocery Store owned by her grandparents Kumu and Leila Kalekilio. She grabbed the second bouquet of flowers, got out of the car and stepped into the grocery story with a loud "Aloha!"

Leila, an older Hawaiian lady, about 70 years old with white hair, was sitting behind the cash register and jumped up. Her face was beaming as she quickly walked up to Lani to give her a hug. "Kumu!" she shouted toward the back, "look who's here!"

Lani, who was still not entirely comfortable with her grandfather who had made her mother leave and give her up for adoption thirty years ago, handed the flowers to Leila, who was so happy that she had tears in her eyes. Lani smiled at her and let Kumu hug her. Lani was trying to forgive him since he genuinely seemed to regret what he had done.

"It's so great to see you. Aloha and welcome, my child!" said Kumu with a smile in his face.

"You and Max will have to come over for dinner on our next day off!" said Leila. "And did you bring the dogs? I can't wait to meet them."

Lani nodded. "I think they don't understand what's going on. But they love Hamoa Beach! I had to pull Lilly out of the water this morning because she just kept swimming and swimming further out into the waves. She's only used to lakes."

"Be careful," replied Kumu, "especially that she doesn't drink the salt water. It's not good for them."

"Yeah, she's never been in salt water. I'll keep a close eye on her. "

A customer walked up to the cash register. "Well, I know you guys are busy right now," said Lani. "I just wanted to stop by and say hello. Maybe I can bring the dogs by the next time or you guys can stop by."

Her grandmother said bye and went back behind the register to ring up the customer. Another customer stepped up to the deli counter and Kumu walked over to help him, while he waved at Lani.

Lani left the store and walked over to the Maui Farms stand where teenagers and young people from all over the world, participating in the "Work Away" program, were working. She chatted a little with them, picked out some fresh fruits and vegetables and found a little lilikoi pie that would be a good afternoon snack for her and Max.

She walked back to the convertible, waved inside the store again, where she could see Leila who was looking out and waved back, and slowly drove back toward Hana, taking in all the beautiful places she was already familiar with, while discovering some new ones. She loved the tall tropical tree canopy and the vines and philodendrons growing all over the trees. Every yard was full of plumerias, hibiscus, poincettias and other flowering shrubs and, as far as Lani could tell, something seemed to be in bloom all year round.

This was certainly a plant lover's paradise. She passed Hana Hotel on her left with the art gallery where her mother's best friend Alana Kalawai worked and Fagan's Cross on her right. She had to go up there for sunrise one of these days. She had heard it was a truly meditative experience. She had soon passed through the little center of the rural town, drove past Henderson Ranch on her right with its wide vast fields with cows grazing and on the left the ocean in the background. She took a left turn toward Koki Beach and slowed down at the Huli Huli chicken food truck to see if her friend Malea was working today. But it was still too early in the day and the food truck was closed.

She looked back at Koki Beach and the red lava rock towering behind it. The ocean was wild and the waves crashed into the red sand of the small beach. In the distance, Lani saw Alau Island that stuck out of the ocean like a huge shark's fin. She had this warm fuzzy feeling seeing all of the landmarks again that were familiar this time. It truly felt like coming home. She turned into the driveway of Koki Beach House and smiled as she saw Max, standing in front of the breezeway, talking to a handyman, pointing up at the roof of the guesthouse. Her smile disappeared quickly though, when she saw the worried and angry expression on his face. Lani walked up to the two men, nodding at the handyman whom she hadn't met yet.

"Good morning," she said as she turned toward Max. "What's going on?"

"Half of the roof shingles are missing. They were delivered and stacked right here, next to the garage. I think someone has been sabotaging our renovations and stealing things. An entire delivery of wood was suddenly gone the other morning as well. This is Tony, by the way. He owns the roofing company. We might as well cancel his crew for today. They're on their way right now and we have no shingles for them to put on the roof. Tony, this is Lani, my girlfriend. She owns the house."

"Aloha." said Tony and shook Lani's hand.

Lani looked at them, upset. "Wow, who would do something like that? People around here surely know that we can barely afford the renovations as it is."

"Yes, that's the strange thing. If it were someone in town, which I don't think it is, we'd eventually find the supplies and I don't think anyone would risk that…"

"Well, I'm going to get going and you let me know when you want to order new shingles," said Tony and tipped his cap to them as he departed.

"Okay, Tony, thanks and sorry that you had to come all the way out here. I hope you guys can find something else to do today. Can you order the right amount of new shingles for us right away?"

"Yes, I'll call you when I have them," answered Tony.

"Mahalo," said Lani and Max while Tony got in his truck and drove off.

"It's not good that our building supplies are disappearing. I can't imagine that there are any haters in town who don't want us to renovate the house…" Lani replied with a worried expression on her face.

"Maybe we have to set up cameras at night or some type of alarm system?"

"Yeah, I thought about that too…" said Max. "I'll ask Keanu and Billy if they can help me with that."

They walked into the house where Max took Lani into his arms. "Despite all problems, it's soooo good to see you!" he said and twirled her around. She laughed and he set her down. They looked into each other's eyes and started kissing each other, but they had forgotten about Lucy and Lilly who were excited that their Mama was back home and wanted some attention, too. The girls jumped up on Max and Lani's legs until they separated and Lani kneeled down to pet them. "Wow, I didn't think you'd be jealous! What's up with that! I guess we need a walk."

Max laughed and walked toward the front door where he had installed some hooks and had neatly hung up the harnesses and leashes. "Okay, let's go…"

Lani followed him and took one of the harnesses and put it around Lilly's broad chest. Max put the other one on Lucy. They stepped out of the front door, walked down the breezeway, then the driveway into the afternoon sun and took a left onto the road leading toward Hamoa Beach. As usual, the girls walked in slow motion and had to sniff every single blade of grass.

"Sorry, that's how they walk," Lani apologized. "In a perfect world, I'd love to fence the entire yard or just a part of it. I'm not sure how much that would cost. But then we could just let them out and wouldn't have to walk them every single time they have to pee…"

"Yeah, that makes sense," agreed Max. "Maybe we can price out some options. It doesn't even have to be a tall fence."

They reached the stairs leading down to beautiful Hamoa Beach and looked down at the waves crashing into the tan colored sand. "Let's keep walking up here," proposed Lani. "That way Lilly won't run into the water and get all muddy again. I've actually never walked past the beach…"

Max nodded and they continued their walk up a slight incline. They had to pull the dogs to the side when cars passed. The street was broken asphalt, quite narrow, full of potholes and there were no sidewalks. Also, there were many puddles from the last showers of the morning. The cars were all courteous, slowed down and drove on the other side of the road when they saw the two pedestrians with the dogs. But suddenly, a sports car came speeding along, didn't slow down and didn't bother veering a bit to get around Max and Lani. Max, who was walking in back of Lani and covering her for the most part, was sprayed from head to toe with puddle water. Lani only got splattered a bit. Max just stood there, watching the sports car speed away, then he and Lani stared at each other.

"Well, that car looks familiar. I'll be damned if that wasn't Joseph McAllen again, that son of a bitch!" Max cursed as he tried to wipe the mud off of his shorts. "And do you know what? If anyone has an interest in sabotaging the renovations, it would be him. Maybe he still wants to buy the house and tear it down...."

"Wow, and he does that after we helped him the other day... but I guess we don't have proof...." added Lani, watching the car disappear around a curve.

Max thought for a second. "I wonder where he's going right now. You know, there's actually been talk at the fire station about someone applying for building permits for a colony of oceanfront condos right past Hamoa Beach," he paused briefly, "actually right down here," he said, pointing at the hills on the left leading down to the ocean. "I haven't paid much attention to that gossip, because I've been off and working on the house, but I should ask around and find out if it's McAllen." He looked at Lani. "Can you imagine how bad traffic would get if that happened?"

"And all those people would go to Hamoa Beach," Lani added.

"Yeah, that wouldn't be good. Hana doesn't need even more tourists than it already has," replied Max.

****

Chapter 6

Lani and Max hadn't had much time for each other since she had arrived yesterday. The dogs were finally tired, and after lunch Max and Lani just hung out together in the big open living-room area on the couch for a while as Lani enjoyed being back in the house. She looked at the big painting on the wall, depicting her mother Luana, painted by her father Paul Kent. The painting made Lani sadly think about how Luana had mysteriously disappeared…

"Even though I just got here, I'm anxious to go back to the nursery in Honolulu and check if Luana might be there…" Lani said. "Do you think you can ever take some more days off and go with me?"

"I can try. I'd feel bad putting off the work on the house, but one or two days aren't going to make a huge difference. Maybe now would be the perfect time since we don't have any roof shingles anyhow. And who knows when the new ones will be delivered? But there are certainly enough other things to repair."

"I think Aaron and William also want me to go to Honolulu with them to check out the gallery there, which will be the next stop on the exhibition tour. I'd love you to join us," she said, while she scooted closer to him, put both of her arms around his shoulders and gave him a kiss while looking into his eyes. "I've missed you so much, I can't just leave you again."

He returned her kiss, which became quite passionate until the jealous Bassets on the couch interrupted yet another tender moment and jumped right onto Max and Lani.

"Wow," laughed Max. "This is how it must be to have kids. No privacy whatsoever…"

Lani laughed as well and jumped up to give the hounds a treat and lure them to a different area of the house, but the romantic moment was over. They were both tired and just sat there, looking out at the ocean and listening to the sound of the waves until they both fell asleep in each other's arms and took a refreshing nap.

They woke up a while later, the sun was already lower and shining into the kitchen windows on the west side of the house.

"Why don't I show you what we've done so far in the house?" Max asked while he jumped up.

Lani nodded, getting up as well.

Max continued. "As you already know, the master bathroom was our main priority so that it can be used again… We've already done some work on the exterior wall over there in the kitchen too. It still needs to be painted or wallpapered. You have to choose which and the color or pattern. Can you tell that the wood has been renewed?"

"Yes, it looks a lot better than before. I'd say painting should do. It will look great! And I really like the fixtures in the master bathroom. You did a great job. I don't even think my dad has to come and help."

"Well, there's still a long list of things we have to work on. But he shouldn't have to work too much when he comes here anyway. Your parents should spend time with their daughter and enjoy their vacation," he said with a smile. "Have they made any plans yet?"

"Yes, they're coming in about three weeks," Lani replied. "I can't wait for them to meet you and to show them around."

Max's phone rang. He answered the call.

"Oh, hi! I totally forgot. But we're home. See you in 10 minutes." Lani looked at him, quizzically.

"Boy, I'm sorry, I totally forgot. Since you and I have to go to Paia for the reception the day after tomorrow and you'll be doing much more traveling, I want you to meet a dog- and housesitter I found. Her name is Kate Sterling. She'll be here in ten minutes."

"That was actually really thoughtful of you. I didn't even think about that!" replied Lani. "I don't know what I was thinking. Even if we took them to Paia, we certainly couldn't take them to Honolulu!"

"She said she's very flexible. She can either sleep here or just come a few times a day and she can even take them to work if it's necessary. It's really up to you. She's actually the perfect petsitter. She's American, but grew up in England and went to vet school in London. She just graduated and is possibly going to start a job at the vet's office on Uwala Road."

"Wow, that sounds perfect! She'll know how to handle these two spoiled babies," she said, grinning. "Shall we have some coffee while we wait for her?"

"Sure. Sounds great."

Lani walked over to the kitchen to brew some coffee and got the lilikoi pie out of the fridge.

A few minutes later, the doorbell rang and the Bassets went crazy, barking and jumping up at the door. Lani walked over to the door and opened it, while Max came down the stairs to join her and Kate Sterling, the petsitter. Kate was a tiny, wiry redhead with curly hair. Her face and entire body were covered with freckles, and it felt like a whirlwind had just entered the house. She was super high strung, talked nonstop and was breathtakingly gorgeous. She immediately loved the Bassets and they loved her. Lani was not so sure. When she saw Max and Kate say hi to each other, they seemed a bit too friendly in her opinion and she couldn't help but feel a slight tinge of jealousy. She tried to hide this feeling and calm down. During her last stay, she had already realized that Max was just super charismatic and everyone felt attracted to him, even 75-year old ladies.

"Thanks for coming over," said Lani. "I'm Lani. And this is Lilly and this Lucy." She pointed at Lilly, then at Lucy. "Would you like a coffee while we chat?"

"Hi, they are just adorable. I'm Kate, and yes, I'd love a coffee," said Kate with a strong (and Lani thought, sexy) British accent.

They all walked over to the kitchen counter where Lani had set up the little lilikoi pie and some forks, plates and napkins. She got three coffee mugs out of a kitchen cabinet, poured coffee into them and offered Kate milk and sugar. Lani stayed on the kitchen side of the counter, while Kate and Max sat down on the bar stools opposite of Lani. Max offered Kate some pie but she said: "No, thank you, just coffee please."

"Well, I don't think there's much to discuss. Obviously, you're absolutely qualified to do this. Have you guys discussed rates?" asked Lani.

"We agreed on $60 per day," answered Kate.

"That sounds very fair."

"So, we can walk them on Thursday before we leave and it's probably okay if you don't come and let them out until noon. Then we'll keep you posted about the exact time we'll be back," said Max.

"Okay," Kate replied. "Can you show me where you keep their food?"

Lani walked over to a little pantry and showed Kate a big bag of dog food that Max had organized before she arrived. She pointed at the dog food. "They both get one cup twice daily, in the morning and evening. And I'll get some treats out and leave them on the counter where you can easily find them."

"Sounds great!" said Kate. "And do you have a hiding place for your house key? I guess you don't have an alarm?"

"We'll put it under a big conch shell by the front door. And no, we don't have an alarm," said Max.

"Okay, sounds good," said Kate.

"Oh, let me show you the guest room in case you decide to sleep here," said Lani. She looked at Max and asked: "The one with the crawl space or the other one?"

"I'd say the other one," replied Max. The one with the crawl space still has some of the fire damage."

"Okay," Lani and Kate walked upstairs and Lani showed Kate the guest room, that was further toward the back, and the bathroom.

"What a beautiful home," mentioned Kate, looking around, full of admiration.

"Yeah, we're pretty fortunate, I inherited it from my great aunt," replied Lani.

They walked back downstairs where Max joined them again. They stood in the foyer for a while and chit chatted about Hana, the veterinary office and life in general, then Kate had to leave and said goodbye.

"Nice woman," said Lani, trying not to sound jealous as Kate walked down the breezeway and into the driveway with springy steps, got in her car and drove away.

"Yeah, the dogs will be in great hands," said Max. "You should check out the vet's office too. You'll have to go there eventually."

"True," replied Lani.

"And now it's time for a swim. Also, I have another surprise for you!" yelled Max and happily lifted Lani up and held her in his arms while he kissed her.

"Great idea! What is it?" she kissed him back happily, freed herself of his arms and jumped up and down a few times like an excited child, holding on to his shoulders.

"Tell me what it is!" she begged him.

"Let's go and change first. It's outside."

They rushed into the bedroom, changed into their bathing suits, grabbed a couple of towels and bottles of water and walked outside. Max led her down the breezeway toward the guest house and said:

"Close your eyes!"

She stood in between the breezeway and the driveway next to the garage, closing her eyes tightly, while he walked into the laundry room in back of the garage through a side door. She heard him rummaging around a little, coming back out and closing the door, but obeyed and kept her eyes closed.

"Don't peek!" he said and then after a few seconds: "Okay, now you can open them."

She opened her eyes and there was Max, standing in the driveway, holding a brand new pink surfboard. His old surfboard was leaning against the garage.

"Wow!" exclaimed Lani happily. "Is that for me?"

"Yup. It's your welcome gift."

She ran up to him and gave him a great big hug. "I looove you! This is so awesome! Thank you, Max!"

"You're such a talent, you need your own board," said Max. "Let's go, sun's going down soon."

They both grabbed their surfboards and walked down the driveway with giant blooming plumerias on both sides. Max stretched to pick one and stuck it into Lani's hair with a big smile. She smiled back at him. They took a left down the road toward Hamoa Beach and after just a two-minute stroll they could see the beautiful perfectly crescent shaped beach beneath them, surrounded by hilly lava rock and lush tropical foliage. Lani's heart skipped a beat. She had missed this so much.

****

Chapter 7

Two days later, Max and Lani were getting ready for their trip to Paia for the opening of the Paul Kent exhibition that mainly consisted of the blown up photos of Luana and him that Lani had found in a crawl space in the upstairs bedroom of Koki Beach House.

Lani's Aunt Malani had either kept them there for a reason or just forgotten about them. Nobody would ever know. The photos had turned out to be very valuable, since Paul Kent, even a quarter century after his presumed death, was a very highly acclaimed artist and obviously also a very talented photographer. Nobody had ever seen this collection of his gorgeous photos taken in Maui in the late 80s that were about to be exhibited by Aaron, his partner Mats and their friend and art dealer William in a touring exhibit throughout the Hawaiian Islands and the West Coast of the US mainland. The fact that Lani, his unknown biological daughter, was going to be present at some select locations, added even more excitement to the exhibit.

Aaron had confirmed that they were going to fly to Honolulu the day after the reception in Paia and stay there for two nights.

Max and Lani were running through the house like headless chickens. They wanted to be in Paia by noon, but it was already ten o'clock and the drive took a minimum of two hours without any stops. They were both in a bit of a bad mood, since something had happened that could have easily been avoided and that could have ended in a catastrophe. Someone had left the back door open, enabling Lilly to escape and run away. They ran out in a panic to search for her since the street in front of the house was the main road leading to Hamoa Beach and could be quite dangerous. Additionally, Basset hounds are not very easily visible to drivers because of their short legs and height. Lilly had run all the way past Hamoa Beach and they had found her down in the bushes on the side of the road heading down to the ocean, exactly where Joseph McAllen was trying to get a permit to build oceanfront condos.

"We should go down there and check that area out when we're back. Look at that, it looks like there's an overgrown trail leading down to the ocean. Maybe somebody's leaving garbage down there that she could smell. It's quite weird that she went straight down there, of all places. You'd think she would have gone to the beach… although she doesn't like those stairs very much…" said Lani, while she and Max were walking back to the house with Lilly, now on her leash, being an unusually good girl. She seemed to know that she had caused trouble…

Max was quiet. He was the one who had left the door open and Lani had snapped at him in a way that he had never seen.

"This is not the first time this happened, trust me," said Lani, trying to make Max feel better. "Do you know what I usually say when one of them has gotten out and run away? At least they got some exercise," Lani added. She was extremely talkative because she knew that she hadn't been very nice to Max.

His facial expression told her he was upset, but at least he acknowledged her words by nodding.

"Max? I'm really sorry for snapping at you like that. It could have happened to me as well. I think we're just both a bit stressed out."

"That's okay," he replied. "Let's forget about it. I'm sorry I left the door open. It won't happen again and we should do some research on fences when we're back. That would make things a lot easier."

"Thanks." She walked over to him and gave him a peck on the cheek. He put his arm around her shoulder, pulled her closer, stopped walking and kissed her gently.

"Let's not get stressed out. It's not like we really have to be there for lunch. It was just an idea. It's more important that we're there at five when the reception starts."

"That's true," she replied. "Let's take our time and just try to leave by noon. I'll call Kate and let her know that she can come later."

"Okay" Max nodded. "We can have lunch at Nahiku Marketplace. I'll tell my friend Ava that we're coming."

Soon they were back at the house, continuing packing and getting the house ready for Kate. Even though they were going straight to Honolulu from Paia, it wasn't so bad after all: there wasn't that much to pack and prepare for three days and nights.

About an hour later, they locked the front door, left the key for Kate under the big Pu Hawaiian Conch Shell by the entrance and they were off, on the road to Paia. They drove the last few curves out of Hana, passed the Island General Store and were now going backwards on the famous Road to Hana which so many people were afraid of, but the more Lani drove on it, the more she loved it. Sure, there were some tight spots and lots and lots of curves, but all you had to do was drive cautiously, not too fast and pay attention to the other cars. In the meantime, Lani had her favorite spots and she loved looking out for them.

Their first stop was almost right after leaving Hana, Nahiku Marketplace, with a few Hawaiian product shops along with the lady who had been a good friend of Max's mom and sold really good coconut candy, Ava Langoorina. She was waiting for them with some really good Thai take-out she had picked up for them because she knew it was Max's favorite. They sat in some old lawn chairs in front of the row of colorful motorhomes and food trucks underneath the thick tree canopy, chit chatting with Ava, who had to leave them every now and then to sell some coconut candy to tourists. The food was delicious and the atmosphere was enjoyable and relaxing.

One of the vendors was playing old Bob Dylan music, and a very old guy wearing a Panama hat was sitting in front of his truck, trying to accompany the music on a harmonica. He was incredibly out of tune, but nobody cared because everybody felt he had the right to have a little fun and on Maui you never knew: It could have been Bob Dylan himself, playing like that on purpose…

Most people were on vacation and the ones who lived and worked here felt like they were on a constant vacation too, because they were happy with the cards they had been dealt, satisfied with their simple life in paradise. Max and Lani finally got up and Ava handed Lani a bag of her coconut candy.

"Thank you, Ava, I'll have to come back with Lilly and Lucy, so you can meet them. You're going to love them."

"Thanks for lunch," said Max and gave Ava a peck on the cheek. "It was great to see you."

"Safe travels," said Ava and waved goodbye as they climbed into Max's old pick-up truck to turn back onto the Hana Highway. They continued their drive on the long and winding road through the rain forest with the dark tree canopy opening up to beautiful panoramic views out onto the ocean in the curves and beautiful waterfalls on the land side. Lani loved the giant African Tulip Trees full of their big red blooms, also known in Hawaii as the "flame of the forest" that you could see everywhere on the slopes leading down to the ocean.

Their next stop was Coconut Glen's famous ice cream stand which was not even two miles away from Nahiku Marketplace and had the best dairy-free, rich creamy and smooth ice cream. They walked up to the stand to say hello to Glen's assistant Tami, who was currently covering for Glen, scooping out some of the delicious ice cream for a group of customers.

"Aloha, Tami, how are you?" asked Max.

"Aloha, guys, Glen already left a while ago, he wanted to have lunch with Aaron and Mats."

"Yeah, we're running a bit late," answered Max. "One of Lani's Bassets got out."

"Uh oh, were you able to get her?" Tami asked worried.

"Yeah, she's fine," replied Max and looked at Lani. "Do you want to get an ice cream?" he asked her.

"I think I'll pass today. I'm sure Aaron and Mats are going to have tons of food there. Or we might go to Mama's afterwards. I can imagine they'll want to go there to celebrate. I'm also really full from the Thai food right now."

"Yah, I'm full too. Bye, Tami, see you next time!" he shouted over at her and Lani waved as well.

"Aloha!" said Tami, waved and continued scooping out ice cream and talking to her customers.

Max turned back onto the Hana Highway. It was still quite early in the day and lots of cars were heading toward them, so he had to really watch the curves and yield when the street became too tight. Lani loved going back from Hana when she could be a passenger in the car, because she was on the ocean side and could enjoy the beautiful views. Max was such an experienced driver that it was a pleasure riding with him, except when he started going too fast for Lani's comfort, but he knew those dirty looks by now and slowed down with a grin when he felt her eyes glaring at him from the side. Lani looked out across the rainforest, at the deep blue ocean and the bright sky. It was a beautiful sunny day.

On the left there was a wall going straight up with gigantic philodendrons, bamboo and other jungle plants trying to grow into the road. This side had to be cut by Hana County on a regular basis or the jungle would just quickly take over the road. Soon they passed Hanawi Falls and then Pua'a Ka'a State Wayside Park. Lani had to chuckle.

"Do you know that this is where I stopped the first time I came here, totally sweaty and desperate to go swimming… I was able to get my bathing suit out of my suitcase and changed in the bathroom, but I didn't have a towel…"

"Oh, no, that's one of the rules on the Road to Hana – always have a towel to go swimming in all of the awesome waterfalls," replied Max.

"Yeah, but I didn't know… Thank goodness for my terry cloth dresses – they are kind of the same thing as a towel," she laughed.

Max chuckled. He knew her favorite terry cloth dresses by now. "Laura Cattleya sets up her stand there sometimes," he said.

"Oh, I should go and see her when I'm back," said Lani, "have you seen her lately?"

"No, not really, I've been so busy with the house."

Lani looked at him and put her hand on his arm. "I really appreciate what you and the people of Hana are doing," she said. "I would have never accepted the inheritance without all of that support."

He smiled, but couldn't take his eyes off of the road.

"Max, I wanted to discuss something else with you…"

"What is it?" he asked a bit nervously.

"Well, you know, when I have to go to Honolulu and Kona with William… will you mind having to take care of the girls while I'm gone? I feel bad that I'm just coming, then leaving and causing you additional work…"

"Oh," he replied, full of relief. "That's really no big deal for me – I can just take them to Hamoa Beach in the morning and let them run – that should tucker them out…. And if I'm too busy, I guess I could always call Kate and she could watch them or take them for a walk."

Lani nodded, but looked out of the window on her right, a bit subdued. There was something about Kate that she wasn't so sure about…

****

Chapter 8

It was 3:30 pm. Max and Lani finally arrived in Paia, parked the car and walked over to the gallery.

Aaron and Mats looked up surprised, as Max and Lani walked in. They had just finished preparing everything and were just getting ready to go home for an hour to quickly freshen up.

"Oh, I'm sorry, guys!" Aaron exclaimed as he walked toward the couple and blew kisses on their cheeks. "I thought I told you that we could meet at our house and we could all freshen up and have a quick coffee before all the craziness begins."

"That's a great idea," replied Lani. "I'd love to take a shower after the long drive. Everything looks great, guys!" Both she and Max walked over to greet Mats, while they looked around, nodding excited. Even without all the special lighting a lighting director had installed specifically for the event, the photos and paintings looked great. Max walked up to a gorgeous blown up black and white photo of Luana, walking through a bamboo forest, which was probably the bamboo forest at Pipiwai Trail. "Wow, this seriously looks just like your mirror image, Lani," he said. "What a gorgeous photo. The lighting with all the dappled shade is amazing." Lani stepped next to him, took his hand gently and nodded. Her father had certainly been a gifted photographer. They just stood there looking at the photo for a silent minute while Mats and Aaron realized what a thoughtful moment they were having and didn't want to bother them. Then finally Aaron had to interrupt: "My friend Jill is setting up catering in the back and Glen went to see an old friend. He'll be back at five. I'll go and tell Jill that we're leaving for a while. Do you guys want to get a head start and drive over to the house? Do you remember where it is?"

"No, I don't know if I'd find it. We can wait a few minutes," replied Max.

So they all drove back to Aaron and Mats' house together, Lani and Max following the couple in their car. They stopped in front of the property with the contemporary three-story house that was so transparent with all the glass they could see the ocean in back of it, right through it. A high-tech gate opened silently. "I forgot how cool their house is," said Lani. Max nodded.

They all drove through the gate, parked and walked into the house. One entire wall was covered with a giant tryptich, a three-paneled painting Lani's father, Paul Kent, had painted and which looked like a tropical rainforest extending to some tropical plants on the back terrace overlooking the ocean. It was stunning in the afternoon sun. Lani and Max just stood there, admiring it, while Aaron and Mats set down some items they had brought home on the counter.

"Let me show you the guest room and bathroom," said Aaron. "Please make yourselves at home. Mats and I are going to take a shower and after that we'll make some coffee."

"Thanks," replied Lani and Max and followed him to the guest room where they took a shower and then came back out to the main area of the house to watch Aaron finish frothing milk for the coffee he had brewed. He also had prepared a little platter with various different local pastries. They were all dressed up now, the men in nice slacks and Hawaiian shirts and Lani in a stunning long muumuu with a beautiful floral pattern and thin shoulder straps, accentuating her athletic arms. "Wow, Lani, you look gorgeous," said Aaron and Mats added: "Yes, absolutely stunning."
Max looked at her lovingly and they gave each other a kiss.

"We all clean up quite well, don't we," replied Lani with a smile. "You guys all look great, too."

They just stood at the counter, sipping their coffee, admiring the view and the mural.

"The bad thing is we'll never be able to move," said Mats in his thoughts.

"Oh, but why would you ever want to leave? It can't get any better than this!" answered Max surprised.

"Well, sometimes I think of trying to get Aaron to move to Gothenburg with me, to be closer to my family. I'm the only son and my parents are getting old…"

"Wow, that is far. I already had a hard time leaving my parents in the Hudson Valley, which is only half the journey! We need them to all move here," replied Lani with a smile.

"My parents would never move away from there, it's cold in Sweden, but beautiful. And my mother actually also owns a quite successful gallery there. They have a big circle of friends…"

"She sounds like you!"

Aaron looked at Mats with a serious face. "Mats' dad was just diagnosed with cancer. He is going to fly over for a while and I'm going to join him when the exhibition is over. Thank goodness, William will take care of the traveling part."

"Oh, no, Mats, we're sorry," Lani and Max both replied simultaneously.

"Thanks. That's another reason my parents would never leave Sweden. Healthcare there is terrific. At least I know he'll be in good hands…"

"Yeah, you can't say that about here, unfortunately…" replied Lani regretfully.

"Lani," said Aaron, "I'd like to bring up one more thing."
Lani turned toward him and riveted her attention on him.

"Regarding the rights of the Paul Kent photos and paintings for the traveling exhibition… we had to do a search for any descendants or heirs of Paul Kent so that nobody ends up suing us or coming forward when the exhibition is already well under way, and we came across a Bridgett Kent, Paul Kent's mother."

Lani held her breath.

"She lives in a town called Clayton, in upstate New York, and she runs a museum and gallery there. I told her about you. She was actually quite speechless, but after a while she was quite excited and happy to have a granddaughter. She would like to meet you whenever you're ready. She is seventy-five years old and doesn't like to travel very much. Otherwise she would have come to one of the exhibitions. She wasn't interested in a share of the proceeds of the exhibition. She confirmed that there are no other descendants and said everything is yours."

Lani's eyes filled up with tears as she thought about the kindness of her unknown grandmother. She stepped out onto the terrace and just stood there for a few moments, facing the ocean, her hair being blown around by the wind, while she tried to pull herself together and not start crying right there. She would definitely have to go and see her grandmother soon. It would be great to learn more about Paul Kent.

The others just stood there for a while and gave Lani some privacy while they finished their coffee. Finally, Aaron looked at his watch and said quietly into the silence: "We should get going, guys, it's already 4:30. I'd like to get there before people start arriving and I want to check out how J.R. adjusted the spotlights."

Max stepped out onto the terrace and gently took Lani in his arms. "It's time to leave, darling."

"Okay," replied Lani as she looked up at him and gave him a kiss.

"We could take one car, since we're all coming here afterwards," proposed Aaron as Lani and Max stepped back into the living room while Lani grabbed her purse.

"Sure, that makes sense," replied Max, "especially with the way parking in Paia is."

They all got into Aaron's old classic Mercedes and were off.

Aaron parked the car in their designated parking lot right in front of the gallery. They all got out and walked in. Glen was already waiting and they all greeted him happily. J.R., the lighting director, was on a ladder, adjusting one of the spotlights hanging from a rail mounted to the ceiling. As he saw Aaron walking into the gallery, he called over to him. "Hey, Aaron, can you help me adjust this one? You can dim it, while I aim it at the photo." Aaron walked over to the lighting director on the ladder, reached his hand up to shake J.R.'s. "Lani and Max," Aaron said, "come and meet the best lighting director in the world, J.R. Aluwai."

They walked over and also reached up to shake J.R.'s hand. "Nice to meet you," they both said. "Everything looks great so far," added Lani.

Lani and Max watched Aaron and J.R. for a while. It was astounding how much the photos' expressions could be changed and accentuated with different lighting. J.R. and Aaron worked together on dimming and adjusting this spotlight and several other ones, while Lani and Max got distracted chatting with William who had arrived in the meantime. Lani had forgotten how tall, elegant and distinguished he looked. He was wearing a white Hawaiian shirt with stitched white flowers, beige linen pants and what looked like hand-stitched very expensive brown leather shoes. He reminded Lani a bit of Hugh Jackman. She nudged Max in the side and said "Doesn't William look just like Hugh Jackman?" Max looked briefly at William and nodded.

Soon everything was ready and Aaron popped a bottle of champagne and poured each one of them a glass before the guests arrived. He proposed a toast.

"May our and especially…" he paused while he turned toward Lani and held his glass up to her, smiling, "… Lani's exhibition become a great success. Without you and your dad this would not be happening, Lani."

Lani smiled back at him and acknowledged the kind words with a blush. She was a bit embarrassed. They all clinked glasses and took a sip. Max gave Lani a hug and they stood closely next to each other, Lani smiling at Max, nestling at his collar, as Aaron walked to the front of the gallery to greet the first guests, who were now arriving.

William walked up to Lani and Max, said briefly "May I?" and stuck a plumeria in Lani's hair that he had pulled out of one of the gorgeous flower arrangements that were plentiful throughout the gallery. "I thought that would be the frosting on the cake. You look just stunning, Lani," he said and then he finally turned toward Max, "and so do you, Max. Beautiful couple."

He had to walk away, because Aaron was making waving motions at him to come and meet a VIP guest that had just arrived.

"Well, that was overstepping his boundaries a bit," huffed Max, a bit indignant.

"Oh, come on, I think he was just trying to be nice," Lani replied. "He just likes to act like an old-fashioned gentleman. And, to be honest with you, I don't even know if he's gay or not." She quickly gave him a kiss on his cheek to calm him down, but had to laugh a little. "I didn't know you're jealous, Max Palakiko…"

"Well, it's hard to keep up with Wolverine…" said Max and grinned.

"He's got nothing on you and you know that," replied Lani and gave him another kiss.

The reception was a big success. More and more people from the Hawaiian art scene arrived as well as locals and friends such as Laura Cattleya; Lenny who owned Mahi Fish Company; the elegant Mama from Mama's Fish House and some other local artists, art buyers and local business owners.

Everyone held their breath for a second when Manolo Wlaschek, the owner of a bigger Hawaiian gallery chain, entered with his beautiful wife Gloria, a renowned actress and artist. To have Manolo come already meant the exhibition was a great success, although he owned a house on Maui and was seen there often.

Some photographers and journalists were there also, not only from Kahului, but also from Oahu, the Big Island and Kauai. Waiters and waitresses were walking among the guests with trays full of glasses of Mimosas and delicious little pupus. There was also a buffet in the back room, catered by Jill, who had received her training as a chef at Mama's Fish House.

As soon as most of the guests had arrived, Aaron tapped a spoon against his glass. Everyone quieted down immediately and listened.

"Aloha, everyone. As you may or may not know, I'm Aaron Alessoni and this is my partner, Mats Lindquist. We'd like to thank you for honoring us with your presence to launch the very first exhibit of Paul Kent, the Photographer." Everyone clapped.

"Also, I'd like to introduce our business partner, William DosSantos, who will be organizing the next stops of this traveling exhibition." William stepped up next to Aaron and everyone clapped again as the photographers' cameras flashed.

"And now everyone… please meet Lani Winters, Paul Kent's daughter!" Lani stepped up, bowed slightly and everyone clapped, full of excitement, while the photographers continued snapping tons of pictures.

They all started whispering or talking to each other, because they could immediately see that Lani looked like she had stepped out of most of the photographs on display. Aaron tapped against his glass again.

"And now, please enjoy the buffet. Have a great time. Mahalo!" Everyone clapped again and lots of people mingled their way over to stand in line at the buffet, set up in the center of the back room, full of sea food, sushi, various salads and Hawaiian specialties such as slow cooker kalua pork and the most beautiful flower arrangements in the middle. Outside, in a courtyard in the back, tables and benches were set up where people could sit down and eat.

Lani and Max were just about to get in line at the buffet when William stopped them.

"Lani, can I kidnap you for a second? I'd like to introduce you to a journalist of the Honolulu Times, Kenneth Buschner." He nodded at Max. "Is that okay with you, Max?"

"Sure, go ahead, Lani, I'll make you a plate and grab us a table," Max answered.

Max continued walking over to the buffet, grabbed two empty plates and picked out a nice mixture of the delicacies on display, as he proceeded to walk forward in the line. He sat down at one of the tables outside and waited and waited and waited, but Lani didn't show up. Frustrated, he started eating his food that had become cold. As soon as he was done eating, Lani rushed up.

"I'm so sorry, Max. At first that journalist took forever asking me all these questions, then I had to have my picture taken with some of the photos in the background, and then William took me to meet Manolo Wlaschek and his wife. They were so nice! They might consider letting us use one of their galleries for the exhibition in Honolulu."

She talked and talked and was so excited that she didn't notice how quiet Max was. He was happy for her, but had wished to be a little less forgotten. Lani ate a few bites of her dinner, but then William was back again. "I'm so sorry, Max… Lani, there's one more person you have to meet, the owner of the gallery in Kona. She has to leave and really wants to meet you… I promise it'll be the last time I interrupt you guys…" Lani stood up and William put his arm around her shoulders as she walked away with him. She looked back at Max and shrugged a bit helplessly.

Max was upset, but thankfully his friend Lenny and Lenny's girlfriend Tammy came up with their plates at this moment and sat down next to him.

"Hey, buddy, looks like Lani is quite busy tonight. What a party in our little town. It's quite the high society gathering," he said and grinned.

"Hey Tammy, hey Lenny, glad you guys could make it. Yeah, quite the party," Max said a bit glumly.

"Hang on a second, guys." Lenny jumped up, walked over to Jill's catering truck and got three bottles of beer out of a cooler that looked like a secret stash. "Tammy and I don't care for that snobby bubbly. Do you want one, too?"

"Sure. Thanks." They opened the bottle caps, clinked the bottles and took a big swig.

Lenny and Max started telling Tammy stories from their high school days and Max didn't notice Lenny switch out his empty bottle for another full one. That plus the champagne didn't mix very well, especially since Max usually didn't drink much at all. When Lani came back, he was already quite buzzed…

"I'm so sorry that it took so long… Oh, hey guys, how are you tonight?"

"We're good, we've been keeping your poor lonely boyfriend company," replied Lenny loudly, who, just like Max, had also already passed his tolerable amount of beers.

"Sure your new friend William isn't going to come and kidnap you again?" asked Max with a snarky voice. He didn't hide how insulted he was. Lani swallowed. She realized she hadn't spent any time with Max all evening. It was her event and she had been busy, but maybe she should have paid more attention to him…

"I'm sorry, Max. I should have included you more. I think I got carried away with being dragged around to meet all these people. You should have come with me…"

She sat down next to him and put her arm around his shoulders, but then she realized that he was quite intoxicated. "Boy, you're drunk, Max… Let's get you home. I'm going to tell Aaron and Mats that we're leaving. Can you guys keep an eye on him for a sec? I'll be right back."

Lenny and Tammy nodded. "I can call you a taxi," offered Tammy.

"You don't have to leave because of me!" said Max quite loudly. People at the other tables turned their heads, wondering who was yelling like that. But Lani was already gone to tell Aaron they were going to leave early and take a taxi home.

Aaron and William were standing in front of a photo, having a conversation, when Lani walked up to them. "We're leaving, guys, Max isn't feeling too well."

William grinned. "Too much champagne?" Aaron saw how upset Lani was as she ignored the comment. "Our code for the gate is 1972 and here's the house key. Just leave the door unlocked."

"Thanks, Aaron and sorry to leave so early. Good night, William."

She returned to the outside table. Lenny and Tammy walked Lani and Max out to the taxi. Max had quite a hard time walking straight. He wasn't used to drinking champagne at all and it wasn't a good mix with beer.

In the taxi, he apologized. "I'm so sorry, Lani. Ohhh, I don't think I feel very well…"
The taxi arrived in front of Aaron and Mats' house and they walked inside. As soon as Max's head hit the pillow, he was out like a light.

Lani just sat there, watching Max snore quite noisily. She adored him and felt bad that the evening had ended like this. She snuggled up close to him, listening to the loud roaring surf and his snoring…

Chapter 9

The next morning, Lani was up before Max, who still hadn't slept off the unusual amount of alcohol he had consumed. It was a beautiful sunny day. Lani laid sideways next to Max for a while, her head propped up on her elbow, watching him sleep with the open windows and the roaring ocean in the background, sparkling in the sunlight. She could see a big sailing boat in the distance. Her heart was full. This was a life she would have never dreamed of leading just six months ago, getting up early every day and doing manual labor in the nursery and flower shop. She had loved her life and certainly wanted to go back to work soon, maybe at Maui Exotics, but this touring exhibit and the party last night seemed like a dream. So many things had changed since she had inherited Koki Beach House.

After a while, she got antsy. Max didn't seem to be waking up anytime soon, so she put on her bathing suit and a short flowing cover-up, grabbed one of the towels in the guest bathroom, went downstairs and stepped onto a beautiful terrace to go down to the beach for a quick swim.

To her surprise, Aaron, Mats and William were already sitting at a table under a covered area of the terrace, having a big breakfast of eggs, fresh bread, a big fruit platter, juice and coffee and all sorts of delicious Hawaiian jams.

"Good morning, everyone! Great evening last night," she said cheerfully.

"Yes, we ended up going to Mama's afterwards. Too bad you guys couldn't join us," said Aaron.

"Yeah, we were a little tuckered out, I'm also still quite jet lagged…" she tried to distract from Max's condition last night while the three men grinned. "I was going to go for a quick dip. Would you mind if I joined you in a little while?"

"We'll be here for a while. We're talking about the next steps of the exhibit. It would probably be good for you to hear this too, but take your time," replied Aaron.

"Where's Max?" asked William as he tried not to stare at Lani's long athletic legs too obviously.

"He's still sleeping, but I'm sure he'll be joining us soon," she replied. "See you in a minute!" She walked quickly down to the ocean and jumped into the rough water and dove down to get past the first wave break. The three men watched her impressed. She was really an accomplished swimmer after being in swim teams almost her entire life.

"Wow, Lani seems to be an experienced swimmer," said William. Aaron and Mats nodded.

Ten minutes later, Lani stepped out of the water, dried herself off with the towel, wrapped it around herself and returned to the table. "I'll go and change into some dry clothes and be right back," she said. The three men nodded.

Max had already been in the shower and was just getting dressed, when Lani entered the guest room. "Oh, hey, honey!" She walked up to him and gave him a tender kiss.

"How are you feeling?"

He was embarrassed. "I have a splitting headache, of course. I'm really sorry about last night. I seriously usually never drink that much and I think I was quite drunk. I hope I didn't say or do anything stupid."

She laughed. "It's fine. You just almost fell asleep in the taxi and then you were out like a light as soon as we got here."

"Sorry," he said. "I guess I kind of ruined your big evening…"

"No worries. I'm actually sorry, I should have included you more…"

"Yeah, I have to admit, I felt a little abandoned. But I guess it was your evening after all. Maybe it's better if I don't come along the next time."

"But I want you to come. I can't be separated from you again for too long…" She took his face in her two hands and kissed him again gently on the lips. He embraced her and returned the kiss. They almost got carried away, but Lani remembered that Aaron, Mats and William were waiting downstairs and let go of Max.

"I just ran into the guys downstairs. They're waiting for us with breakfast," she said, while she started taking her bathing suit off and drying off a bit more, then looking through her carry-on bag for something to wear. "We should go, I'll take a shower later."
A few minutes later, Lani and Max stepped onto the terrace and joined Aaron, Mats and William for breakfast.

They were just laughing about something funny and William looked up at Lani, making motions for her to sit down next to him after nodding at Max. "Good morning, Max! Sit down next to me, Lani! I wanted to tell you what a star you were last night. The press loved you. They couldn't stop talking about how much you look like your mother."

Lani sat down next to William and Mats and Aaron pushed their placemats around a bit and scooted their chairs over so that Max could sit next to Lani.

They all ate a few bites of their breakfast, drank some coffee and then William started complimenting Lani again: "Lani, you looked great in the ocean, like you're a really good swimmer. Did you swim in high school or college?"
Lani replied: "Yes, I actually was always on the swim team and for a short time I also played water polo, but then I couldn't do both and chose swim team… But I guess I'm not that great…" She smiled at Max and put her hand on his. "The first time I went for a swim at Hamoa Beach I almost got pulled out by a rip current and Max had to come and rescue me…" Max smiled back at her, thankfully. His blood pressure had just started rising a little bit because he felt that William was paying a little much attention to Lani again, but she was handling it well and made him feel better…

Lani looked at Aaron and asked "So, did you book the afternoon or evening flight to Honolulu for all of us?"

"I chose the 1 pm flight so that you'd have a bit more time in Honolulu," he replied.

"William is flying at 11 and we'll meet him for dinner at Jimmy's, so you guys can explore a bit this afternoon and maybe go to the nursery again if you're up for it…"

"I was definitely planning on going, but I wasn't sure when…." began Lani, "…maybe that would give me a chance to go twice if she's not there again today."

She looked at Max and asked: "Would you mind?" meaning she wanted to go by herself because it was a very sensitive situation. If indeed her mother Luana owned Blue Tropics Orchids in Palolo Valley and was purposely giving her employees instructions to tell people that she wasn't there, it would be an awkward situation to confront her directly by going there. It could backfire badly. After all, Luana had abandoned Lani in the hospital 30 years ago. But Lani had to find out. She had to find out if the woman in the newspaper article she had found six months ago was her mother or not…

"Of course not," replied Max. "I already assumed you'd want to go alone and, even if Luana isn't there, spend hours looking at thousands of orchids," he grinned, "so I made plans to get together with some old friends that live on the North Shore."

Lani grinned back at Max. Of course he knew how excited she was about just going to a professional orchid nursery the size of Blue Tropics Orchids.

"Can we talk briefly about the schedule for the exhibit?" asked William. "I have to make arrangements with the gallery owners. How long do you want to keep the photos here in Paia?" he turned toward Aaron and Mats. "Both gallery owners of the two potential locations in Honolulu are ending exhibits in the next few days and are anxious to show our photos as soon as possible. But if we don't firm dates up with them soon, they would start something else and we wouldn't get a window of opportunity for weeks… Honolulu should definitely be our next longer show…"

"It's totally fine. I can send you the photos whenever you need them. The lighting is a pain, but we can just keep the spotlights up where they are now and work around them or use them for other artwork, and we can do a longer exhibition in Paia again in the end," replied Mats.

"Okay, I'll inform the gallery owners in Miami. One of them is Manolo Wlaschek by the way. He's very interested since last night. His wife was thrilled. And of course he owns galleries everywhere, even on the mainland."

They all looked at each other full of excitement, holding their breath.

"It might be easier just dealing with one gallerist, but it might also be a pain working with such a big shot. He even has his own legal department, so the contracts are probably much more complicated and… he needs to make more money with such a big overhead. Sometimes it's easier dealing with small up and coming galleries."

They all understood and nodded, but Manolo Wlaschek was certainly a big deal.

"So, everything else really depends on who we end up working with in Honolulu, because we might just get an exclusive deal with Manolo," William continued.

"Our appointment with him is tomorrow at 9:00 am and after that we have another meeting with Yoko Arnold who owns a smaller but really "in" gallery in Waikiki. The appointment with her is at 11:00. You met her last night, Lani. Are you going to come, Max?" he said, making an attempt to try and include Max. "Maybe you could help Lani make a decision?"

Max nodded and smiled, happy that William was involving him for once. "Sure."

"Okay, then I should start packing up and getting ready for my flight." He got up and picked up his silverware and plate. "Can I help you guys clear off the table?"

"No, please don't worry about it," replied Aaron. "Maybe we'll graze a little more," he said, pointing at the fruit platter. "And we can clean up. Shall we plan on leaving for the airport around 9:30?"

"You don't have to drive me. I'm sure you have enough to prepare yourself."

"That's totally fine. Mats will take care of the gallery and there's not much to pack for two nights."

"Okay, thanks. I'll just take my place setting then, see you guys later and thanks for breakfast," said William as he took his plate and cup and headed back into the house.

As soon as he was inside, Aaron said: "Guys, this man knows his shit. To have William on board is really big. He knows the art scene. He's the one who talked Manolo Wlaschek into coming."

Lani and Max nodded. "Does he really look like a mirror image of Hugh Jackman, or is it me?" Lani asked.

Aaron and Mats looked at each other and grinned. Mats replied: "He does. He's one of Honolulu's most eligible bachelors... and he's quite hot. Too bad he's not gay..."
They all laughed - except Max.

****

Chapter 10

Just a few hours later, the Boeing 717, en route from Kahului to Daniel K. Inouye International Airport in Honolulu, was already descending for its landing. Lani, Max and Aaron all had seats next to each other on this plane, that was unusually large for a flight between the islands. Max, in the window seat, had a great view onto Diamond Head and Waikiki, Lani was asleep and Aaron was reading something on his laptop. Just a few minutes later, the plane touched down and taxied to one of the gates. Lani woke up and stretched. "Wow, I must have been tired if I slept through the entire flight and landing," she said, smiling at Max.

Max looked at the time on his phone and turned around toward Lani, while they were walking down the aisle getting off of the plane. "It's almost two o'clock. Why don't I take your carry-on to the hotel and you can take a cab straight to the nursery? I'm sure they close at four or five, right?"

She smiled. "That's an awesome, idea, thanks, honey! I didn't even think about them probably closing early. Yeah, I'm sure they do close at five at the latest."
Since they all only had carry-on luggage, they didn't have to stop at baggage claim and were able to go to the transportation exit right away. Lani had forgotten how beautiful the Honolulu airport was with orchids on display everywhere. Max and Lani gave each other a kiss as they reached the taxi stand. Aaron and Max, now with two carry-ons, went to one taxi and Lani went to another one in back of it.

"I'll see you later, guys. I'll text you when I leave the nursery, Max."

"Okay, good luck."

"I'll be crossing my fingers too," said Aaron. He also knew how important this visit was for Lani.

Lani got into the backseat of the taxi. "To Blue Tropics Orchids in Palolo Valley, please. I'll give you the street name in just a second," she said.

"Oh, I know," the young Caucasian taxi driver with a long pony tail answered, "most of the nurseries are on Waiomao Road. I'll find it."

"Thanks," Lani replied while she looked out of the window at the beautiful surroundings. They were on the H1 freeway, and at first it looked a little industrial around the airport, but soon she could see the lush hills in the distance with the mountain ridges, typical for Hawaii. Just 20 minutes later, they reached an area with one nursery next to the other, Palolo Valley, a suburb of Honolulu. In the meantime, Lani had found the house number and the taxi driver stopped in front of the gate that already looked familiar to Lani from her last visit.

She paid the driver, got out of the taxi and read the big sign: "Blue Tropics Orchids". She walked down the dirt driveway and found the entrance with another sign that said "*Aloha! Orchid addicts, please enter at your own risk*". Lani had to laugh out loud. She hadn't seen that sign before. The little chuckle was good for her, because she realized how nervous she was and that she had a bit of a lump in her throat. What if she indeed ran into her biological mother, Luana? What if Luana didn't want to see her and had everyone "screen" Lani? Or, even worse, what if it wasn't her at all and the painting in the office just hung there for some other reason or was just a coincidence? They could have just bought it at a flea market? She walked up to the office. It was empty, so she walked around the desk and walked up to the small painting that was still hanging on the wall, very obviously depicting Luana. It was signed by Paul Kent.

Someone behind her cleared his throat. "Can I help you, Miss?" Alex, the young man who was obviously the owners' assistant or worked in the office and Lani had met before, walked into the office. His voice didn't sound too happy, since he felt that Lani had intruded in his workspace.

"I'm really sorry, we've met before. I just had to take another look at the painting." Lani replied. "Remember me?"

Of course, Alex remembered Lani from her last visit. How could he not remember her since she looked exactly like his boss? He immediately became uncommunicative and nervous, obviously not knowing how to handle the awkward situation.

"Let me call my boss," he said curtly.

He went behind his desk, pressed a button on an intercom system and said: "Patrick, I need your assistance in the office, please."

A few minutes later, a tall, very pale and skinny but friendly looking middle-aged Caucasian gentleman with dark blonde hair walked up, wearing a blue t-shirt with the logo of Blue Tropic Orchids on it, baggy shorts and sneakers. As he walked toward the office, he took a pair of gloves off. He looked at Lani and froze for a second, but tried to hide any emotions or surprise. He looked at Alex with a quizzical expression in his face. "What's going on?" Then he looked at Lani. "Hi, I'm Patrick Brinkmann. Is there something I can help you with?"

Lani recognized the man from the photo belonging to the newspaper article.

"Hi. My name is Lani Winters." She pointed at the painting. "I'm looking for the woman in that painting. Can you see the resemblance? I think she might be my mother. Luana Kalekilio from Hana."

He was silent for a moment and just looked at her. He was quite shocked about how straight forward she was, but even more shocked about the obvious resemblance.

"I do see a certain resemblance to my wife in younger years, but that must be a coincidence. She doesn't have any children and never did. And her name is Ana."

Lani felt her heart dropping into her stomach. She was very disappointed. The painting, the resemblance with the woman in the newspaper article, and then it wasn't her? Lani didn't want to give up immediately.

"Is she here by any chance? Could I talk to her? Or do you know where you guys got that painting? Because my father painted it…"

"She's not here, sorry. She's at an orchid show on the mainland. She's always had that painting. I don't know where she got it…"

"Oh, that's too bad. Well, okay." There was nothing else Lani could do right now. "Do you guys mind if I look around anyhow? I collect orchids also."

"Of course," Patrick replied in a professional manner. "That's what we're here for. Let me know if I can help you find anything. The greenhouse to the far left is the species house, the next one the Cattleya house with primary hybrids and hybrids and the two closest to us are the Vanda houses. It's bicolor time right now and most of them are blooming. I'm sure you'll enjoy them if you like bifoliates…"

Lani almost didn't feel like looking anymore, she was so disappointed, but now that she was there... It was quite the trip and she'd regret it if she didn't. And she did love bifoliates. They were actually some of her favorites…. She walked over to the species house first and saw what Patrick had meant. She had never seen so many bicolor or other bifoliates in bloom at the same time. Even though bicolor were usually rather scraggly plants, they were big and well grown here. Most of them were staked and looked like rows and rows of soldiers. She took her time and walked through the aisles.

She picked a big amethystoglossa and a guttata, both in sheath, that she decided to take with her on the plane. She wanted a memory and didn't care if she'd have difficulty getting them on as her carry-on.

Finally, she came up to an aisle that was taped off with thick orange tape. The orchids in this aisle all had a piece of orange tape, either on the pots or on the mount that said NFS. Lani knew that this meant "not for sale" and was obviously the owners' private collection.

She ducked underneath the orange tape that separated the jungly "not for sale"-aisle from the rest of the nursery and crawled into the aisle. She could barely walk down the aisle, because the plants here were so big and growing right into the aisle. They were mostly the mother plants that the owners used to create new hybrids and crosses or took for orchid judging. There were stunning Cattleya species and other big specimen plants. Lani was in heaven, she looked at almost every plant, pulled the tags out, looked at them and was excited when she found out that she had guessed the name right. Even though she was upset about her mother, being surrounded by all this beauty was quite distracting for her and made her happy again.

Her favorites were definitely the waxy spotted hot pink bifoliates and the waxy dark red Chocolate Drop hybrids that bloomed in big clusters of large flowers. She spent almost an hour in just this one aisle.

At the very end of the aisle, she found a quite unusual big plant that looked like a cross between a Schomburgkia and a Cattleya, a Schombocatt, mounted onto a very big piece of wood with long healthy roots almost flowing down to the ground. Again, just like all of her favorites, the flowers were very waxy, but these were dark orange with brownish-red spots. She looked for the tag that was stapled to the back of the mount. It said: "Cattleya Paul Kent". Lani's heart skipped a beat. "Wow," she said out loud. She couldn't believe what she had just found. Who would have made a Paul Kent cross, if not Luana… and she seemed to still care for him if she named orchid crosses after him…

She tried to turn the tag around to see if she could find the name of the nursery that had made the cross, but it was stapled to the wood and she had to pry one of the staples out of the wood with a fingernail. She felt bad and looked around if anyone was around, but she seemed to be the only person in the greenhouse. Her fingernail broke. "Ouch!" she exclaimed, but the staple was out and she was able to pull the tag around and look at the backside. *"Blue Tropics Orchids Hilo"*.

So, Blue Tropics Orchids also had a second nursery in Hilo, which Lani had never seen advertised…

"Miss, can I help you? These are not for sale. They belong to the owners' private collection. You're not allowed in there…" An employee had come up in the aisle next to the one Lani was in and noticed her. It seems she had been hidden behind all of the big plants all this time and no one had seen her. Lani startled and looked at the older Hawaiian woman.

"Oh, I'm sorry, I know they are not for sale, but I thought I could at least take a look. Do you mind if I take a picture of this one? I really love it…"

Without waiting for an answer, she got her mobile phone out and took a picture, not only of the blooms, but also of the tag from both sides. Thankfully, the woman didn't care, had turned away and was pulling some weeds out of a bigger pot. Lani walked back to the front of the aisle and ducked back down under the orange tape.

She grabbed her two orchids and walked back to the office to pay for them. It was getting quite late and Max and Aaron might be wondering where she was.

"Can I please check out?" she asked Alex who was sitting behind his desk again.

"Yes, sure. I'm sorry that Ana wasn't here again, she travels a lot."

Lani didn't want to make him uncomfortable again and therefore didn't ask any more questions. She just looked at the painting on the wall behind the desk for a while and then at Alex.

"That's okay, I guess that's what's going to happen if I show up like this without calling first. I'll try to call next time and see if she's around. I'm not that far away, I live in Maui now…"

Alex just nodded and swiped the credit card she had handed him. He put the two quite large plants into a nice Blue Tropics Orchids paper bag and handed it to her.

"Oh, I forgot!" she hit her forehead with her hand. "I came with a cab. Would you mind if I call a cab and use the restroom while I wait?"

"Of course not, take your time, it's only 4:30. We don't close until five."

"Thank you."

She called a taxi, which arrived a few minutes later. She got in and was off to the hotel in Waikiki. While she sat in the backseat of the cab, she remembered her broken fingernail, and looked at it. She got a little cosmetic bag out, opened the zipper and looked for her nail clippers, but couldn't find them. Then she took out her phone and looked at the pictures of the "Paul Kent" Schombocatt she had taken, especially the front and back of the tag. *Blue Tropics Orchids Hilo*…

Another trip she'd have to take very soon…

****

Chapter 11

Lani's taxi pulled up to the Royal Hawaiian Hotel. She was speechless. She had seen it briefly during her last trip to Honolulu, but had never stayed here. It looked like a tiny pink castle surrounded by huge skyscrapers, even though it was quite a large hotel. It was no surprise to her that its nickname was "The Pink Palace of the Pacific" with the bright pink hue of its concrete stucco façade and its Spanish/Moorish styled architecture. It was nearly 100 years old and Lani, Max and Aaron were staying in historic rooms with beautiful dark wood furniture.

Lani grabbed the bag with the two orchids and her purse, walked into the lobby, was greeted by several bellboys and looked for the elevator to meet Max upstairs in the room.

He was already waiting for her on the balcony overlooking the beach and the sparkling ocean with countless surfers bobbing up and down on the waves. It was an amazing view, like on a postcard. Waikiki Beach was shaped like a crescent and the hotels were built right up to the sand. Diamond Head, the landmark of Honolulu, was towering in the distance.

Lani's heart skipped a beat as she gazed upon Max standing there on the balcony, looking out at the ocean, lost in his thoughts. He hadn't noticed her yet because the surf was so noisy and she just stood there for a moment looking at his tall muscular body and broad shoulders, thick black curly hair, his hawk nose and chiseled chin. She fell in love with him all over again.

She snuck up to him quietly, gently lifted his arm closest to her, squeezed between him and the railing and started kissing him. He was pleasantly surprised, kissed her back and held her as if he never wanted to let go. She put her arm around his neck and felt the little curls at the bottom of his hairline that made her knees weak…

"Finally, you're back," he said quietly.

"I know. We've barely had any time for each other, between the crazy Bassets and the gallery…"

They just stood there, kissing each other in the glow of the setting sun, Lani's long hair blowing in all directions from the slight breeze of the trade winds, blending in with Max's curls. Somewhere a musician was playing ukulele and singing a traditional Hawaiian tune…

Unfortunately, once again, they didn't have much time for each other. Lani's phone started ringing.

"Ignore it," whispered Max in her ear. But Lani couldn't. She knew it was Aaron in the room right next door and he was probably calling to make dinner arrangements for the evening. She freed herself from Max's arms, stepped inside to grab her phone and stepped back onto the balcony while she answered. At the same time, Aaron was also stepping onto his balcony, which was right next to their's, and they just stood there, holding their phones up to their ears, looking at each other. They all burst out in laughter.

"Haha, hey Aaron," laughed Lani as she ended the call. "I guess we don't need our phones…"

Aaron and Max laughed too, as Max put his arm back around Lani's shoulder.

"Hey, guys," replied Aaron cheerfully. "Lani, any luck with your mom?"

"Yeah," added Max. "How did it go?"

"Not too well," replied Lani, a bit bummed. "She was either really not there again or she is hiding from me and gives everyone orders to tell me she's not there. I actually met her husband, Patrick, but he didn't give me any news either. He insisted she's never had children…"

Max and Aaron frowned. "That's too bad," said Aaron.

"Oh, but guess what I found…" She picked up her phone again, unlocked it and scrolled through her photos. "An orchid named "Paul Kent." Is that just another coincidence, like the painting in their office?"

She showed Max the photo of the tag from *Blue Tropics Orchids Hilo* and then also held it up to Aaron. "You'll have to show me later," he replied. "I need my glasses and I'm too vain to wear them, haha," Aaron laughed.

"Well, that's quite a lead," said Max. "I guess that means you have to go to the Big Island?"

"Yup. But William and I are going there anyway next week to check out the gallery in Kona," Lani replied.

Max felt a slight twinge of jealousy again, but didn't show it. He nodded.

"I made dinner reservations at Jimmy's at eight. Is that okay with you guys? If you're hungry already, they do have some great happy hour snacks downstairs on the terrace around this time," said Aaron. "William and I are meeting downstairs for drinks. There's a luau around sunset on the back terrace. But feel free to just relax or do whatever you want," he said with a grin on his face. "It looks like I interrupted some snuggle time…" He stretched out his arm toward the beach in a theatrical manner. "Oh, I just love this place! Isn't it beautiful?"

Lani and Max both smiled at him and nodded. They felt the same way. The sun was slowly setting, the light over the ocean couldn't be more romantic and they felt very blessed to be where they were, in one of the most beautiful places in the world…

About two hours later, after a long and refreshing nap, Max and Lani met Aaron in the lobby and grabbed a taxi to the popular hotspot Jimmy's Restaurant. William was stuck on a conference call and was going to meet them a bit later. Lani was surprised as the taxi drove into an industrial area close to the ocean and stopped there. Aaron paid the taxi driver. They all got out and walked toward an old warehouse with no windows, just an elevator door and a little inconspicuous sign that said "Jimmy's" under the elevator button.

"Wow, if you didn't know this place is here, you'd never find it," exclaimed Lani, surprised.

"Wait until you see it," replied Aaron, "it's really fabulous."
He pressed the button and after one or two minutes the door opened with a "bling". A young elevator operator in a suit greeted them and took them up to the rooftop. Max and Lani were absolutely amazed by

what they saw when the door opened and they stepped out and saw "Jimmy's":

It was a separate little building on the roof of the warehouse right on the ocean, built entirely out of glass, probably with a steel frame. Even the ceiling was made of glass. The interior was very contemporary and rather simple, with some longer tables and benches, but also a number of "four top" tables. The lighting in different warm tones and the cascading orchids everywhere on tall metal stands made up for the simplicity. Lani gazed at the orchids full of delight. On the back wall was a giant seafood bar all the way across the room with an enormous lobster tank full of live lobsters and a wide variety of fish, scallops, crabs and oysters on display. A quintet was quietly playing modern jazz, and a few couples were dancing. Some male and female waiters in black tuxedos were walking back and forth, taking care of the guests in a very professional manner. The entire atmosphere was quite glamorous. They walked up to the hostess stand and were immediately seated at a nice four top with a water view. They had just received their menus and the waiter was telling them about the catch of the day, when William walked in.

He had such charisma and was so strikingly handsome, that half of the restaurant stopped their conversations and looked up at him. He seemed to be used to the attention but he seemingly didn't care and certainly didn't let it bother him. He stepped up to the hostess stand, shook the maître d's hand, and was greeted by him and the waiters as if he were an old friend. The owner, Tony, who was quietly observing, stepped up to greet William.

"Hey, William, good to see you. We already seated your party at your regular table," said Tony.

"Thanks, Tony. How've you been? How's business?"

"Everything's great, especially when you're here," replied Tony.

"Hey, buddy, where have you been?" asked another waiter who walked by as William continued on his way through the restaurant.

"Long time no see, William," said a busboy carrying a tray full of dirty dishes to the kitchen.

"Hey, Angelo," replied Tony. He seemed to treat everyone the same, whether owner or busboy. Lani and Max were impressed.

William arrived at the table. Everyone took turns getting up and giving him a hug, except Max who remained a little cool and shook his hand. William also shook the waiter's hand, whose name was Keanu. William automatically took over as the head of the table.

"So, what's the catch of the day? Onu? Shall we just get a mixed fish platter with some giant crabs and some oysters as an appetizer?" he looked around and everyone nodded approvingly. "We'll go over to the seafood bar and make a selection. Would you like to join me, Lani…?" After a brief moment of hesitation he added: "…and Max?"

Without even waiting for an answer, he continued: "Did you guys already order wine?" He looked at Keanu. "Do you still have your great Far Niente Chardonnay, Keanu?"

"Yes, we do. One bottle?"

"Sure. And please bring us two of your oyster appetizer platters. And does anyone like salad? Their Cesar salad is really good, with fresh anchovis, and they make the dressing fresh from scratch at the table…"

"I'll have some," said Lani. "Me too," added Max.

"I'm fine, I'm on a diet," said Aaron.

They completed the order and the waiter left to get things started. A second waiter came and filled the glasses with triple filtered water and left a pitcher on the table, a third waiter came and brought some fresh bread with olive oil and marinated garlic cloves.

William made signs for Lani and Max to get up and follow him to the seafood bar.

"You can actually just pick and choose what you want and then they prepare it for you and make a custom seafood platter," William explained on the way over.

The lobster tank was gigantic and the seafood bar was amazing. There were rows of fresh yellowfin tuna, mahi mahi, shark, ono, hapu'upu'u (the fish that you can only get locally in Hawaii), opakapaka (Hawaiian pink snapper), mussels, giant crabs, shrimps and oysters. The variety was amazing. All they had to do was pick and choose, which was the hardest part, because they wanted to try everything.

Back at the table, Lani looked around very impressed and commented: "What a nice place."

"Yes, it's wonderful," replied William. "They are actually working on getting their first star. The owner Tony is an old friend of mine, he went to the Culinary Institute of America in the Hudson Valley."

"Wow, what a coincidence. Do you know that's where I'm from?"

"No, I didn't. What a small world. I'll have to introduce you later." He continued: "How did your day go, Lani? May I say you look lovely?"

Just like in Paia, William doted on Lani, constantly complimented her and paid a bit too much attention to her. She was aware of it and tried to involve Max in the conversation as much as possible, but - to say the least - Max was quite irritated. After William had very obviously tried to flirt with Lani again a couple of times, Max had to get up and go to the bathroom because he had to bite his tongue and was afraid that he would say something he'd later regret. Lani got up, followed him and caught him before he walked into the bathroom.

"I'm sorry, Max. I think he's just like that with everyone. He just has an extremely charming personality. Don't you notice how he flirts with Aaron the same way he tries to flirt with me? And you're actually a little like that too, Max... you flirt with everyone..."

"Yeah, maybe, but I don't flirt with a woman whose boyfriend is sitting right next her. I'm about to tell him off. It's a bit rude, don't you think?"

With these words, Max just walked into the bathroom and left her standing there. He walked into a stall and felt like punching the wall, but he controlled his temper. He wasn't going to show that arrogant Lothario that he was jealous.

When Lani and Max returned, they didn't know whether Aaron had spoken with William about his behavior, but he was quite restrained the rest of the evening and tried not to flirt with Lani anymore.

"Let's get back to Manolo Wlaschek," William said, now all business. "I talked to him earlier today and he seriously doesn't have a bad deal for us. And we wouldn't even have to go and preview all of the galleries, because they are basically all the same, which is perfect. The only place he doesn't have a gallery is in Kona, but I'd still like to include all major Hawaiian Islands."

Lani perked up when she heard Kona. She was really anxious to go the Big Island.

"When are you planning on going to check out the gallery in Kona, William? Sorry to be rude and change the subject, but I really have to go to Hilo soon. It's not that far from Kona, is it? I showed Max and Aaron earlier…" she got her phone out of her purse, "look what I found at the nursery today." She scrolled through her photos and showed them the photo of the Cattleya Paul Kent and the tag with the name of the nursery: *Blue Tropics Orchids Hilo.*

"I totally understand," William replied. "You don't have to apologize for being anxious about finding your mother, Lani. I think we all understand. It's a two hour drive from Kona to Hilo." He looked around the table.

"It's quite amazing that she doesn't seem to be there, although all the hints point to her and now even to your dad and to that nursery. What did they say about the painting today and about the "Paul Kent" orchid?"

"I didn't even ask," she replied a bit subdued. "I met her husband, and he was adamant that she never had kids. Kind of shut me up right away and changed the subject."

"Sounds like they have all been instructed to keep her under wraps." said Max.

"Yeah, but what do I do? I can't just start stalking her and showing up all the time unannounced."

"You could hire a detective or one of us could go," proposed Aaron.

"Yes, but then I'll know she's alive and doesn't want to see me. That might hurt even more." She continued: "Well, since William and I have to go to the Big Island anyhow, I might as well go and check out that nursery first. Who knows what I'll find there. There is obviously someone who loved Paul Kent enough to name an orchid after him."

"We can go to Kona anytime, even the day after tomorrow, if you can change your flight. The sooner we check out the galleries the better, because they need to be pinned down. They organize their exhibitions months in advance, so I'm anxious to get on their schedules as soon as possible," said William.

Lani looked at Max, who of course was not too happy about Lani changing her flight and going to Kona with William, but that was what had been discussed and it was business. He nodded. "You should do that while you're here, Lani. There's a flight to the Big Island about every hour from here and afterwards you might be able to fly straight back to Maui, it's actually closer to Big Island than Oahu…"

Two waiters came and brought a tray of desserts and coffee, and they all became quiet for a while just enjoying and sharing the treats while they looked out of the window at the dark ocean, illuminated by the waning gibbous moon and the star-studded sky. They all couldn't stop thinking about whether the mysterious woman working at *Blue Tropics Orchids* was Lani's mother or not and why she was never there when Lani showed up…

****

Chapter 12

The next morning, they all met for breakfast on an oceanfront terrace, but had to rush a bit since dinner had gone quite late last night tiring them out, so they had slept in a bit. They had to be at Manolo Wlaschek's gallery at 9:00 am and it was already 8:15 am. Thank goodness it was just about a ten-minute walk down the road on Kalakaua Avenue. The sun was already high up in the blue sky and there was a pleasant breeze coming from the ocean. They could almost touch the people on the beach, walking down to the ocean with surfboards, lying in the sand or just strolling about. Lani looked up, closed her eyes and just held her face into the sun for a minute.

"Oh, I don't think I'll ever get tired of this sun. It really puts you in a good mood," she said with a smile.

The three men nodded and smiled. "Yeah, you sure get spoiled here," replied Aaron, "I don't know what I'll do if Mats insists on moving to Sweden…"

They had lots and lots of Kona coffee, fresh tropical fruit, pancakes with coconut syrup, eggs Benedict and omelettes made to order. Too much, thought Lani. The buffet was only worth it if you could sit there and eat for three hours, but it was delicious and a treat just to sit there and enjoy the location.

They got the check, charged the breakfast to the rooms and walked through the beautiful lobby to Kalakaua Avenue where they took a left and walked away from Diamond Head toward Manolo Wlaschek's gallery. There were tall skyscrapers on both sides of the road and traffic was quite heavy this time of day: the sidewalks were full of tourists with cameras or phones taking pictures of everything they saw. But that was Waikiki: a busy tourist hotspot. William walked in the front, behind him Aaron, then Lani and Max, he weaved in and out of groups of people, walking as fast as he could. He stopped at a gallery with a sublime glass façade, on the ground floor of an upscale hotel, and walked inside.

"Hey, guys!" Manolo Wlaschek himself happened to be in the gallery currently, talking to an assistant. He walked toward them, blowing kisses onto everyone's cheeks. He was an older gentleman in his early sixties and might have been from Czechoslovakia or Poland. He was tall, had a receding hairline with white hair, combed back and held in place with gel, was dressed all in light grey linen, a casual button-up shirt, wrinkly linen pants and expensive looking light grey leather shoes. He stopped in front of William and put his hand on his shoulder.

"Thanks for organizing this meeting, my friend. I'm so honored to see Paul Kent's daughter again. Lani, you look gorgeous my dear. I'm so excited about the opportunity to possibly work with you. You know, I tried to have an exhibition with your dad about 25 years ago. I had just met him, but then I heard the news of his accident and could never reach anyone responsible for his work and portfolio. He never seemed to have a manager. I even tried calling the University in New York, but nobody had any information about what had really happened…"

"Wow," said Lani. "I had no idea that you met him. Yeah, it's like he disappeared from the face of the Earth and even off of the Internet. You can't find any information about him."

"I'd love to add some of his paintings to the exhibit if you can spare any on a temporary basis. Also, of course, if you'd like to sell any."

She nodded and remained silent. She didn't think she could sell any of her father's paintings, but she also wondered how desperate she might become with the renovation and all the disappearing building supplies.

"Let me show you around," Manolo continued. The gallery was huge, the backside was all glass over two stories looking out onto the ocean. A wide spiral staircase in a back corner led up to the second floor and a big balcony with a metal railing overlooking the back part of the gallery and the ocean. There were several contemporary sitting areas on the balcony and a bar or café, which invited people to sit down, have a drink or a coffee and just enjoy the atmosphere.

"I wanted this place to be modern and sleek, but also inviting and comfortable. Let's go upstairs and have coffee or juice…"

"We just had a giant breakfast at the hotel, Manolo," replied William, "maybe in a bit?" The others nodded. They were still stuffed.

He led them from room to room, pointing out certain paintings or artists to them. "We are currently exhibiting the Polynesian artist Saito Alaniki. He was born and raised in Hawaii, but lived in Tahiti for a while and did a lot of painting there. He reminds me a bit of Gauguin. What do you think of these magnificent colors?"

The paintings were amazing and they all enjoyed the tour. "We also have some of the work of Judy Macintyre, Thomas Kawai and Julio," he explained as he led them through two more rooms, "last but not least," he led them into the last sunny room which was so close to the ocean that they felt like they were on a ship, "the carved surfboards of Lilly Palapaloa. These are my favorites, I just love the intricate designs." Some of the surfboards were on display hanging from the walls, some were on stands in the middle of the room. They were just gorgeous, some were entirely carved with intricate ornamental designs, some were simply half carved and the other half had been left as the original wooden surfboard.

"Gorgeous," said Lani and they all admired the beautiful carvings.

"Oh, and let's not forget some VIP paintings that we have on display over here," he looked at Aaron and grinned. "I'm sure our humble friend hasn't told you," he laughed and led them to a corner off of the oceanfront room where they discovered some of Aaron's paintings. "Wow, Aaron," they all said surprised. "Why didn't you tell us?"

"Well, I didn't want to brag," Aaron replied. "And it was a fun surprise, wasn't it?" he grinned at his friends.

"Yes, congratulations, they look great," said Max and Lani added "That's no surprise, you're very talented, Aaron!"

"Well, let's have some coffee or tea upstairs and we can discuss my proposal. Do you guys still have a moment?" Manolo asked. William looked at his designer watch and nodded. "We're fine," he replied. "Our next appointment is at 11:00."

They walked back to the main room where Manolo's assistant Ally was sitting behind a giant counter, talking on the phone. "Ally, would you mind bringing the proposal for these guys upstairs?" They all walked up the spiral staircase. Manolo walked over to the "bar" and looked around at them. "What can I get you to drink?"

"It looks like you have a nice coffee maker there, I'll have a coffee please," said William. "Me too," said Lani. Aaron and Max just asked for water.

While Manolo, who obviously enjoyed taking care of these things personally, got a carafe of water out of a sleek fridge, some glasses and three elegant white coffee cups out of a contemporary open shelf, turned on the coffee maker and brewed a pot of coffee, Ally came upstairs in her six inch heels and brought Manolo two elegant looking folders. They sat down on the couch and he handed one of the folders to William. "Sorry, guys, I only have one copy, would you like Ally to make some more copies?"

"That's fine," replied Aaron. "We can look at William's copy. And William is the businessman in the group anyhow," he added and grinned.

William opened up the folder and scanned through the document, holding it so that Aaron could view it as well. They both held their breath for a split second. "That's quite a generous offer, Manolo," he said and handed the folder to Lani, who was sitting next to Max.

Lani and Max also held their breath for a second. They had no idea that the exhibit would be so lucrative.

They chatted a bit longer, drank their coffee and water and enjoyed the beautiful view. Manolo's wife Gloria came up the stairs and greeted everyone. She was very friendly and charismatic, but seemed to be in a rush. It looked like they had an appointment and she had come to pick him up. "Are you ready, honey?" she asked with her deep voice.

William stood up, and Aaron, Max and Lani followed his example. "Well, thank you very much for your time, Manolo," said William. "We have to get to our other appointment and will be on our way."

"It was great to see you all. Please take a closer look at the proposal and let me know what you think," he replied.

"Thank you very much, Manolo, nice to see you again, Gloria", said Lani and they all air kissed each other again and walked down the spiral staircase, waved goodbye at Ally and exited the gallery.

Back on Kakakaua Avenue, they grabbed a taxi that took them to Ko Olina on the leeward, west side of Oahu. It took about 45 minutes to get through the busy Honolulu traffic. Some people thought Ko Olina was one of the prettiest areas on Oahu. It was a resort style preplanned community, so it had a bit of an artificial vibe that was definitely not "local" Hawaii, but still beautiful. It was home to some of the island's loveliest beaches and hotels such as the new expansive Disney Hotel Aulani and the Four Seasons. The gallery they were scouting had a very different atmosphere than Manolo's. It was smaller and more intimate, which was not a bad thing. The gallerist was a lovely Polynesian woman named Yoko Arnold, who was also an old friend of William's and had been to the opening in Paia the other day. She had long black hair that was braided skillfully around her head and she was dressed in a beautiful handpainted muumuu with a tropical motif along with comfortable pretty sandals. William and Yoko greeted each other with a long hug.

"Yoko, remember my friends Lani, Max and Aaron? You met the other day and I think you even have some of Aaron's paintings in your gallery, don't you?"

"Aloha and welcome to my gallery. Yes, I've known Aaron for a long time. Hello and welcome back, Aaron, and hello Lani and Max," she said with a deep calm voice. "It's an honor to have Paul Kent's daughter here. He was such a great artist. I actually own a few of his prints that I bought way back when. I couldn't afford originals back then," she said with a smile. "Let me show you around a little and then I have some refreshments." The gallery was a stand-alone contemporary building with an ocean view and a glass façade in the back. It was flooded with sunlight and consisted of two big rooms with some room dividers made of beautiful giant timber bamboo. Some paintings hung from these dividers. The spotlights were also custom-made slices of giant bamboo canes. It was much more rustic than Manolo's gallery with a more natural vibe, but it was beautiful and made a very authentic island impression.

"So, how long are you planning on keeping the photos and paintings in your gallery in Paia, Aaron?" she asked.

"We are totally flexible. I already told William that we could dismantle them anytime and postpone our exhibition until after the traveling exhibit. That would allow us to keep them as long as we want, since nobody would be waiting for them."

Yoko continued: "I am finishing my Yuki Kannaka exibition in a few days and have another artist on hold, but she doesn't care if we add another artist in between. She had some possible travel plans with her family come up and is waiting to hear from me before she makes a decision…" She led the way into the first main room and pointed at the Yuki Kannaka paintings that were all giant-size fish paintings, some really beautiful koi close-ups, some dolphins swimming in a pod in the ocean, some whale close-ups. "Aren't these just gorgeous? I will miss them. Every exhibition feels like a part of me and I really miss the paintings until I get used to the new ones."

They walked into the second room where she had an exhibition of a renowned Polynesian glassblower. Just like in the other room, all the stands and cases were made of giant timber bamboo. It was quite unique and complimented the beautiful local artwork in a very creative manner. Lani was blown away.

Yoko offered them lilikoi and guava juice along with tiny little homemade cinnamon rolls and to everyone's surprise they realized that they were all hungry again. Just like Manolo, she handed them her proposal in an elegant folder and the amount she offered was not very different from his.

They said goodbye, thanked Yoko and walked around Ko Olina a bit, touring some of the beautiful resorts.

"So, what's your first impression of those two galleries, Lani?" asked William.

"Boy, that's a tough decision," she replied. "I really like Yoko's gallery because it seems more Hawaiian and authentic, but then I think this area is kind of out of the way. Waikiki is so much more old Hawaii, in my opinion."

"I agree," said Max and Aaron chimed in too. "Yeah, this is a bit in the boonies."

"And then, as much as I like Yoko … and Manolo seems so much more like a cold businessman… I really like him and the fact that he knew my father and already wanted to have an exhibition of his work 25 years ago. That would be kind of cool for marketing."

"Wow, Lani, I didn't know you're such a PR person! That's a great idea," exclaimed Aaron.

"True, that's a great idea, Lani. Well, let's all sleep on it," said William. We don't have to sign contracts right away. But don't forget that the logistics will also be much easier with Manolo. All of his galleries are similar and we don't have to go and check every single one out."

Lani nodded. That made a big difference, since she wanted to start helping Max with the house and her parents were coming in about three weeks.

They walked up to a really nice hotel. "How about some lunch?" asked William and held the door open for the other three.

****

Chapter 13

"Wow. This glamorous world of art exhibitions and galleries is quite intriguing and exciting, but I'm glad that we can just hang out and relax with some old friends of yours now," said Lani to Max as they both climbed into the back of an Uber after lunch.

Max nodded. "Yeah, I can't wait to finally just relax and stop small talking with these upscale gallerists." They both laughed. Everyone had been very nice and it had been an exciting morning, but it also seemed like a different world…

Max had made plans to meet some of his old friends at Heeia Boat Harbor to go out to Kaneohe Sandbar with them.

"Are you sure you wouldn't rather go to the nursery again and see if you run into your mother?" asked Max in a caring manner.

"No, she wasn't there yesterday, my next chance to find her will be in Hilo and after that I'll be back in Honolulu when the exhibition opens here in a few days. I want to spend some time with just you now. You've been so patient with all the gallery business and now I'm looking forward to a fun afternoon together. That is, if I'm allowed to come…" she said with a grin. "Who knows how many of your old girlfriends are going to be there."

He laughed. "Don't be silly. Of course I want you to come. Wait until you see the sandbar. It's a raised strip of land in the middle of Kaneohe Bay. At high tide the water is just above the waist and at low tide the sand is actually exposed. Being out there is like a day at the beach, except you're in the middle of the ocean. It's the coolest feeling. And my friends will have beer, food and music."

She grinned. "What? We're going to eat again?"

"You'll see, we'll be hungry again in two hours from being in the water and swimming."

Lani laughed. "I guess…"

She was a bit tired, but excited. She snuggled up against him in the backseat of the Uber and he put his arm around her. They both sat there quietly, looking out of the window at the beautiful deep green mountain ridges in the distance.

Despite quite heavy traffic, they soon arrived at Heeia Boat Harbor. Max's friends were already waiting for them in the boat. "Sorry, guys, traffic wasn't great on a Friday afternoon," said Max and gave the three guys and one girl high fives.

"Bianca, Charlie, Conor and Nick, meet my girlfriend Lani," Max introduced Lani to his friends. Lani shook their hands while Bianca, a beautiful blonde in a tiny bikini, gave her a strange look. Lani wondered briefly, I hope this isn't some other stalker ex-girlfriend of Max's, but she'd find out soon that Bianca was staring at her for a different reason…

"Hey, guys, would you mind waiting for another five minutes? I think it's more comfortable if Lani and I change in the marina than on the boat," said Max, pointing at their nice clothes that they had to wear for the meetings.

"Sure, no biggie," answered Charlie. "I was actually wondering why you guys are so dressed up. Take your time."

"We had some meetings, we'll explain later," replied Max.

Max and Lani went into a building in the marina that had changing rooms and changed into their bathing suits they had brought in a beach bag.

"Wow, I can use a refreshing swim now after walking around galleries and being in taxis and Ubers all day," said Lani as they walked back to the boat.

"Yeah, it's hot today," replied Max. "It'll be nice and breezy out on the water. My friends usually also bring snorkeling gear. That might be fun too."

"It's great to see you guys," said Max to his friends as he got into the boat and stretched out his hand to take Lani's as she climbed in after him. As soon as they had all sat down and the boat had departed the harbor, Bianca looked at Lani again and said:

"Wow, Lani, it's really crazy, you look like the mirror image of someone I work for every now and then, except that she's older. It's like you two are sisters. I'll have to see if I can find some photos on my phone later when it's not so bumpy..."

Lani swallowed. Of course she immediately wondered whether Bianca meant Luana or, as she seemed to call herself, Ana...

Bianca knew what she was talking about when she said bumpy. The boat had left the no wake zone around the harbor and Charlie, the captain, put the engine in full throttle, catapulting the boat out toward the open ocean. Lani, Max and the other passengers had to hang on for dear life, but they enjoyed the wild ride as the boat sped away from the bay out toward the sandbar. They all looked like excited children on a roller coaster ride. The wind and the spraying salt water felt cool and refreshing in Lani's face. She had to twirl her hair in a ponytail to keep it from whipping into her own and Max's face. Max put his arm around Lani and she felt safe and comfortable leaning against him, as she watched the wake of the boat and the rugged dark green mountain ridges move further and further away. She loved being out on the ocean.

It took them 15 minutes to drive from Heeia Boat Harbor out to Kaneohe sandbar. Charlie dropped the anchor and they all took their t-shirts and cover ups off, lathered each other with reef safe sunscreen, climbed down a small ladder and got into the water – Lani was amazed. It was only about knee deep and she could clearly see the shadow of the sandbar that stretched about three miles long and one mile wide. Lani could see all sorts of fish darting around in the clear shallow water and the small ripples at the sandy bottom.

"How does it feel to be standing in the middle of the ocean?" asked Max with a big smile in his face as he waded toward her in the knee-deep water. She walked toward him and gave him a big hug. "Oh, Max, I'm so glad I came with you. What a fun day!" She looked up and gave him a kiss which he returned as he also held her in a tight embrace.

"Hey, hey, guys," interrupted Charlie, "you're not alone here..." The others giggled as he handed Lani and Max each a bottle of beer. Lani and Max had to laugh as well and clinked their beer bottles with Charlie and the others who had all waded up. Bianca had a tray of – what else could it be: homemade Huli Huli chicken - and passed it around to share. Lani, who had thought she could never eat again after the giant breakfast and lunch, had worked up an appetite again, grabbed a piece of chicken and took a hearty bite. It was delicious and the beer was ice cold and tasted great.

They waded around and hung out for a while enjoying their beer, the food and the reggae music coming from the boat. The water had become a bit lower and Bianca got two lightweight folding chairs out of the boat, set them up in the shallow water and offered Lani a seat, while Max was wading around a bit in the distance, talking shop with his buddies.

"Here, Lani, I wanted to show you some pictures of the woman who looks exactly like you…"

Lani sat down next to her and asked: "Does she happen to own a nursery?"

"Yup. In Palolo Valley."

Bianca had brought her phone from the boat and was scrolling through her photos. "I work there sometimes to pay for college. I live about ten minutes from there and during the orchid shows I can make some pretty good cash." She found some photos of Ana in her phone, just fun photos, working at an orchid show, selfies of them together, posing with blooming orchids. "She's really nice, more like a friend than a boss. She's actually a bit like a mother to me, since mine recently passed away…"

That comment hurt Lani a little. Even though her adoptive mother had been great and Lani hadn't lacked anything as a child, her biological mother Luana had given her away as a baby, obviously never wanted her and now she was being "motherly" to other people…

"She has actually mentioned a few times how much she wanted kids but never had any…"

Lani rolled her eyes. "Well, she obviously has a daughter that she abandoned and that's me…"

"Wow, are you serious? So, there's really a connection between the two of you?"

"Yeah, it really seems that she's my biological mother and gave me up for adoption when I was a baby. There's more and more evidence to suggest that… I've been trying to get in touch with her, but she's never there when I show up at the nursery and when I spoke with Patrick yesterday, he was quite adamant about her not having kids as well… I think she's purposely avoiding me…"

"Well, I guess giving your baby up for adoption isn't something to be proud of," Bianca answered carefully. "Maybe she's ashamed of herself for doing that and doesn't know how to react. I don't know. I wonder if I could make a contact."

"Hmmm… Are you that close?"

"Quite close, but she is actually really out of town right now, I think."

"Let me think about it, okay? That's very nice of you to offer…"

Bianca nodded. "So, how did you and Max meet? He's a great guy."

"It all has to do with my family… I inherited a house in Hana from my great aunt and Max happens to live in the guesthouse. I guess his mom and my great aunt were best friends… and how could I not fall in love with him?" she sighed and looked over at him adoringly.

Bianca laughed. "I'm so happy for him. That Mandy… she's quite the nut case. They weren't even really together, but she sure thought so…"

"Oh, yeah, I met Mandy a few times… I wasn't sure whether they had been a couple or not. For a while, she seemed like quite the stalker."

"I wouldn't trust her as far as I can throw her…"

"The last time I saw her in Waikiki, she seemed to have a new boyfriend, which I have to say I was quite happy about…"

Before they could continue their conversation, they got interrupted by Max, who was wading up with two sets of masks, fins and snorkels and handed one set to Lani as he gave her a quick kiss.

"Hey, I thought we'd go snorkeling a little bit while we're here. Do you mind, Bianca?"

Lani jumped up. "Sure, great idea!" She smiled at Bianca who pretended to be upset. "Well, I guess I'll have to get another beer then and hang out with Charlie and the guys…" They all grinned. Max took Lani's hand and pulled her into an area that was a bit deeper. "There are some better reefs closer to shore, but there's a lot to see here too," said Max. He put his mask on, dipped down into the water and started floating right underneath the surface. They both floated next to each other calm and relaxed, sometimes holding hands, while they pointed out the various colorful fish to each other. They even came across a nurse shark hovering right above the reef and Lani, a bit nervous, squeezed really close next to Max, but the shark didn't seem to be bothered by them and just went about his or her business, scanning the bottom of the ocean, probably looking for something to eat. They swam back to shallower water and again couldn't keep their hands off of each other. Lani wrapped her arms around Max's neck and neither wanted this day to end…

Unfortunately, the sun was slowly going down and the wonderful afternoon was coming to an end.

"What about you taking scuba diving lessons?" said Max, looking deep into her eyes as they slowly floated back toward the boat. "It would be so great to do that together. It feels like flying under water."

"I've always wanted to learn how to dive," replied Lani. "Maybe we'll have some time when the house is done…"

They both nodded. They had both totally forgotten about the house and all of their responsibilities during this little half-day vacation.

As if on cue, Charlie asked, as they all climbed back into the boat and started getting ready to head back to shore: "So, what's going on with the house? How's the renovation going?"

"It's actually been going really well, except for the fact that someone has been stealing our building supplies," answered Max.

"What?" They were all flabbergasted. "Who would do that and why??"

"Do you have any enemies?" asked Bianca.

"There's a builder who was trying to buy the house when Lani inherited it and didn't know whether she could accept the inheritance or not, because it came with some conditions and isn't cheap to fix up…

This builder obviously wanted to tear it down and build condos on both sides of Hamoa Beach and might not be too happy that Lani refused to sell…"

Charlie replied: "Hmmm… That's really weird. Doesn't seem worth it… I've been hearing about the controversial construction project that some builder is planning all along the coast past Hamoa Beach. That's awful. That beautiful countryside shouldn't be destroyed for luxury condos… I heard somewhere that some people are planning a demonstration in Hana next week. You should get in touch with them. One of the leaders is my friend Michael, the manager of the Henderson Ranch Restaurant."

Max looked at Lani and they both nodded. "Oh, yeah, he's a good friend of mine… I'll definitely get in touch with Michael and find out what they're planning. Thanks, Charlie."

"Okay, let's get back, I have to work tonight," said Charlie, "unfortunately I'm not independently wealthy," he added with a grin.

"Charlie is a manager at a restaurant in Waikiki. He can also take us back," explained Max to Lani while they put their t-shirts and cover-ups back on. Their swimsuits were almost dry again in the meantime.

They made sure they had all of their empty bottles and garbage, packed them away neatly, pulled up the anchor, put their bags under the seats and were ready to go. Out of courtesy to the other boats on the sandbar, Charlie started the engine very slowly, but then he put the engine back into full throttle and they sped across the water, toward beautiful Koolau Range, the mountains that paralleled the eastern coast of Oahu.

As they drove toward Waikiki, they all became silent just watching the beautiful moon, that was still a waning gibbous, going up above the ocean behind the skyscrapers on Kalakaua Avenue. The busy tropical tourist hotspot was quite the amazing sight.

****

Chapter 14

It was a beautiful new day in Waikiki Beach. The sun was rising, filling the sky with shades of orange and pink. A taxi was standing in front of the Royal Hawaiian Hotel. Max held the door for Lani, as she joined William in the backseat. The cab was going to take them to the airport, where they were going to fly to Kona and check out another gallery. After that, Lani was going to visit *Blue Tropic Orchids Hilo* and check whether she could find her biological mother or some information about her there.

"Have a great flight," said Max and leaned in to kiss her one more time, then he closed the car's door and waved goodbye. Lani waved back and said: "I love you" through the open window.

She knew he wasn't too happy about her traveling alone with William and that jealousy was gnawing at him. She would have felt the same way. She looked at William who was on another business call, looking so elegant and self-confident and always seemed to do and say the right thing except that maybe he was a bit *too* charming and confident. She felt a bit insecure and stiff, but this was only for two nights and it was business. It was going to be okay. And she was really looking forward to going to the Big Island, another place on her bucket list that she could check off and another chance to find her biological mother, Luana. Lani felt more and more the urge to find her and to find out why Luana had abandoned her as a baby. Even though Lani had her adoptive parents, she felt like a part of her was missing now that she had found out more about her biological parents and really wanted to meet her mother and also get more information about her father.

The taxi driver stepped slowly on the gas pedal and merged into the stop and go traffic on Kalakaua Avenue, while Max turned around and walked through the hotel to meet Aaron on the back terrace for breakfast. Their plane back to Maui didn't depart until noon.

William ended his call. "I can't wait to show you the Big Island," he said and smiled at her. "You're going to love it."

Lani was a bit taken aback, because she thought he was just going to the gallery with her and from then on she'd be on her own. "It's okay with you if I rent my own car and drive to the nursery, isn't it?"

"Oh, you don't have to rent a second car," he replied. "I'll just hang out at the hotel by the pool or work while you're on the road. We both have been upgraded to really nice suites, so I'm sure I won't even want to leave the hotel, besides maybe showing you some nice spots in Kona later today. I am a little worried about you since the drive to Hilo is two hours from Kona, but I guess it's not as bad as the road to Hana that you're quite used to, correct?"

"Yes, that doesn't bother me at all, I think… I'd hate for you to be stuck without a car all day, but I guess we can play it by ear," Lani replied.

"I'm serious. The resort is super nice and if I have to go somewhere I can always take an Uber."
She nodded. "Okay, thanks."

Twenty minutes later they were at the airport. The taxi driver got out and opened the door for Lani. William had already exited the taxi and was retrieving their carry on suitcases from the trunk. While they walked inside the terminal, Lani's phone rang. It was her mother. "I have to take this," she said to William as she answered the call, still walking up to the counter with William and handing the airline attendant her ID while William did the same.

"Hey, Mom!"

"Hi, honey, I just wanted to check if everything is okay. I haven't heard from you in a while."

"Yes, sorry, we've been in Honolulu checking out galleries and right now I'm at the airport with William. We're on our way to the Big Island."

"Wow, it sounds like you're having quite an amazing time. I'm so happy for you."

"Mom, I'm at check in. Can I call you back in a few hours when I get to the hotel?"

"Of course, Dad says hi. Call whenever you can, no rush. We're up late."

"Okay. Bye, Mom."

She ended the call and William handed her boarding pass to her with a smile on his face.

"Well, Shelley here was so nice to upgrade us to first class. What do you think about that?"

"Oh, wow, thank you very much!" exclaimed Lani surprised.

"No problem, William flies with us so much that he's kind of a VIP," replied the airline attendant and smiled at him, flirting.

He winked at her and said: "Thanks again, Shelley, and see you next time."

They walked through security and to the gate, William with his arm on Lani's back in a way that was almost a bit too intimate as they boarded the plane. She didn't think much of it though, since she had many male friends that hugged and touched her all the time...

Lani and William's seats on the plane were amazing – four people would have had enough space in them. As soon as they sat down and were settled, a flight attendant brought them each a glass of champagne and a dish of macadamia nuts. Lani was quite happy with this treatment. They proposed a toast, clinked glasses and drank champagne while the plane took off. They flew over Oahu, saw Diamond Head from above, a bit of Lanai and were soon over the harsh west coast of Hawaii that was made up of black lava rock and descended into Kona International Airport, which was on the dryer and sunnier side of the Big Island.

Lani was already a bit tipsy from all the champagne and she and William were laughing and having a great time. He was certainly a fun guy and was very obviously flirting with her. While they walked down the jet bridge to the gate, he mistakenly - or maybe not - bumped slightly into her. She staggered a bit and had to hold onto him with both hands to not fall.

"Whoa, whoa, whoa," he said, "careful."

"Oops, I'm sorry, William, I almost lost my balance for a second," said Lani and they both had to laugh while he held her for a second too long. She looked into his blue eyes and blushed a little as he stared back into hers. She looked down for a second and did her best to pull herself together. She didn't like the feeling she had just had as he held her.... After that, while they walked through the terminal to the car rental, she remained distanced and businesslike. She got out her cell phone and called Max to let him know they had landed.

"Hi, Lani!"

"Hey, honey, I wanted to let you know that we landed and everything's fine here. Are you guys already on your way to the airport?"

"No, not yet, we're just going back to our rooms to pack and check out... Shall we call each other tonight? I'm sure you'll take a while to get to your hotel and then you have your appointment pretty soon, right?"

"Yeah. Love you and miss you! Have a good flight."

Lani ended the call and followed William to the car rental booth where he gave the pretty car rental agent his reservation number. She also seemed to know him and beamed as she saw him. "Oh, hi, Mr. DosSantos! It's great to see you!"

"Hi, Tanja! You look lovely as always..." Lani was surprised that he remembered the car rental agent's name.

The agent basked in William's compliment. "Let me check in my computer what we've got here…" said Tanja and paused, while she typed in all the information. "Oh, it's your lucky day, you have a reservation for a Jeep Wrangler, but it looks like I can upgrade you to a Range Rover today, Mr…" She paused and looked at Lani, "…and Mrs. DosSantos."

"That's awesome, thank you," replied William and didn't bother correcting her. He smiled at Lani. "You're like a good luck charm, Lani."

After putting their luggage in the back of the brand-new beautiful Range Rover in British racing green, William entered the hotel's address into the car's GPS and they left the airport behind, heading south toward Kona.

"Wow, what a smooth ride, I'd love this car at home," exclaimed William. It was definitely very classy.

"You know, William," replied Lani, "I don't even really know where you usually live. Do you spend more time in Honolulu or San Francisco?"

"I live in San Francisco in the summer and right outside of Honolulu in the winter – it's the best of both worlds. San Francisco gets quite chilly in wintertime. I can't handle that anymore," he looked at her from the side and grinned.

"Yeah, I get that, I could get used to being in the warm all the time too… the winters in the Hudson Valley were pretty rough," she replied.

"Oh, I know, I'm originally from New York City. Brrrr… it might be fun to visit for a few days, but boy, do I hate that cold weather. Well, I don't think we have to worry about that right now," he grinned. "Look at that…" They both stopped talking and Lani just took in the beautiful view, as William had to watch the quite heavy traffic. They were almost at their destination, the luxurious resort on the coast south of Kona, in which the gallery was also located, and they could catch first glimpses of the beach, engulfed in black lava rock and the ocean. The resort was beautiful. The property sprawled out over several acres right on the ocean, they felt like they were in a tropical garden as they walked on a path along the bungalows and finally found their two villas right next to each other with balconies overlooking the ocean.

"Our appointment with Jill in the gallery isn't until two," said William, while he looked at his watch. "It's 11 now. Do you want to relax a bit and then meet for lunch at one? As far as I remember, the bungalows are always stocked up with fruit and snacks."

"Sure, good idea."

"See you at one."

Lani opened the front door leading into her bungalow and stepped inside. It was a dream. She could look straight out onto the ocean and the entire bungalow was furnished and decorated with dark French-Polynesian furniture and Hawaiian artwork. She stepped out onto her balcony and was surrounded by lush plumerias, hibiscus and palm trees that provided shade. The beach was about ten feet away and instead of taking a break, she quickly changed into her bathing suit and went down to the water she swore she heard calling her name. A refreshing swim always cleared her mind. She kept feeling the butterflies she had had in her stomach when William kept her from falling at the airport and couldn't stop thinking about Max. She wondered how she could have these feelings for someone else… She jumped into the waves and swam as hard as she could. Soon her head was clear and she started relaxing while she opened her eyes, looking down at the wonderful underwater world.

Half an hour later, Lani stepped out of the water and walked back up to her room, enjoying the beautiful surroundings. She thought of her biological father. Being in this beautiful resort was another thing she had to thank him for, because his artwork was taking them to all of these amazing places. She wished she could have met him….

Back in the room, she laid down on her bed to relax a little and fell into a deep sleep with wild nightmares. She saw her mother and father, both sitting in the little cabin near Waioka Pond. Her father was painting her mother, but then they were suddenly in an old pick-up truck driving off of the cliffs of Puu Pehe on Lanai, never making it to the water or the ground. They just kept falling and falling, which made Lani toss back and forth and then snap awake. She was breathing hard and had broken out in a sweat since she hadn't opened any windows or turned on a fan. She walked over to the sliding-glass door, opened it to let the fresh breeze in and walked over to the small kitchenette to pour a glass of water. Then she looked at the time on her phone. It was 12:30. She just had enough time to take a shower and get ready to meet William at one.

"Hey, William," said Lani, as she rushed toward William's bungalow. He was already standing there, waiting. "I saw you went for a swim," he said with a smile. "I'm sure that felt great."

"Yes, over the years it's become a great way to clear my mind and relax," she replied.

They walked up to the hotel's main building where Jill's gallery was located. There were a few restaurants to choose from, a nice upscale oceanfront one, a more casual one as well as an outside pool bar with a full menu. "Let's go inside, with our nice clothes. We'll just get all sweaty and wrinkly if we sit outside," proposed William. They had a nice lunch and then it was time to walk over to the gallery. The gallery was beautiful just like all of the other galleries they had seen. This one again was full of local Hawaiian artwork and the meeting took just about twenty minutes.

"I think this would be the perfect location," said Lani to William quietly while Jill had to answer a business call.

"I agree, it reminds me of Aaron and Mats' gallery and you saw how great the photos looked in there," replied William.

"Here's my proposal," said Jill as she stepped back up to William and Lani and handed them both an elegant looking folder. They were impressed since she was the only one who had bothered making several copies.

"Thanks, we'll take a look, but we have to say that we really like this location," said William.

"I'd like to take you guys out for dinner tonight if that's okay? The restaurant is one of the best on the island and there's a great Luau on the terrace, if you're interested." said Jill.

Lani was relieved since she was a bit nervous about spending time alone with William, especially in a romantic setting which was basically everywhere in Hawaii…

"I'd love to watch a Luau," she said and looked at William, "and I'd appreciate if we could stay close by, since I have to get up early in the morning…"

"Sure, I agree. This restaurant is really good, I've had dinner here before." He looked at his watch and turned toward Jill. "We have a few hours to kill. Can you recommend something typical in and around Kona that I could still show Lani?"

"Pu'uhonua o Honaunau National Historical Park is really interesting and the Painted Church is my personal favorite. They might close at four thirty or five, but it's not far, you might be able to look around for forty-five minutes or so."

"Let's get going then," said William with a smile. "Thanks, Jill, and shall we meet you in the lobby at 7:30 or is 8 better?"

"Let's say seven or 7:30 so we can eat dinner before the dancing part of the Luau begins. Or do you guys want to take advantage of the buffet style Luau dinner as well?

"I'd say we just get some dinner a la carte, the entire Luau including buffet probably takes about three hours, correct? And that way we can just eat a light dinner and watch the dancers?"

Lani nodded. "Sounds good to me."

They shook hands with Jill and walked back to their rooms.

"Do you want to change?" asked William.

"I'm actually fine," replied Lani, "This dress can go as formal and casual... I can be ready in five minutes, how about you?"

"I'll just drop off my jacket and put a different shirt on," he said. "See you out here in five minutes."

****

Chapter 15

Since William and Lani's hotel was South of Kona, it was only about a twenty-minute drive south on the Mamalahoa Highway along the coast to get to Pu'uhonua o Honaunau National Historical Park, also called the Place of Refuge. They passed lots of antique shops, some coffee farms, local fruit stands and the beautiful ocean on the right, all belonging to historic south Kona, took a right onto 160 and then the ocean was suddenly on the left because they were driving north again.

They drove into the parking lot with long black lava rock walls on the left and lava fields on the right leading all the way down to the ocean.

Walking into the park was like stepping back in time: They entered the Royal Grounds first and walked through an entire field of tall coconut palms on sandy ground that had been planted to commemorate chiefs that had passed on.

Lani read in her guide: "The Hale o Keawe Temple, guarded by carved wooden Ki'I, symbolizing Hawaiian gods, is a very sacred site. Inside rest the remains of 23 Ali'I – which means rulers or chiefs – The Temple and Royal Grounds are protected and separated from the Pu'uhonua by a Great Wall, constructed over 500 years ago in the 1500s using uhua humu pohaku – it looks like that's a type of dry stack masonry with lava rock. Over 80% of the original wall was still intact when this site was reconstructed and restored in the late 1960s. The wall measures up to 12 feet tall, 18 feet wide and 950 feet long."

William brushed slightly against her while they walked through a gate from the Royal Grounds into the Pu'uhonua. Lani felt the tension between them and she slowed down a bit to let him walk ahead.

She continued reading in her guide. "When you visit the Pu'uhonua, you can walk in the footsteps of those who sought refuge here over the course of centuries, and see where the Ali'I and Kahuna who pardoned them resided. The Pu'uhonua was not only for those who had broken a law, but a safe place for women, children and elderly during times of war. As you walk through the Pu'uhonua, you will the see the foundations of older heiaus (temples), and the great wall that separates the Pu'uhonua from the Royal Grounds. Visitors to this special place will notice the peaceful energy and spirit of forgiveness that can be felt throughout the park to this day."

They walked toward the ocean. "Wow, those statues look scary," said William and grinned. "They look like giant tikis, don't they?"

Lani nodded. They were very impressive. She took some photos and William told her to stand next to the statues while he took some pictures of her.

"You look gorgeous, like a Hawaiian goddess," he said, while she blushed a bit and quickly continued walking.

Too soon it was 4:30 and the park closed, but that was okay and a chance for both of them to see the Painted Church and then return to the hotel and get some rest. As they left the park, they spotted a sign leading to Honaunau Bay. Lani read in her guide that it was voted one of the 10 best snorkeling places in the world. "Wow, that would be a place to return to," she said.

The road leading to the Painted Church, also called St. Benedict's Church, was one of the most scenic roads on the island. One priest had painted the entire inside of the church by himself. He only had green, white and brown house paint. He had made the remaining colors by adding natural pigments found in the plants growing nearby. "Wait until you see this," said William, "you will love it with your artsy background."

Lani was speechless. It was unbelievable. The ceiling was painted with pastel colors, from blue with white fluffy clouds in the middle to a very blush pink, then a very light yellow, then a darker pink and a darker blue than the one in the middle. Palm trees painted onto the ceiling looked like they were growing out of the columns on the sides. The walls on the sides were depictions from the bible and the lives of the saints. It was all very intricate, ornamental and just beautiful.

She looked at William to thank him. "Thanks for taking the detour and coming here. I'm so glad I saw this."

He smiled at her. "I knew you'd love it. If we had a bit more time, we could go to Galaxy Gardens, a beautiful botanical garden, and Kealakekua Bay where Captain Cook first landed and where he was also killed. It's beautiful down there." He briefly put his hand on her back while they walked back to the car and again she felt this mix of being attracted to him, but also a bit uncomfortable, with a guilty conscience.

"Let's stop here and get something to drink." William stepped on the brakes and took a right into an unpaved parking lot in front of a small roadside farmer's market. There were only two vendors, one with bountiful fresh fruits and vegetables from lilikoi to pineapple, coconuts, guavas and bananas, to cucumbers, tomatoes, Maui onions and even fresh taro, the other with tropical bouquets of flowers and beautiful orchids, mostly Phaleonopsis with cascading spikes of blooms. They didn't seem to have any drinks, but the first vendor offered: "I can cut you a couple of coconuts and you can drink the water." Lani and William looked at each other and nodded. That was a great idea. They watched the vendor pick up a big machete and skillfully chop the tops of two coconuts off and stick bamboo straws into the openings. William handed Lani one of the coconuts as his hand brushed against hers seemingly by coincidence and they strolled down to the orchid stand, sipping their refreshing drinks.

The orchid vendor smiled at them, but he had to do a double take as he saw Lani and just stood there, staring at her. Lani thought she knew why he was staring at her, but she didn't say anything. He probably got some of his orchids from Blue Tropics, knew Luana and saw the striking resemblance.

"We should probably get going," said Lani to William who also noticed the vendor's stare.

"What was that all about?" asked William, as he steered the car back onto the road.

"I'm used to people staring at me like that in Hana," Lani replied. "I look so much like my mother, only younger, that people think they've gone back in time or something like that when they see me." She had to laugh briefly about her own explanation. William looked at her and nodded. "Well, I sure hope you find her tomorrow."

As soon as they were back at the hotel and Lani in her room, she called Max. She needed to hear his voice to feel secure in her love of him after William had flirted with her in the car again.

After they had spoken a while, Max came out with the latest bad news: "Someone has stolen some more of our wood and an entire toolbox. It looks like somebody is definitely trying to slow us down."

Lani couldn't believe it. Again.

"Have you spoken with your friend Billy yet about setting up cameras?"

"I will tonight and I'm also going to speak with Michael from Henderson Ranch about the demonstration against building the condos behind Hamoa Beach. Glen found out that someone has inquired with the county about changing the zoning code. We need to find out who it is. It might be the same person who's messing with the house…"

That really put a damper on things. "I really hope my parents arrive soon, the more people we have to watch the house, the better."

"Yeah, it might be a good idea to have your parents come earlier if they can change their flights. It would make a difference if someone was always home. Also, they might be able to help with the dogs. I just paid Kate. That will be getting expensive…"

"Yeah, I can't wait to get home," replied Lani. "After a while, all of the galleries look the same. But I did have quite a fun afternoon. William and I went to Pu'uhonua o Honaunau National Historical Park and this beautiful hand painted church. It's awesome. I wish we could come back together. You can even touch sea horses and go night diving with manta rays here and there's a bay where Captain Cook first landed and was also killed…"

Max was not too happy that Lani was doing all these fun things with William and not with him, but he tried not to show his jealousy.

"Sounds awesome. We'll definitely go on a vacation there. I actually know someone in Hilo we can stay with."

"Okay, I'm going to let you go now. I have to call my parents before it gets too late in the Hudson Valley," she said.

"Say hello to them. Good night."

"Love you."

"Love you."

Lani ended the call and pressed her parents' number that she had on speed dial. Her mother picked up immediately. It was late, but she had been waiting for Lani's call.

"Hey, love, how is everything going?"

"Great, the gallery was beautiful and we had an interesting afternoon at a historical park. I have some bad news though… Someone seems to be stealing building supplies from the house. When Max got home today, some things were missing again."

"You've got to be kidding me? This is happening in a small town like Hana? Who would do that?"

"We have no idea, but we think maybe the same guy who wanted to buy the house to tear it down and build condos on the ocean."

"Well, let me know if there's anything Dad and I can do."

"Funny that you should mention that. I actually wanted to ask if you could change your flights and come earlier. Not sure if Dad is currently working on anything, but we just think the more people are here, the less intruders will dare show up."

"I'll check our flights in the morning. I'm not sure if they can be changed, but you never know. Here's Dad. He wants to talk to you too. I'll call you in the morning, okay?"

Lani and her Dad chatted for a while and he agreed that they would try to come earlier, even just to help as a handyman, since the renovations were getting more and more delayed. They hung up with a "love you" and Lani blew a kiss into the phone. "Love you, Dad."

An hour later, Jill, William and Lani were seated at a nice table that was situated in a way it gave them a great view onto the stage, where the dancers were going to perform, but still were set back a bit and had some privacy.

They all looked at the menus.

"Is there anything you can recommend?" asked Lani.

"The Ono is my favorite, but I've had fish a few days in a row, so I'm going to order a steak, which is really good here. All the beef on the island is grass-fed and really good quality." She paused for a second while she looked at the menu… "You guys should try the lilikoi cocktail as an aperitif. It's really good," recommended Jill.

They all ordered and as soon as the waiter had brought them their aperitifs, William proposed a toast and everyone raised their glasses.

"I think Lani and I are in agreement that we would like to go ahead and work with you, Jill. So, cheers and to a good cooperation."

"Thank you, guys. This exhibition is very special to me, since I met your father about 25 years ago in Hana. He was a very kind and special man. I had a flat tire right outside of Hana once and he helped me change it and we had a nice conversation. I have to admit that I had no idea how to change a tire back then. That was a lesson. Of course, I had no idea who he was back then – I would have been quite star struck, since I was taking painting classes myself…"

Lani looked up. "Wow, that's amazing that you met him. Do you remember by any chance what year it exactly was? Because that's right around the time he had the accident on the Road to Hana."

They all had a sip of their cocktails and Lani had to cough a bit since it was extremely strong.

"Let me think about it, I might be able to figure it out, since I already lived here and wasn't in Maui that often…"

"Thanks," replied Lani. "This is a strange question, but did you find that he seemed depressed?"

"No, I can't say that, he didn't talk that much though. He was just very courteous and nice. But our conversation didn't go that much in depth…"

She drank another sip of her cocktail, looked at Lani and said: "You know, I remember now. I was there to participate in a weekend painting workshop, but it got cancelled because he suddenly wasn't available anymore. I remember being quite disappointed, but nobody really mentioned the reason it was cancelled… And I also remember wondering why he was driving *away* from Hana, if he was giving the class in Hana the next morning."

Lani stared at her. Her mind was racing. What a coincidence if Jill had met Paul Kent on the Hana Highway right before his accident. And why had he left Hana right before teaching a weekend painting workshop? Although that didn't mean much. Some people went back and forth to and from Kahului constantly.

Right in this instance, their conversation was interrupted by two drummers walking out onto the stage. The audience started clapping. The drummers sat down on the edge of the stage and started drumming in a rhythmic manner.

Four luau fire dancers stepped onto the stage. They were dressed in short loin cloths, "malo", with grass bracelets below their knees or anklets (kupe'e), headdresses with red flowers on one side and giant bone necklaces around their necks. Two of the men had Polynesian tattoos on their shoulders and arms. They were all holding sticks with fire on both sides and twirled them at an incredible speed, accompanied by fierce rhythmic drumming. They passed the fire sticks between their legs, changed the direction they were spinning them in and became faster and faster to the rhythm of the music, which looked incredible, like a lit up circle, in the dark. They threw the fire sticks back and forth to and from each other, until they then climbed onto a pedestal and formed a human pyramid, jumped back down, the drums slowed down and the fire dancers bowed for the audience that was going crazy with wild applause.

The next performance was a bit more laid back. A group of beautiful barefoot hula dancers with knee length grass skirts and beautiful flowers in their flowing long black hair walked on stage and started dancing to calmer Hawaiian music. Lani could finally relax. She just sat back and watched, as they danced the hula with their many hand motions signifying aspects of nature, such as the swaying of a tree in the breeze or a wave in the ocean, a feeling or emotion, such as fondness or yearning.

The show went on for a while, with various other groups and a solo hula dancer. Their food had been served and they ate as they watched. When they were done, they all got up and walked down toward the ocean to enjoy the beautiful scenery, lit up by the waning moon and the starfilled sky.

"Jill, if you can ever remember any more details about my father, I'd really appreciate it. As you can imagine, I'm looking for any information I can find, any little detail about him would help me, since it's so hard to look at his beautiful work having never met him…"

"Sure, I'll think about it…" said Jill and gave her a sincere hug. She really liked Lani.

"I'm going to get going, since I want to get up really early tomorrow morning and drive to Hilo," said Lani looking at William. "Could you stash the car keys somewhere before you go to bed?"

"Oh, I can come and give them to you," William offered who still had a glass of wine in his hand.

"No, no, no, you guys drink your wine and stay here," Lani replied quickly. "Just put them under the door mat or somewhere where I can find them and let me know. Thank you very much for dinner and the great evening, Jill." And she rushed down the path leading to the suites.

****

Chapter 16

The next morning, Lani drove the almost two hours to the nursery in Hilo, going straight across the island on the Hawaii Belt Road and Saddle Road. She started the drive through the Kona side, which was like a desert, dry and unpopulated, with very few rolling green hills. It reminded her a bit of the back road past Hana and Upcountry. At first, it was all flat with brownish grass on both sides and mountains in the distance, then it became greener with rolling hills, some dead looking little trees with lava rock on both sides, then there was more and more lava rock on both sides. It was surreal, like driving on a different planet, she passed a native tree sanctuary and nature trail called Kipuka Pu'u Huluhulu – oh, she'd have to come back here, that was right up her alley!

She didn't stop though and put this on her to do list for the next trip, because she wanted to have as much time in Hilo and the nursery as possible. An endless road led straight through lava country with Mauna Kea in the distance, its observatory on top that Lani could actually make out… There was snow on the summit. Mauna Kea's peak was 4,207 meters above sea level, making it the highest point in the state of Hawaii. Suddenly she realized she was high in the clouds as they were on the same level as the road. The clouds around her shrouded everything in darkness, making it feel like evening, even though it was still mid morning. She saw patches of tiny red flowers growing in the lava that almost looked like heather. I'll have to find out what they are, she thought to herself. Giant lava fields came up on both sides. It was amazing, but then she briefly thought of Jill and the flat tire, hoping she wouldn't encounter the same fate…

The closer she got to Hilo, the more she drove down from the high elevation. The countryside became vibrantly green and lush again with taller trees and some farms on both sides with white fences, rock walls or hedges. Lani started seeing tunnel style greenhouses on both sides of the road. She wondered if there were orchids inside. The entire area was full of palm trees and tropical plants.

She had to take a break and drove into a beautiful rest stop. It was Wailuku River in a gorge, surrounded by beautiful tropical foliage.

According to her GPS, Lani was getting quite close to *Blue Tropics Orchids* in Hilo. She had to leave the main road and take a left into a smaller side road that was paved in the beginning, but soon turned into a dirt road, surrounded by overgrown tropical foliage, shrubs, palms and vines. The road was so narrow, Lani wondered if she was lost. But the foliage ended abruptly and she stood in front of a giant field containing several greenhouses.

The tallest greenhouse was closest to her and appeared to be the main building and entrance. A big sign on it read *Blue Tropics Orchids Hilo.* Lani parked the Range Rover in a designated spot, got out and walked into the building.

"Aloha!" Lani said to a gentleman who was just leaving and held the door for her. They both took another look at each other. It was the vendor from the roadside orchid stand near Kona. He said: "Aloha, you must be Ana's sister. I just saw her and thought I was seeing double!" and stepped outside with a smile and a quick wave. Lani held her breath for a second. So, Ana was here... If only she knew where. She wanted to rush inside and just start looking for her, but then she realized that she would make a bad impression, so she tried to calm down, take deep breaths and act normal, even though her heart was pounding in her chest, knowing that Lu/Ana was so close.

She stepped inside and looked around the giant foyer with a big water fountain in the middle, surrounded by beds of lush tropical flowers and shrubs – and of course orchids everywhere. There were some benches on two sides of the foyer, inviting guests to sit down, relax and enjoy the beautiful fountain. The next room was a big sales room with hundreds of blooming orchids on display. Lani stepped into the room and looked for an employee to ask about Ana, but they all seemed busy with customers, so she took her time and browsed. For most people, every orchid nursery looks the same, but not for an orchaholic like Lani. She immediately found some hybrids she had never seen before and walked from greenhouse to greenhouse for at least an hour, immersed in the wonderful selection this place had, but never fully concentrating and keeping in mind that her mother Lu/Ana might suddenly pop up in front of her. It almost drove her crazy.

As she was walking from one greenhouse to the next, Lani bumped into a tall sympathetic looking Caucasian gentleman who must have been at least in his early to mid seventies. "Aloha," he said with a friendly voice and looked down at her with a smile. She could tell that he worked at the nursery, because he was wearing the same t-shirt that Patrick had worn in the Palolo Valley location. "Aloha." "Can I help you find anything?" Then he took a second look at Lani and froze. "Well… I'm looking for Ana," she started carefully. "I guess so.... Are you related to her?" he asked in an upbeat manner. "I can definitely see the family resemblance…"

"Yeah… possibly…" Lani was trying not to blurt it out this time and alienate him so she remained a bit reserved. He thought for a moment. "I think she is on the early lunch break today which starts at 11." He looked at his watch. "She might be gone for an hour or so. I'd be happy to lead you around until she's back." He looked at Lani again, who was a bit pale. "Can I get you anything to drink? It is very hot in here and you should stay hydrated. Usually one of the employees walks around, passing out guava juice."

He looked around, saw a girl with a tray full of little paper cups and waved at her. "Hey, Conny, can we get some juice, please?" The girl came over and Lani took one of the cups off of the tray. Tom took another one and handed it to Lani.

"Mahalo," she said. The girl just nodded and kept walking toward some other customers.

"I'm Tom, the greenhouse manager, by the way," said the gentleman.

"I'm Lani. Thanks."

"Would you like to sit down for a second? People tend to get a bit dizzy from the heat in here sometimes."

"I'm fine, thanks, I actually used to own a nursery myself and I'm used to being in greenhouses. I collect orchids too."

"Well, then… how about I show you Patrick and Ana's private collection?"

"That would be awesome. I'm particularly interested in Paul Kent hybrids, if you have any…"

"Oh, trust me, we do," he grinned as he led her to another greenhouse with a roped off aisle, similar to the one in Palolo Valley. "So, how do you know about the Paul Kent hybrids? They're usually not talked about much. You must have heard about them from Ana?"

"Umm, it's a long story…" Tom realized that she didn't want to talk about it, and didn't ask additional questions, but he could tell that there was a special connection. This young lady moved and talked just like his boss, Ana. She was possibly her sister or maybe even her daughter, even though she said she had never had one… Tom was a very wise man and knew Ana's story and how she had suddenly come to *Blue Tropics Orch*ids one day without a past or ever speaking about it… There was an immediate connection between Tom and Lani, almost like between a grandfather and a granddaughter or between fellow orchid lovers.

"Follow me," while he stepped up to an aisle and unhooked a thick rope that was closing off the aisle with the private collection to the general public. They both walked into the aisle and he hooked it back up. "The Paul Kent hybrids are all the way in the back. We can work our way up to the front," he said, while he made his way past the overgrown orchids, trying to grow into the aisle from both sides, making sure Lani was following him, as he held big growths and inflorescences up that were in their way. He stopped at the end of the aisle. "This is where Ana keeps the Cattleyas that are dearest to her. Look at this one." He pointed at the same Schombocatt cross, Cattleya "Paul Kent", that Lani had found in Palolo Valley with several inflorescences with the beautiful waxy orange-brown spotted blooms and the hot pink lip.

"Do you mind if I take pictures?" asked Lani. "These are just breathtaking."

"If they're only for your private use it's fine, but I don't think Ana would like you to publish these. For some reason, she never sells or has these Paul Kent crosses judged and keeps them under the radar."

He looked for something in the far back of the orchid bench, reached through a jungle of big Cattleyas and grabbed two pots that he picked up and showed Lani, while he took the tags out and handed them to her. The first one said *Cattleya Paul Kent "Wellesley Island"* and the other said *Cattleya Paul Kent "1000 Islands"*. There were a few other Paul Kent crosses.

"Wow, interesting that she always makes the connection to the 1000 Islands. That's where he's from," said Lani.

"Who? Paul Kent?" asked Tom. "Do you know him? She never told me about him. Who are you, Lani?"

"He's most likely my father…"

She looked into his old wise face and knew she could probably trust him. "And she's my mother. I've never met him or her, but I have reason to believe that he's my biological father and she's my biological mother. I was given up for adoption as an infant and adopted by very nice people who raised me in the Hudson Valley, upstate New York. Out of the blue, I inherited this beautiful house in Hana and have been finding out more and more about my biological parents, for example that my mom disappeared right after I was born and my dad was a very renowned artist but possibly died a few years later. There is a beautiful giant painting of a girl right in the center of the house and I assume it's my mother Luana, or now Ana as she calls herself, because she looks exactly like me…" She continued: "It's crazy. When I walk through Hana, people recognize me and think I'm her and time has stood still..."

"Hmmm…" replied Tom in his thoughts. "The story would kind of work out with your age… How old are you?"

"I just turned thirty."

"I remember just like yesterday how she suddenly came to Blue Tropics Orchids thirty years ago. I was the greenhouse manager in Palolo Valley back then. She had just come to Oahu and by coincidence met the owners' younger son who was working as a bellboy at a hotel on the beach. The Brinkmanns were able to give her a job and she stayed in a little guesthouse which employees or business associates sometimes lived in. Sadly, the younger son fell in love with her, but she and the older son Patrick hit it off and eventually got married. The younger son never got over that and left the islands and has been estranged since…"

They were both getting hot and dehydrated, standing in the back of the aisle in the hot greenhouse and Tom said:

"Let's go and sit down on a bench. We should drink some water. There's a water cooler right over there."

They stepped out of the aisle and sat down on a bench near the exit of the greenhouse. There was a water cooler with a big jug of water and little paper cups in a dispenser. Tom filled two cups and handed one to Lani. The two new friends just sat there for a while, resting and talking.

"Eventually Patrick and Ana took over the nursery from his parents and opened this place in Hilo. Ana travels back and forth a lot between both nurseries. I think because she loves to work on cloning new hybrids, which we only do here in this location. And Hilo seems to be her secret retreat when she needs some alone time. She is quite a loner and definitely never talks about her past…" He hesitated and looked at her with big eyes. "I hope I'm not telling you too much, but I just feel like I can trust you, Lani. And I feel like you belong here…"

She smiled and looked in his old wise eyes. "I feel the same way."

"Maybe we should go check and see if Ana is back from lunch."

Lani nodded. They both got up and slowly made their way to the front of the nursery. Tom was walking a bit slower than in the beginning. His age was telling now.

"I'm a little nervous about confronting her," said Lani. "It's going to be quite the shock…"

"Well, if you were already in Palolo Valley twice, she might know that you're looking for her and be expecting you at some point…"

The girl at the front desk informed them that Ana had a doctor's appointment and had left for the day.

Lani's jaw dropped. She had a hard time holding back her tears. "So, she was here and I missed her again..." she said.

Tom had never heard of any doctor's appointments or that Ana was going to be out in the afternoon, but he kept that to himself and it wasn't any of his business. That's typical for Ana, he thought. She always avoids any confrontation. And this was quite the confrontation. Tom didn't voice his opinion, but he trusted Lani... It all made sense...

"Do you want me to speak with her about you?" he asked as he walked Lani out to the car.

"I'm not sure... let me think about it. It might be too much pressure from all sides. She must think I'm stalking her..."

"Okay, just let me know. I have quite a good connection with her."

Lani gave him a hug, got into the car, started the engine and rolled down the window. "It was great to meet you, Tom. Thanks for everything."

She started the long drive back and even though she wasn't hungry at all, she had to look for something to eat. It was way past lunchtime.

****

Chapter 17

After the long drive back to Kona, Lani returned to the resort in the late afternoon, disappointed and hungry. She couldn't stop thinking about how close Ana must have been this time and was very obviously avoiding her. She was very glad she had met Tom though. What a great guy. She had been trying to reach Max the entire afternoon. Just as she was stepping back into her suite, someone finally picked up the phone. But it wasn't Max. It was a woman, laughing and giggling. It sounded like they were hanging out together and this girl had taken Max's phone away from him.

"Hello? Hello?" said Lani.

"Helloooo," answered the woman with quite the seductive voice.

Lani could hear Max's firm voice in the background saying "give me the phone".

Lani said "Can I speak with Max, please?" but the other person ended the call.

Lani tried to call again, but this time there was no answer. Lani felt the blood rushing out of her head and had to sit down. Was she going to start having those doubts again, as soon as she turned her back on Max? All that nonsense with Mandy six months ago, was that going to happen again? Was he still not fully committed to her? Even though she was quite hungry, she changed into her bathing suit, just grabbed a bottle of water, a cereal bar and a towel and walked down to the ocean. A swim would clear her mind after the disappointment regarding Luana and now Max. She ate while she was walking, dropped her towel on the lava rock and walked into the ocean through a little path leading into the water that looked like it had been cleared for visitors. She started swimming faster and faster parallel to the shore and all worries were washed away. She relaxed and floated on her back, slowly treading water, facing the sky with her eyes closed. When she came back to her towel, William was sitting there. He looked up at her cheerfully with his perfect smile and asked: "So, how was your day today?"

Lani had mixed feelings as she saw him sitting there. On the one hand, she was happy to see him, he was always charming and in a good mood. On the other hand, she constantly felt that she shouldn't be alone with him, because truthfully she knew she had a bit of a crush on him, despite her love for Max. But now if Max was hanging out with other women...

"Not so great, to be honest with you," she replied. "Luana wasn't there again. I'm pretty sure she's going out of her way to avoid me. She was actually there and when I asked for her, she suddenly supposedly had a doctor's appointment and was gone…"

"Wow, I'm sorry to hear that. Did you gain any new insights?"

"Yes, I actually met the older greenhouse manager who was a sweetheart and who has been working there for thirty years. He told me how she showed up at the nursery one day, got a job and moved into a guesthouse. He said she never talks about her past and has no family ties. It must be her."

"I'm really sorry about that. Maybe you can return soon, also to Honolulu."

Lani nodded. With the exhibition in Honolulu starting so soon, she probably would.

"I have a nice surprise to cheer you up." William said. "Jill recommended a really nice place called "Henry's" right on the ocean for dinner tonight. It's supposed to be one of the best places in Hawaii."

"Sounds great, thanks. I'm actually starving. I haven't eaten all day. When do you want to leave? I'll go and get ready."

He looked at his watch. "It's six now. How about I make the reservation for 7:00 and we leave at six thirty?"

"Okay, see you then." She smiled at him and walked up to her suite.

Henry's was an oceanfront fine dining restaurant just a few miles up the road from the hotel. William and Lani were led to a nice table by a hostess, which was so close to the water that they could see the entire coast of Kailua Bay and Kona Harbor. Tall palm trees on the side of the property were swaying in the wind and they could hear the gentle waves lapping against the black lava rock underneath the wooden deck. The restaurant was built on stilts on top of the black lava rock.

The waiter ignited a candle. The perimeter of the property was illuminated by burning tiki torches, bathing the entire restaurant in a beautiful warm glow. Lani looked out across the ocean, saw a pod of dolphins and pointed: "Look, how beautiful," she exclaimed. William only had eyes for her. She was wearing a long flowing yet body-hugging floral dress with spaghetti straps that showed off her figure, she barely had any make-up on and seemed like a natural Hawaiian beauty. "You look stunning, Lani," he complimented her. She blushed a little.

"You look great too, thank you," she replied.

"So, tell me about your drive across the island," he requested.

"It was unreal, like driving on a different planet, there are just fields of lava on both sides for miles and miles, then you can see Mauna Kea in the distance and it seems you're simply driving through the clouds…" Then she told him about her day at the nursery and meeting Tom. William was a good listener and very empathetic.

"You know, Lani, I was adopted too. That's why I can totally relate to how badly you want to find your mother and get more information about your father…"

She looked at him wide-eyed. She had no idea they had something like that in common. "Wow, I had no idea. How interesting… and… did you ever meet your biological parents?"

"No, my adoptive parents told me at a young age that my parents both died in a car crash. My adoptive parents are actually my godmother and godfather. They were all best friends. So, I didn't have to look for them. They were always very open about it and still talk about my parents a lot. They were all doctors, but now my parents are retired."

A pretty middle-aged waitress came to their table and poured them two glasses of water, brought some complimentary puu puus and took their drink order. They ordered two Mai Tais. William immediately flirted with the waitress in his charming manner and Lani watched him. She noticed the similarity to Max's flirtatious personality. They were so different, yet quite alike.

Lani drank way too much. She was tired from the long day, the Mai Tai was way too strong and the wine went down incredibly easy with the interesting conversation and the delicious dinner of sesame and ginger glazed tuna, rice and mango cole slaw. She hadn't eaten all day and had a hearty appetite. William a very entertaining charmer, the atmosphere was quite romantic under the Hawaiian half moon and the clear sky studded with millions of stars. William told Lani how he became an art dealer even though his parents had wanted him to follow their footsteps to become a doctor and how he had met Aaron and Mats. He had such a fun and charismatic way of telling stories that she hung on his every word and they both laughed a lot. The waitress came around again and William ordered dessert with cappuccino and two cognacs. Lani thoroughly enjoyed someone just taking charge and ordering for her. It made things so easy and she was tired. They lifted their glasses. Lani took a sip and shuddered a bit. The cognac was much too strong for her, but tonight she didn't care and she downed it way too fast.

They just sat there, gazing out at the ocean, drinking their coffee and cognac. After a while, a local band started playing a mixture of Hawaiian music with reggae and some locals started dancing on an outside dance floor close to Lani and William.

"Shall we?" asked William.

"Nooo, definitely not," said Lani determined, "I'm a really bad dancer."

"Oh, come on…" He got up and took her hand. She didn't put up a big fight, stood up and let him take her into his arms, while the band started playing a faster reggae song. Lani hadn't danced in ages and it was quite fun. William twirled her around and she had to hold onto him, as she felt a bit tipsy. They both laughed while the band switched to a slower song. William was a great dancer and continued to hold her close while they danced slowly across the dance floor. Lani's face was buried in his chest and she almost felt like she was floating. Being so close to him was a bit intoxicating. She couldn't bring herself to look up into William's face as she felt his eyes gazing down at her and recognized the familiar erotic tension between them. The song ended and the band's leader announced a fifteen-minute break. Lani and William stood on the dance floor, clapping, when another couple came up to them, complimenting them on their dance style.

"You guys have great form. We have these dance evenings here once a week and even competitions if you ever feel like coming again," the Polynesian woman said.

"Oh, thanks, but we're only here for one more night," replied William. "We usually live in Oahu and Maui."

They walked back to their table and Lani said: "It's getting quite late, I guess we should head back?"

"I could dance forever, but I guess you've had a long day," replied William.

They drove back to the hotel in the Range Rover and parked in the parking lot.

William placed his hand lightly on her back again in an intimate manner while they walked along the narrow path among tropical foliage leading to their suites. They stopped at a little outlook on the ocean with a railing and a few benches and looked at the moon shining down on the sparkling ocean. William put his arms around Lani, she looked up into his blue eyes, her heart beating faster and faster as their lips were about to meet each other for a kiss. All of a sudden, Lani snapped awake, like out of a dream. Max! She pulled away abruptly from William and said "I can't," ran ahead to her suite without even looking around one more time.

With shaking fingers, she got her room card out and was barely able to stick it into the opening in the door and let herself in.

She saw her phone on the counter that she had obviously forgotten, picked it up and saw that there were five missed calls from Max...

****

Chapter 18

What a day to wake up to. Lani looked out of the window across the ocean that was glistening in the morning sun. Even though she was in paradise, her stomach was in knots. She was going to have to face William, and Max was already calling her and she didn't feel like answering the phone. She also had a headache from all the drinks last night. She looked at the clock on her phone. There was still enough time for a morning swim before she was supposed to meet William for breakfast, then check out and head back to the airport for their flights to Honolulu and Kahului. At least we're on two different flights, thought Lani.

The swim made her feel a bit better. William was just returning from a walk on the beach as Lani stepped out of the water and walked up toward her suite.

"There's nothing better than getting some fresh air after a bit too much alcohol, isn't there?" he said and grinned at her. He didn't seem upset about last night.

"William, I'm sorry about last night…"

He made a waving motion and played it down. "No worries, Lani, I'm sorry too. We both drank a bit too much last night. Yes, I'm quite attracted to you and we'd make an awesome couple, but I know you love Max. I'll get over it."

"Thanks, William," she replied. "Yes, I like you too, but that should've never happened. Max and I… we belong together…"

"Not another word about it. We'll handle it like adults," he said. "I'll see you at breakfast. We should leave by 9:30 at the latest."

"Okay. See you at breakfast." Sighing a sigh of relief, she picked up her towel and walked up to her suite where she took a hot shower. Her headache was gone. Maybe I should call Max now too, she thought. She still didn't feel ready to talk to him, but then her phone rang and the display said "Max". With a sigh, she answered. There was no use in avoiding him. Sooner or later she would have to talk to him and ask him about last night… She didn't waste any time and cut right to the chase.

"Hey… So, what the heck was going on last night?"

"Hey, Lani… Umm… do you mean Layla answering my phone? Sorry, I was just hanging out with a few coworkers in the bar of Hana Hotel and Andrew's girlfriend drank a bit too much…"

"Okay…"

"She was just seriously being silly… Hey, I have a surprise for you. I'm picking you up in Kahului and I want to take you to meet someone in Kihei…"

"Who is it?"

"I'm not telling… It's a surprise. I'll see you around 12:00. When exactly does your plane land?"

"At 12:10. I can't wait to see you."

Lani's thoughts were racing. Who was he going to take her to meet in Kihei? And: was he telling the truth when he said the girl on the phone was his coworker's girlfriend?

Lani stepped out of the terminal and looked for Max's truck. But he wasn't driving the truck. He was in his friend Danny's Mustang convertible that Lani had been driving. She was excited. It would be fun to drive back home on the Road to Hana in the convertible. He drove up a few feet to stop right next to Lani, got out of the car, walked around it and gave Lani a big kiss.

"I've missed you," he said and gazed deep into her eyes.

"I've missed you too," she said, but couldn't shake off her guilty conscience and gave him a hug to hide her face.

Max took Lani's carry-on case, put it into the trunk and then got back into the driver's seat. He looked at her while she got into the car and asked "Are you hungry? Shall we have lunch first or would you like to see your surprise first? It's about a twenty minute drive…"

"I'm not hungry and I can't wait! William kept getting these upgrades to first class, so I had snacks hanging out of my ears during the flight. Let's see the surprise first!"

"Oh, how is Mr. Jackman?" asked Max, a bit irritated to hear about William.

"He's fine," and she quickly changed the subject. "Boy, the Big Island is beautiful. I'd really like to go there with you…"

Max nodded. "I'd love to go…"

They headed out of Kahului and down the coast toward Wailea and Kihei on State Highway 31. Soon they could see all the resorts in Kihei, strip malls, shopping centers and the beautiful deep blue ocean on the right. Lani was excited to be back in Maui and felt as comfortable with Max as she had from the first day on. She looked at his dark curly hair and classic profile. William might be hot, she thought, but Max looks like a Hawaiian god. She immediately felt bad again for having these thoughts comparing Max and William and tried to shake it off.

Max felt right away that something was wrong. "What's the matter? Why so gloomy?" he asked.

"Oh, nothing," she replied and looked out at the ocean.

Max turned into a shopping plaza and parked.

"What are we doing here?" asked Lani.

Max took her hand and led her through the parking lot up to a little shave ice stand called "Peace Love Shave Ice". The name was written on the little building in colorful psychedelic 70s letters and there was a VW beetle parked in front of it full of peace stickers, 70s flowers and a big yellow sun on the front hood. They walked up to the window and a lovely middle-aged blonde lady with her hair piled up on top of her head and held by a wide colorful bandana beamed at them with a smile that could melt the ice on the counter.

"Aloha, guys!'

"Lani, I want you to meet Allison," he said. "She used to be a friend of your mom's. Glen and Allison went to college in Honolulu together about thirty years ago. But that's not even the biggest news, she also knew Luana by coincidence… Allison and Glen just happened to reconnect and he told me about her."

Allison couldn't take her eyes off of Lani. "Hey, Lani. Wow, you do look like a mirror image of Luana back then," she replied. "Okay, but first I'm sure you'd like to try a shave ice, guys? I can really recommend lilikoi, it's one of my favorites and made with fresh local lilikoi…"

"Sure," answered Lani excited, "lilikoi is my favorite."

"How about you, Max?" asked Allison.

He looked at the long list of choices. "I'll have tiger's blood," he replied.

"Okay, let's do it!"

They sat down on two wooden bar stools in front of the stand and watched Allison work her magic. She took a big clump of ice and fed it into a big professional shave ice machine. Then she carefully stacked the shave ice into a big paper cup, grabbed a bottle of lilikoi syrup and poured it evenly over the ice. She handed the cup with a spoon to Lani.

"There you go!" She turned back around and started making Max's shave ice.

"Mahalo," said Lani and tried it. It was delicious and refreshing, had the perfect consistency and the flavor tasted just like fresh lilikois. She fed Max a spoonful. "Boy, that's delicious," he said as Allison put his cup in front of him.

"So, Allison, how do you know Luana?" asked Lani, eager to hear what Allison had to say.

"I used to hang out with a bunch of hippies in Waikiki when I went to college in Honolulu. That's where I know Glen from, by the way. One day, this girl suddenly showed up. She was very forlorn and didn't really belong there, but she didn't seem to have anywhere else to go, so she hung out with the hippies on the beach for a while until she got a job at an orchid nursery in Palolo Valley…"

Lani looked at Max. That was definitely Luana.

Allison continued: "After that, she and I both met at the beach from time to time and hung out. We had a good connection. I actually majored in biology and was also into orchids back then. I helped out at the shows sometimes. I haven't seen her in years though. Would love to reconnect…" she said thoughtfully. Then she snapped out of her thoughts and looked at Lani. "I had no idea she had a daughter though. But you certainly look like her."

Lani smiled at her. "I was given up for adoption as an infant. She must have had me just before she went to Oahu."

"Wow, I guess she would have just been eighteen or so…"

"Yes and she had run away from home because her father didn't want her to have me…"

"Oh my goodness. Poor thing. She seemed a bit blue sometimes, but she also handled it quite well, I guess. Does she still live in Palolo Valley?"

"Yes, but I can't get a hold of her. It's driving me crazy. I've gone a few times but she seems to be avoiding me… She doesn't seem to want to see me…" said Lani sadly and stared into thin air.

"I wonder if I could contact her and try to find out," proposed Allison, "I'd love to see her again. Please refresh my memory - what's the name of the nursery again?"

"Blue Tropics Orchids and she calls herself Ana now," replied Lani and added nervously: "Please don't mention me yet, let me think about it. I feel like she must be thinking I'm stalking her. I don't quite know how to approach her…"

"You let me handle it, but I won't mention you," said Allison in a motherly manner and put her hand on Lani's arm. They looked at each other and smiled.

****

Chapter 19

As they got back into the car, Max told Lani that he had another surprise for her.

"I thought we could use a break from all the galleries, your mom and the house renovations… and since you've never been up to Haleakala, we're going to drive up there tomorrow morning for sunrise and bike down. My buddy Noa does the tours and is taking us for free. He says he owes me a favor and Pike got me a good rate at the hotel in Paia…

Lani looked at him with big eyes and smiled. That sounded exciting and she was really happy to spend a little 24-hour vacation with Max.

Instead of taking a left to go back to Paia, Max turned right and said: "And now we're going to have lunch and do some sightseeing. You brought your bathing suit, didn't you?"

Max was always so spontaneous and full of surprises. Lani loved that about him. "Of course, I did," she said with a smile and had to hang on to her seat as he turned and accelerated a bit too fast. She gave him that look from the side and he slowed down with a grin.

Their first stop was 5 Palms, a really nice oceanfront restaurant right on Keawakapu Beach. "My friend Ben is the assistant manager here and got us a really nice table," said Max.

They parked the car in the parking lot of a big resort and walked all the way down to the ocean. As usual, everyone knew Max and the host greeted him with a fist bump and a high five. The assistant manager, a tall Polynesian young man walked up to them and Max introduced Lani to him. "This is Ben, Pike's grandson. He's training to become a firefighter in Paia, but works here whenever he can."

"Hey, Lani, nice to meet you. Now, enjoy and have a great lunch." She grinned liking the fact that everyone on the island seemed to know them, but since Max often taught classes in the other fire departments, he was well known all over the island and he wasn't shy about calling in favors to save money when he could.

"Let's not eat too much," said Max, as they sat there with their feet in the sand, looking at the menu. "Lenny invited us to come and eat at Paia Mahi House tonight."

"Okay," replied Lani, but she was starving and so was Max. They almost fought over the bread that was served and ordered crab cakes, seared ahi brushetta, coconut crusted shrimp and a kale salad with watermelon, strawberries, almonds and feta. "We're crazy," said Lani, "but it all sounds so delicious…"

It was delicious. While they were eating and just enjoying the view, Ben came up and asked: "How is everything, guys?" "Delicious," replied Lani, "Thank you, this place is great." As Ben walked away, Max watched him leave and gazed through the restaurant. "Well, look at that." He put his silverware down and had to do a double take.

He leaned slightly over toward Lani and said: "You're not going to believe who is sitting back there…" She looked up from her plate. She couldn't look because she'd have to turn around in a very obvious manner to see who Max was looking at. "Who?"

"I think that's our friend Joseph McAllen having lunch with nobody else than Kate Sterling… I wonder what those two have to do with each other, but I'm not too impressed about her choice of people to hang out with…"

Lani looked at him surprised. "I thought she's watching the girls? What would she be doing here?"

"Alana and Billy offered to watch them overnight and I accepted. It's getting quite expensive if we have to pay Kate $60 per day every time we go somewhere…"

Lani tried to turn around inconspicuously, but she couldn't really without being too obvious, so she got up and went to the ladies' room. Just as she was walking by, still a few tables away from Joseph McAllen and Kate, she saw him hand her quite a big pile of money. They didn't see her.

"That was really strange," she said to Max after she had returned to the table. "He gave her a large amount of money. It almost looked like a drug deal. I don't trust that Kate as far as I can throw her, especially now that she seems to be doing business with McAllen…"

"Yeah, that's really weird. Now I wonder if she has something to do with our supplies disappearing. She could have totally scoped out the house while she was staying there."

"Ugh, that's creepy to imagine that she was staying there all by herself. She might have even let him into the house." Lani shuddered to even think about that possibility.

Joseph McAllen and Kate got up and left the restaurant without seeing Max and Lani who looked down to not be noticed.

"Well, we'll have to keep an eye on her, but let's not let that ruin our day," said Max and waved at their waiter. "Let's order some coffee."

They enjoyed some Kona coffee and then it was time to continue their sightseeing tour of South Maui. Max had an idea. "Lani, should you go and get your bathing suit and change into it here? There won't be any bathrooms at the beach…"

She started to say "I can change in the car…" but then she remembered that they were driving the little convertible…it wouldn't be easy in that car. So she walked out to the car to get her bathing suit out of her carry-on case. Just by coincidence, she saw that Joseph McAllen and Kate were still there, standing in front of a big new pickup truck, looking at some giant blueprints that were spread out over the hood. They didn't notice her.

Of course, Lani couldn't see what the blueprints were, but she wondered if they were for the proposed construction at Hamoa Beach…

After lunch, Lani and Max went "beach hopping". He showed her some of his favorite beaches along the south coast including the Black Sand Beach in Makena that could only be reached on a very narrow and bumpy dirt road. The usual lush tropical vegetation became dry and dead looking. Max explained: "This part of the island gets less than ten inches of rain per year." In the back of the beach were black/reddish hills of cinder cone. They continued to Max's favorite beach in this area, Big Beach, with beautiful white sand where they got some cold drinks from a stand in the parking lot, frolicked in the water and hung out for a while. They got back into the car and Max drove all the way south to La Perouse Bay in the Ahihi Kinau Natural Area Reserve which ended in a single lane road with some private homes on the left and the beautiful ocean on the right with a very rocky shoreline. The last stretch to the bay was unpaved and riddled with lava rocks. Max had to drive around several bigger boulders and finally stopped. "I can't continue with this car. We'll have to come back with my truck or even better a Jeep. I think the swimming and snorkeling area is closed to the public right now anyhow. But you can see how beautiful and lonely it is here. I just wanted you to see how nice it is."

Lani looked out across the lava rock at the roaring dark blue ocean. "It's beautiful," she said.

They turned around and drove all the way back to Paia without stopping, which took a little over an hour because it was rush hour and traffic was heavy. Neither of them cared – they were together in paradise. They finally arrived at the bed & breakfast in Paia and checked in. Just as they were entering their room, Lani's phone rang. It was Tom from the nursery in Hilo.

"Hi, Tom."

"Hi, Lani. I wanted to let you know that I made an attempt to talk to Ana about her past. She will not open up about it and it seems there is a bitterness and guilty conscience that overshadows her. I think you should just confront her. Otherwise, she will never get over the past. I wanted to let you know that she and I are flying to Honolulu the day after tomorrow to get ready for an orchid show next week. I don't know if I'm doing the right thing, but I think you guys have to connect. Maybe you can come to that orchid show…"

"Thanks for caring so much, Tom, let me check my schedule and call you back. I do think that I'm scheduled to return to Oahu next week. So, is the orchid show in Oahu?"

"Yes, in the Convention Center. It's huge."

"I'd love to go there anyhow. Let me check my schedule and I'll let you know when the photo exhibition in Oahu begins. I'm supposed to be there for the opening night…"

"Okay, I'll wait to hear from you," replied Tom.

Lani and Max were finally alone. Their room was beautiful. Lani remembered the beautiful view from her last visit here six months ago and stepped onto the little terrace to take a peek. She couldn't help it, but her thoughts wandered off to William and what she had almost done. She had tried all day to forget about last night… She tried to talk herself into thinking that the alcohol had made her almost kiss him, but she had to admit to herself that it was also his charm. Even though she loved Max more than her own life, she was charmed and attracted to William. She had to avoid William… but how, with several gallery openings coming up? She shook off the thoughts and tried to enjoy the moment. When she walked back inside, Max was sprawled across the bed, fast asleep. She grinned. She was awfully tired too, cuddled up against him and was also asleep within minutes.

When they woke up, neither knew where they were at first as it was already dark. "Oh, boy," said Max, looking at his watch. "We barely have enough time to take a shower and rush over to meet Lenny and Tammy."

Lani quickly jumped in the shower and Max followed her.

Twenty minutes later, Max and Lani came jogging up to Paia Mahi House, out of breath and walked inside. Lenny and his girlfriend Tammy were already sitting at the best table in the house, outside on a little patio. They got up and hugged Max and Lani and Lenny waved at the waitress to bring a few more beers.

They all lifted their bottles and proposed a toast. "Cheers," said Kenny. "To good friends."

Max started telling them about Joseph McAllen and Kate Sterling immediately.

"So, I told you about the builder who wants to build condos all along the coast in Hana and that that someone has been stealing our construction supplies and tools, right?"

Kenny and Tammy nodded.

"It turns out that our housesitter is obviously secretly meeting this same builder as far away from Hana as possible. We happened to see them at 5 Palms during lunch today."

"Wow, that's weird," said Kenny. "Do you think she's helping him by staying at your house when you're gone?"

"I can't imagine why of all people the new veterinarian in Hana would do that, but maybe that's just a cover."

"You should create a trap for them and try to catch them red-handed." proposed Lenny. "Tell them you're going somewhere and then don't and have the girl watch the dogs, and while she thinks you're out of town, they might plan another ripoff. Have you informed the police at all yet?"

"Yes, I've reported the incidents because I have to for the insurance."

"Then have Josh from the Hana Police help, he's cool. Tammy and I will be glad to come over and help too."

Max and Lani looked at each other. "That's a good idea, Lenny," said Max. "We can pretend that we're going to Oahu for another exhibit and then we just stay with someone. I should really work on installing cameras."

"So, what else is new?" asked Lenny while some appetizers were being served.

"We're biking down Haleakala tomorrow morning."

"Oh, wow, so you guys have to get up early, like at 3 am?"

"No, we have to be there at 3 am… I guess we can't stay too late tonight…"

****

Chapter 20

The alarm on Max's phone rattled, tearing them out of a sound sleep at 2 am. It felt like they had just fallen asleep but since they were excited, their adrenaline pumping, they jumped out of their beds and got ready to drive over to the check-in location for the Haleakala bike tour in Haiku. "Don't forget your fleece jacket, hat and gloves," Max reminded Lani.

It was slow going at the check-in. People were yawning and still sleepy, but everyone was in a good mood. Max walked up to his friend Noa and they bumped fists.

"Hey, Noa, this is my girlfriend Lani. What's up with this torturous time?"

"Gotta get there on time for sunrise! Aloha, Lani, nice to meet you." He shook Lani's hand. Then he looked at them, assessing their sizes in his mind, turned around, grabbed two heavy-duty motocross helmets, two sets of rain jackets and rain pants and handed everything to them. "I'll chat with you guys in the van, I'm actually driving today. Go ahead and grab some coffee and pastries for breakfast. There's nothing up there," he said and grinned at them. "Oh, and don't forget to sign the release form and let my buddies over there size you for bikes."

"Okay, thanks," they both said simultaneously and Max added: "See you later."

They got in a line to sign release forms and be sized for bikes and then they walked over to get some coffee, breakfast muffins and fruit, but soon it was time to get in the vans and depart for the crater.

It was still pitch black and for half an hour or so they just drove through the hilly countryside which suddenly became a steep uphill climb with more and more curves. The countryside went from trees on both sides to volcanic rock and sparsely populated low shrubs. It looked like they were on a different planet. Noa, who was driving the van, informed the passengers through an intercom system:

"It's a 37 mile drive from sea level to the 10,023 foot summit with the world's highest elevation gain in the shortest distance. On our drive, we're going to pass through just as many ecosystems as you would driving from Mexico to Canada. Sit back and enjoy the warmth, guys. It's going to be about 37 degrees on the summit when we get out in about…." He looked at his watch, "twenty minutes." Finally, the vans arrived at the summit and everyone disembarked. "We still have about half an hour until sunrise, so use the restroom, take your time and look around or relax in the warm van," said Noa. "You can walk around in the roped off areas, please don't step outside of the ropes. Some of the plants are protected and we want to avoid them being trampled. The ecosystem up here is very delicate as you can imagine."

Max and Lani got out and braved the cold. The moon, now a waning crescent, was still out, but the stars were fading fast as the sun was about to rise above the horizon. They walked up to the crater and looked down. It was unreal. The entire crater was 7.5 miles long, 2.5 miles wide and had a circumference of about 20 miles. Its floor was about 2,300 feet below the Haleakala Visitor Center, situated 9,740 feet high on the rim. Reddish cinder cones were scattered across the floor of the crater as well as black lava beds… It looked surreal in the twilight right before sunrise and was already bathed in a shade of brownish-red.

Max and Lani found a prime spot to watch the sunrise and stood looking across the crater. Lani found the cold to be a perfect opportunity to cuddle up against Max. They held each other, looked into the distance across the crater, and Lani snuggled closer against Max's chest to defer the cold. They locked eyes and leaned in for a kiss.

"Pretty good method to warm up," joked Noa, as he stepped up and patted Max's back. They both looked at him and grinned. "Hey, it's great to see you, man," said Max.

"You too, you look great," replied Noa. "Now watch guys, the sun is coming up…"

Everyone stood there, oohing and aahing as the sun slowly began to rise over the crater and bathe everything with a bright red light. It was amazing. "Just beautiful," said Lani as she took picture after picture. "Let me take a picture of you guys," said Noa and Lani handed him her phone. They both posed for Noa with a smile and gave each other another kiss.

After a while, everyone got back into the vans and they drove down to the spot where the bike ride would start. All of the bikes had been unloaded out of the dedicated bike van into the parking lot and everyone suited up in their rain gear, helmets and gloves and climbed onto the bikes. It felt a bit awkward to have the big chunky motocross helmet on, but they got used to it.

"Wow," yelled Lani at Max, who was in back of her, while she pulled the hand brakes as hard as she could and stopped for a second. The speed the bike quickly rose to was incredibly scary with the steep road heading downhill and took her breath away. "Just pace it at your own speed," said Max. "I'll stay behind you to watch and make sure you're okay." "Okay, let me try again," she replied. The others were already ahead, but the van with Noa was always in back of them, keeping an eye on them. She started coasting down the road again and felt the cold wind in her face, but it was such an amazing experience that she got distracted and started enjoying the ride. She simply coasted, having to press the breaks the entire time, but she got up to a good speed and it was extremely fun. A few Hawaiian nene (geese) walked across the street and they had to stop. Some curves were extreme hairpin turns and she often felt like stopping again, but she hung in there driving extremely slow when she felt like it. She laughed at Max, both of them enjoying the ride and they stopped to take pictures. Soon the side of the steep road lined by nothing but lava rock turned into pineapple and sugar cane fields as the sun became so warm that they had to remove their gloves and jackets.

After about an hour, they arrived at the Kula Lodge where Max took the lead, taking a left into a driveway and making signs for Lani to follow him. "Time for breakfast," he said.

They parked their bikes and walked toward the old cozy wooden lodge. To Lani's delight, there was an entire field of yellow-brownish Paphiopedilum (lady's slipper) orchids. She took picture after picture and was beside herself with excitement "To think I could grow these outside in Hana. It probably never gets colder than 55 degrees…" she said. They stepped into the dining room of the lodge with a beautiful view onto a tropical garden, with fields, mountains and ocean as a backdrop and ordered coffee, pancakes with coconut syrup and an omelette to share.

Lani beamed at Max. "This is so much fun, Max, thanks for doing this with me."

"Of course," he replied. "You have to see more of Maui rather than being stuck in Hana all the time."

"There are so many things in and around Hana I haven't done yet. I'd love to go up to Fagan's Cross or to the Red Sand Beach…"

Max nodded. "We'll change that once the house is done and all the craziness with the exhibitions is over," he replied.

That comment reminded Lani of William. She froze and her guilty conscience returned. She wished she didn't have to go back and meet him in Oahu, but he was the head of production of the whole traveling exhibition. There was no way she could avoid him…

"What's the matter, Lani? Why suddenly so glum?"

"Oh, nothing," she shook her thoughts off and quickly made an excuse. "I was thinking of my mom who doesn't seem to want to see me…"

Max reached over the table and put his hand on hers. "Well, you'll find out. Maybe she'll change her mind if either Allison or Tom talk to her. Or even Bianca. I think that might be a good idea…"

Lani nodded and looked out of the window at the mountains and the ocean in the distance. Now she was lying to Max. What was she going to do? Or was it maybe not even that big of a deal and she was making a mountain out of a molehill?

****

Chapter 21

After dropping off the bikes and gear at the shop, Lani and Max drove straight back to Koki Beach House and stopped, hoping for some Huli Huli chicken for lunch, but the stand was closed with a sign "Closed due to demonstration at Community Center".

They had been so busy during their little 24-hour vacation that they had forgotten about the demonstration and the community meeting at noon regarding the construction at Hamoa Beach and the request for an alteration of the building code. They parked their car, ran into the house to quickly let the dogs out and drove back over to join the demonstration.

Cars were parked all the way down the road to Hana Bay and past the Hana Hotel. At least one hundred people were there, which was a lot for a little town like Hana, with signs like: "No construction on Hamoa Beach", "Don't let Hana become the next Waikiki", "Go away, bulldozers", "Our land is sacred", "Stop Hamoa Beach Mega Development". Two police cars were there with several officers, making sure that the demonstration remained peaceful.

Inside the Helene Hall Community Center, the mayor of Hana was listening to the group of builders and their leader, Joseph McAllen, describe the oceanfront community they had planned as they projected the blueprint onto a screen and argued with the young Hawaiian lawyer George Kimono, who the protestors had hired to represent them. He was originally from Hana and had just finished his internship in a big law firm in Honolulu. The demonstration had just ended and the demonstrators were entering the building, filling the seats.

"This is a win-win for the whole community. The project will bring wealth and prosperity to the area," continued Joseph McAllen in his presentation.

The residents in the audience all started mumbling simultaneously and one of them yelled: "People in Hana don't want condo complexes! They want nature!"

Another one yelled "We have enough tourists in the area stampeding through Hana!"

The major interrupted. "Okay, folks. We need to let Mr. McAllen finish his presentation. Then Mr Kimono, and only Mr. Kimono, can present your arguments. Everyone else who interrupts the meeting will be escorted out of the building by security…"

Joseph McAllen's plans were worse than anyone had expected. They would even require a further entrance to Hamoa Beach through the hills in back of it, because the new community was supposed to have direct beach access and an entire area of over twenty acres past the beach would have to be bulldozed. He continued explaining there would be a promenade along the ocean, a restaurant, a café and another grocery store, even though the small town of Hana already had an overkill with three…. Max and Lani looked at each other. Their remote paradise was extremely endangered. George Kimono started listing the arguments against the construction to thunderous applause.

The mayor thanked both parties and ended the meeting. "I will take all arguments into consideration and the town of Hana will make a decision for our next meeting on September 15."

Everyone threw dirty looks at Joseph McAllen. He definitely wouldn't be very popular if he succeeded with implementing his plans. They all filed out of the meeting room and stood outside for a while, talking amongst themselves. Lani looked around to see if Kate was there with Joseph McAllen, but she wasn't. She walked up to her friend Malea from the Huli Huli chicken stand. "Hey there, Malea, are you going to open the stand back up this afternoon?"

"No," Malea replied. "My boss is going to let me have the rest of the day off, so the stand will be closed. Sorry."

"That's okay, enjoy your day off." Lani looked at Max. "Shall we get some Thai food instead?

"Is the Pope Catholic?" Max asked and laughed. Thai food was his favorite. Lani laughed as well. "Yeah, what a question, I guess."

They went over to the Thai food truck, which was within walking distance and they didn't seem to be the only ones who had that idea. The benches were already full and there was a long line at the table where orders were taken. Joseph McAllen was sitting at one of the tables, accompanied by Kate and his Barbie doll girlfriend Dolly. Kate seemed to be embarrassed when she saw Max and Lani. "Hey, guys," she said, got up to say hello to them and walked up to the line. She wanted to say something about her opinion on the construction at Hamoa Beach and having lunch with the obvious enemy, but Max interrupted her.

"Hey, Kate," replied Max. "Oh, Lani, shall we ask Kate about Tuesday? We have to go to Oahu again for a quick trip and wondered if you could watch the dogs again?"

Kate smiled. "Sure, I'd love to. Those girls are my favorites."

"Okay. Lani or I will call you. We haven't booked our flights yet, so we're not sure when we have to leave," said Max. Lani nodded.

"Great. Talk to you then," Kate replied and walked back to her table. Joseph McAllen made sure to wave at them, remembering they had rescued him and Dolly on the Road to Hana. "Hey, my rescuers! Maybe I'll get your house in the end after all! You can sell it and move to a quieter spot once the condos are done! Hahaha!"

They were broiling but turned away, pretending not to hear Joseph. Kate was again embarrassed, her face flushing and looking down sadly. Finally, it was their turn to order and Joseph and his party left. "Maybe it's an advantage that it always takes so long here… At least we don't have to listen to Joseph anymore while we're eating," said Max relieved that they didn't have to put up with any more annoying comments.

****

Chapter 22

Lani and Max were incredibly happy they had no plans for the rest of the day. Lani felt like she had been on the road constantly since she had returned, which was actually true. She couldn't wait to spend some quiet time in and around Hana, her new home, for the next few days. As soon as they were home, they packed up their swim gear, harnessed the dogs that were happy to finally see them, grabbed their surfboards and walked down to the beach.

"It's not easy to hold a dog and a surfboard at the same time," grinned Lani, since Lilly was pulling hard, following some scent she had picked up. Max laughed as he watched Lilly pull Lani down the road. "Maybe we should switch," he replied. "I think Lucy is a bit easier to handle." "It's fine, we're almost there," said Lani. They had already arrived at the stairs leading down to Hamoa Beach. She looked down at the beautiful ocean, unhooked Lilly's leash and let her run down the stairs, which was not easy for the plump short-legged Basset Hound. Lani watched her, worried. "I don't think I can let them do that on a regular basis. It's really bad for their joints."
"We'll have to build them a little lift," laughed Max and watched Lucy jump down the stairs. She had a bit of an easier time since she was younger and thinner than Lilly.

They reached the beach, set their beach bag onto some rocks in the back and Max took his t-shirt off and Lani her terry cloth dress. They started slathering each other with reef-safe sunscreen, but the young lovers got distracted as their eyes met and their lips closed in for a kiss, but, once again, Lilly had enough of the water and had returned, jumping up on them.
"There we go again," laughed Lani and ran down to the water with her surfboard. She patted the surfboard, trying to make Lilly jump on it with her, but she had no luck. Lilly ran away and galloped down the beach along the shoreline. Lani laughed and watched her run away. She

turned her surfboard toward the ocean, stretched out on it and started paddling past the first wave break. Max followed her, while Lucy just sat in the sand wagging her tail, watching them paddle further and further out into the deep blue water. They loved surfing together in the roaring waves, forgetting the world and all worries around them. Max kept a sharp eye on Lani, since the water was very choppy, giving her pointers, but she had quickly become quite adept. "Now start paddling as hard as you can!" he yelled against the noisy surf, as he saw a perfect wave approach. They both paddled simultaneously next to each other and finally, just as the wave was about to break, they both rose up on their surfboards to ride the wave, as its momentum pushed them most of the way to the shore.

"That was epic," said Max with a big smile and held his hand up to give Lani a high-five. She was also beaming and walked up to him to join him on the high five. She hugged him, looked up into his face and stroked back his curly black hair that was hanging into his eyes. They just stood there in the afternoon sun gazing into each other's eyes with the waves lapping around their feet.

Finally, Lucy trotted up and barked. Lani let go of Max and chased her down the beach, clapping playfully. Suddenly, she realized that Lilly was nowhere to be seen. She looked around and walked over to Max who was drying himself off at the rocks. "Max, I don't see Lilly anywhere, do you?" He looked up and down the beach and couldn't see her anywhere either. They walked up to a couple sitting in the sand and asked "Have you guys seen another beige-white Basset Hound, a little bigger than this one?" The couple shook their heads. "No, only that one," the man replied and pointed at Lucy. "She is adorable," added the woman. "Thanks," replied Lani and said to Max as they walked away: "That crazy dog is going to be the death of me. I hope she didn't drown! She could have swum straight out into the ocean. I should have been more careful…"

"I'm sure she's fine," replied Max who was able to remain calmer than Lani. She was quite upset. Max proposed: "Why don't I take Lucy home and check if Lilly's there while the you walk the other way down the road and look. She could have gone up to the street and toward the same area as the other day…"

"Yeah, she probably did, it looked like she found something there last time…" Lani repied. "Call me if Lilly is home and if not, come back and join me?"

"Okay," replied Max while he put Lucy's harness and leash on.

"Can we leave the surfboards here for now?"

"Yeah, nobody steals anything here," replied Max. He hesitated and added grinning: "except building supplies, I guess… I'll see you in a bit. You should walk over that way, there's another path leading up to the street at the end of the beach. She might still be there…" He pointed to the right of the dark hills surrounding Hamoa Beach.

"Okay, got it." Lani took Lilly's leash and harness and walked down to the other end of the beach calling Lilly's name. She wished she had worn sneakers, but unfortunately, she was only wearing flip-flops. She carefully walked up what appeared to be a former asphalt access road for boats or cars, but it was quite overgrown. The asphalt was broken and barely walkable in her flip-flops. She finally got up to the road, took a left and had to walk a few hundred yards past some black lava rock hills until she arrived at the wooded area with the overgrown path that Lilly had run to the last time.

Suddenly Lani stopped. She thought she had heard Lilly's typical Basset Hound baying and continued down the narrow path straight toward the ocean, which was totally overgrown and barely a path. She pushed tree branches out of the way, ducking down and squeezing past thick bushes full of thorns that were scratching her up almost losing her flip-flops several times. It was absolutely quiet with the exception of the roaring ocean in the distance and some birds screeching from time to time. She turned around and wondered whether she would be able to find her way back. The path was barely recognizable and quite steep going downhill toward the ocean. Finally, she came to a small clearing and discovered Lilly, who was digging in a rocky area. "Lilly!" called Lani, "come here right now!" She walked closer to Lilly and realized they were standing in what might be an ancient cemetery! There were some toppled overgrown gravestones, mostly just remnants, but Lani could still recognize them as gravestones and realized this must once have been a cemetery. She quickly hooked Lilly's leash onto her harness and held her while she tried to read the inscriptions, which was made difficult by many years of neglected overgrowth and plant debris. She wasn't sure if she should even touch anything, but she pulled some weeds off of a broken gravestone, wiped the old debris off with her hand as best she could and read 181, the last number was broken off. She just stood there, in awe of what Lilly might have found: an ancient Polynesian gravesite? Wow, she thought to herself. Nobody's going to be building any oceanfront condos with this here.

Finally Lani heard Max yelling: "Lani! Are you here?" She replied: "Here, Max! I have her!" After a few more minutes, he stepped out into the clearing and saw what she had found. His mouth was hanging wide open. "Wow, that seriously looks like the remains of old burial grounds. That's a game changer. There won't be any oceanfront condos here if this is what we think it is. It might be sacred and will be protected. Good job, Lilly. I wonder what led her here?"

"Me too. She was digging. I hope she wasn't trying to dig up some old bones," replied Lani. "But it's weird… It's already the second time she's come here."

"We need to contact a local archeologist or someone who knows how to handle this properly,"said Max, deep in his thoughts. "I wonder if Ana Kamealoha, the old healer, would know what to do. She is the oldest person in the area I know… Or maybe we can ask my old history teacher from High School…"

He looked at Lani and saw how scratched up she was, since she was only wearing her sundress and flip-flops. "First we need to get you home. Your arm is bleeding…" He walked up to her, checking his pockets for tissues, which, of course, he didn't have. "We need to get home and wash that," he said in his nurturing manner. "Let me take Lilly." He stretched his hand out to take Lilly's leash and they made their way back up the jungle path. He looked down at Lilly and said, as if talking to a child, "and you, young lady, are going to be famous for what you discovered…" Lani grinned.

"I guess we don't have to mark this area, do we?" Max asked Lani as they had arrived back at the street. She shook her head. "No, I'd recognize it. You can tell it used to be an old path…"
She took a closer look at Lilly. "Max, do you notice that Lilly is limping?"

"Yeah, you might want to check if she has something in one of her paws. There were lots of thorns down there…"

Lani bent over Lilly and lifted all four paws, stroking over them to see if she had stepped into something, but she couldn't find anything.

They slowly walked back to Koki Beach House where Max immediately started making some phone calls. First he called Pekelo Kamealoha, Ana Kamealoha's granddaughter, who ran the Thai food truck close to Charles Lindberg's grave. Ana was the 95 year-old wise Hawaiian healer who might remember things that had happened in and around Hana no one else knew about anymore.

"Sure, I will ask Ana, but why don't you guys stop by and talk to her. She might enjoy seeing Lani and maybe she will have some ideas about her mother as well."

"Okay, I actually have to work tomorrow, but Lani can probably come over." He looked at Lani and she nodded.

"Of course. I'll let Ana know. Late morning is good or early afternoon, after Ana's nap."

After he had ended the call, Max called Hana Mikelai, another very elderly lady who lived in town; she had been his history teacher in High School but was now retired. She was quite excited and explained to Max: "There is a strict Hawaiian tradition called hūnākele, in which a person is buried in total secrecy and the location is never to be disclosed. King Kamehameha was buried that way. The Hawaiians believe it was necessary to protect his mana, his power. I'm not saying that one of the graves you found could be King Kamehameha's – that would probably be a bit more elaborate – but, you never know, it could be some other important person's or even a ruler's…"

"Hana, do you know if there are any archeologists on the island?"

"No, but if there are old graves, there might also be an overgrown temple, a heiau, close by. That also means that many people would have to go down there to do research and open up the area… but I guess that's better than dealing with oceanfront condos…"

"I agree… do you have any idea who in the town I'd contact regarding something like this?"

"Probably the mayor's office, but if you have any reason to think that the mayor is on the builder's side, you might want to find someone who'd be in a position to confirm that the graves you found are to be protected beforehand."

"Yeah, good point. Okay, thanks, Hana, you've been a great help."

"Bye, Max, I'm glad you're doing so well. Keep me posted. I'll try to think of someone who could help you, maybe one of my old colleagues. One of them belongs to the Hawaiian Historical Society. Oh, and you could check at Kahanu Garden, of course."

"That's a great idea. Thanks, Hana."

Max told Lani what Hana had said and she marveled at the information and what Lilly had possibly discovered.

"And I think it's a really good idea if you go and see Ana. She can see you tomorrow in the late morning or early afternoon. Pekelo said she might also have some new insight on Luana."

"Great, thanks."

"Oh, and don't forget the roofers are coming back tomorrow. They finally have new shingles. You will want to avoid being home anyhow, it will be quite noisy…"

She nodded. "Yeah, I remember how annoying it was when my old house got a new roof. Maybe I can go and visit my grandparents. I also might take Lilly to the vet if she doesn't stop limping by tomorrow…"

Chapter 23

The next morning Lilly was still limping and Lani couldn't find the reason, so she decided to take her to the vet's office and see Kate or another one of her colleagues. Afterwards, she'd stop by her grandparents and still have enough time to go see Ana in the early afternoon. Max had left for work early.

First, she greeted the roofers who arrived early and were already banging and hammering, replacing the old shingles on the roof. She sighed a sigh of relief. She was happy that the work was finally continuing. Not much had happened since she had returned from the Hudson Valley and there was a fixed date in Malani's testament that the house had to be finished by. They had to finally figure out who was stealing the supplies.

She harnessed and leashed the dogs, then was confronted with a new situation she hadn't thought about yet. It was about time to get her own car, since Basset Hounds really didn't belong in a Mustang convertible. For now, she just closed the soft top so that they wouldn't jump out while she drove. The girls were pretty good passengers as long as Lani let them stand next to each other with their front paws on the middle console. The problem was that the roads weren't usually as curvy as they were in and around Hana, but she drove very carefully until she could get some type of car, like a station wagon, where she could put them in the rear hatch.

After taking a right onto Haneoo Road, she followed the road toward the left past the Huli Huli chicken stand where she briefly honked, waving at her friend Malea who was already working. "Hey there," she yelled as she looked up from the grill full of juicy Huli Huli chicken. I'll have to stop on the way back and get some of that for dinner tonight, thought Lani. The girls had their noses up in the air, sniffing furiously. They could obviously smell the delicious Huli Huli chicken.

Lani continued through picturesque "downtown" Hana, drove into a little side street and stopped in front of the vet's office, a little building in the back of a big lawn. A sign above the front door said: "Hana Veterinary Clinic". Lani walked inside with the Bassets and Ashley, the receptionist, jumped up as she saw them, ran around the reception desk and bent down to pet the girls, who were jumping up on her, full of excitement. They loved the attention and sensed when someone was a dog lover.

"Oh, my goodness, who do we have here?" asked Ashley.

Lani pointed at Lilly. "This is Lilly," then she pointed at Lucy, "and this is Lucy. I'm Lani. I had called about Lilly. Nice to meet you," she said while she shook Ashley's hand.

"Nice to meet you. I'm Ashley. We don't have too many Bassets around here. They're adorable."

Lani smiled. "Thank you."

"Could I have you fill in some new patient forms?" asked Ashley, handing her a clipboard with some forms.

"Sure," replied Lani as she sat down to start completing the forms, but she was quickly called into a treatment room and got up again, taking the clipboard with her.

Lani had to wait a few minutes in the treatment room, but then Kate came in, as usual like a whirlwind. She almost reminded Lani of Pippi Longstocking, her red curly hair popping out of her ponytail, sticking wildly up in all directions, her face full of freckles and a broad smile on her face. Lani had a hard time thinking she might be cooperating with Joseph McAllen, helping him steal their building supplies... "Hey, Lani, hey, girls…" She kneeled down to pet Lilly and Lucy and while she was down there, she started examining Lilly's legs and feet. "So, when did this limping start?" she asked. "Yesterday, she ran away and walked down this jungle path with quite a lot of thorny bushes. I thought she stepped into something, but I can't find anything."

"I guess if we don't find anything, we might have to take an x-ray."

Kate reached out for Lilly's leash, hooked it back up to her harness, opened the door of the treatment room and had her walk up and down the hallway to see how badly she was limping. "She's definitely favoring the left front paw," she said, taking a closer look at that paw again. And there it was, a sliver of a thorn, very deep between two pads. Now it was a very easy fix. All she needed was a pair of tweezers and it was out. She showed it to Lani. "That must have hurt quite a bit," said Kate.

Lani looked at it and couldn't believe that she hadn't been able to find it.

"I'll give you some antibiotic ointment that you can put in between her pads, but it will probably heal without any problems."

"Thank you."

"How is everything else going? Are you still going out of town the day after tomorrow?"

"Yup. We're still planning on it if you're okay."

"By the way, regarding Joseph McAllen..."

Lani perked her ears. What was Kate going to say about him?

"I just wanted to let you know that I definitely don't agree with what he's planning here in Hana. It's a bit of a tough situation for me, because he's my uncle. We actually hadn't spoken in a while, but he asked me to take care of his old German Shephard who's blind and deaf. He's paying me really well and I need the money. You can say what you want about him, but he is an animal lover. He thinks it's better for the dog to stay with me since he has to travel to the mainland so much. But other than that all he thinks about is making more and more money."

"Wow, that must be a tough situation," replied Lani.

"Yeah, my father asked me to help him out with his dog."

"Well, maybe we won't have to worry about the construction too much longer if the people of Hana win the case," said Lani, "and he'll move on to a different location."

"Yeah, I hope so. Hana is certainly busy enough."

"Well, thanks Kate and thanks for letting me know about your uncle! I have to go..."

"Okay, see you soon. Bye girls, be careful where you walk, Lilly!" she said, grinning at Lani.

Lani squeezed the big stout Basset ladies back into the little car, drove further out of town and stopped at the Island General Store close to the Maui Farms Stand on the edge of Hana. The Island General Store was the place people stopped to get some last snacks and sandwiches on their way back to Kahului or Paia or the first stop they made after driving all the way from Paia to Hana which most people usually did as a day trip to stop at all of the beautiful sights on the way. Lani's grandparents, Kumu and Leila Kalekilio, were already waiting for her. They were having their employees take care of the store for a couple of hours and had prepared an early lunch for Lani and themselves.

Kumu and Leila were just walking out of the store when Lani drove up, parked the car and let the dogs out. They ran toward the elderly couple.

"Ohhhh, you guys are so sweet!" said Leila while Kumu bent over to pet them as they almost knocked him over. "Let's go inside, they can play in the courtyard. They can't get out there," said Kumu.

As soon as they were inside, they all hugged each other again. Lani was always a bit restrained toward Kumu since she didn't quite know if Luana would ever forgive him.

Leila and Kumu had not only made a terrific lunch for Lani that they now took out to a table in the courtyard, but they also surprised her with two old photo albums Leila found from the time when Luana was growing up. The courtyard was a beautiful little retreat full of potted plumerias and specimen orchid plants. Lani admired the beautiful overgrown orchids.

"Wow, these are unbelievable…"

"Some are Luana's, so imagine how old they are," said Leila. "I think I've given half the town of Hana divisions of these in the past thirty years. That's how well they grow…"

While she walked around the courtyard, Lani stopped in front of a gigantic old Cattleya George King "Serendipity" that was in full bud. It was on a big stand in a gigantic wooden basket. "I'd love a division of this," she said, "it's one of my favorite orchids."

They had wonderful mahi sandwiches with homemade cole slaw and afterwards Lani's favorite, lilikoi pie with coffee. The Bassets were on guard the entire time, hoping that some crumbs or bigger nibbles would fall under the table.

"I'm stuffed," said Lani. "Thank you very much. That was delicious."

"My pleasure," replied Leila. "Why don't we go inside and look at the albums. It's too sunny out here."

Kumu and Lani nodded, got up and took the dishes inside the small but comfortable house. Lani and Leila sat down on the big overstuffed couch, while Kumu paced nervously back and forth, staying within eye and ear contact of Lani and Leila so he could hear and see everything. Lani could tell that the Luana subject still made him very nervous.

"Have you been able to get in touch with her yet?" asked Leila.

"No, I've been to the nurseries three times already and she's never there. I have also spoken with some of her old friends and the nursery manager who has known her since she first started working there, but no luck yet."

"Maybe Glen could try to get in touch with her…"

"There are so many people who want to talk to her already, that I feel like I'm pushing her away. She must feel overwhelmed."

Leila nodded. Lani was probably right. She opened up the first photo album and Lani felt as if she was looking at her own baby pictures. Photos of happy days at the beach, at Seven Sacred Pools, birthday parties, Luana's first day of school and other important events in her life, her confirmation, her and her friends, among them Glen and Alana. It looked like Luana had had a happy carefree childhood. Only her father's fear of what the neighbors would think had driven her away. Lani looked up at him in her thoughts. He was such a kind looking fragile old man that she couldn't imagine he had been so harsh thirty years ago, but times changed and people did too.

****

Chapter 24

Soon Lani had to leave, because she was still scheduled to go and see the old Hawaiian healer Ana Kamealoha.

She stopped briefly at Koki Beach House and walked the dogs a bit to give them some exercise. Then she continued her way on the "Road past Hana" as she and Max called it. For a while the road curved along oceanfront meadows and private residences but then it became extremely narrow, pavement long worn away. Lani drove down a narrow rocky area in the road with a 180 degree wall going up on the inside and a 180 degree drop on the ocean side, wishing she had a different car than a Mustang convertible with small wheels. Thankfully nobody came toward her and she could take her time without feeling pressured. She drove as slowly as she was comfortable. The gorgeous waterfall Wailua Falls came up in the steep curve. Lani rolled down the passenger window, enjoying the noise of the roaring waterfall and watching the spraying water with thousands of gallons constantly pounding down toward the ocean. On the left after the curve was a little parking lot where the artist Laura Cattleya set up her stand sometimes, but she wasn't there today. Lani continued on the curvy road until she arrived at Haleakala National Park, passing over a bridge with the bottom of the Seven Sacred Pools underneath. She passed the big parking lot on her left and continued a few more miles until she came up to the sign for Charles Lindbergh's Grave pointing to the left and the Thai Food Truck next to the old rusty antique car on the right. She pulled in front of the food truck and walked over to greet Pekelo, the old healer Ana Kamealoha's granddaughter, who ran the food truck and was a superb chef.

"Aloha, Lani," Pekelo greeted her and said: "wait, I have something for you." She was working on some chicken satay scewers and handed a couple to Lani. "Mahalo," said Lani and, even though she was still stuffed from lunch with her grandparents, she took the scewers and tried them. "I just had a big lunch, but I'll never turn down Thai," she said with a broad smile.

Pekelo smiled back at her. "Ana is already waiting for you. Can you find your way to the back? I have a whole tour group arriving shortly."

"Sure, thanks." Lani walked down the driveway and around the house into a beautiful tropical garden, where Ana was sitting just like the last time Lani had been here: She was wearing a haku, a tropical Hawaiian flower crown, on top of her long white hair, a long wide flowery mu'umu'u and open-toed sandals. She seemed to be meditating again, sitting by the fire pit containing smoldering black lava rocks. She saw Lani, but didn't interrupt what she was doing. She made signs for Lani to sit down across from her. Lani sat down with her legs crossed, watching Ana full of tension. Ana kept staring into the fire pit and finally said:

"I see Luana. She seems to be running away from something, but she is also curious and keeps turning around, slowing down more and more. I think she is ready to see you, but she is scared. You must go and try to see her again. This time you need to go to Oahu. I see lots of orchids…"

Then she got up, walked around the fire pit and gave Lani, who had risen from her seat as well, a hug while she examined her face. "You truly remind me of Luana, you both are so gorgeous."

"Thank you, Tutu," replied Lani. "I am returning to Oahu in a few days and will look for her."

"Pomaika'i," replied Ana, "good luck. Let me walk you up front."

They walked slowly through the beautiful tropical garden and Ana pointed out several herbs to Lani in her herb garden. "These are the herbs you should grow in your garden, Lani." She pointed at the first one. "This one is kava, pounded and then soaked in water and drank as a tea, it helps against headaches and joint pains. This one is Mamaki." She snapped off a cutting, gave it to Lani, pointing at the big shrub. "You harvest and dry the leaves. You can also use them in a tea. It's for a cough and sore throat." The next plant had deeply veined shiny dark leaves. It was a noni plant. "It's very good for high blood pressure, heart disease and diabetes," explained Ana. "You can also use it for skin infections." She pointed at a leafy green plant lower to the ground. "This is turmeric. I'm sure you've heard of its healing powers." Lani nodded. "I'll give you some roots and some of the other cuttings the next time I see you." They continued walking through the garden, "and this is a candlenut tree. It's used for sores or as a mouthwash."

"Wow, that's very good to know, Tutu, I'd love to grow these at Koki Beach House. Mahalo," said Lani, thankfully. "I see, you also have some beautiful orchids."

Ana nodded. "Yes, these two are divisions your grandmother gave me. I think they're from Luana's plants. She loved orchids."

"Well," replied Lani, "if I found the right Luana, this one even owns two nurseries, one in Oahu and one on the Big Island."

"So, she fulfilled her dreams." Ana's face beamed. She was happy for Luana.
They had arrived back at the food truck. "Mahalo, Tutu, for taking the time."

"Oh, anytime, my child."
Now Lani brought up the graves Lilly had found. "Tutu, I wanted to ask you something else…" They both sat down at one of the tables near the food truck. Pekelo, who was busy but also very attentive, brought them both a glass of Thai tea.

Lani continued. "My dog Lilly ran away yesterday and went down a little overgrown path right past Hamoa Beach. She found some really old overgrown graves. Do you think they could be important?"

Ana perked her ears. "Yes, definitely! There are still some graves of important leaders missing. We won't find out what it exactly is until an archeologist has taken a closer look at the inscriptions, especially the years might be very important…"

"I think they were from around 1810… I could make out three numbers, but the fourth was broken off. Do you know anyone locally who could look at them?"

"Go to Kahanu Garden and look for the manager Kaipo. I hope he still works there. He might be retiring soon. His father is about my age and used to be a historian who was one of the people who helped establish Kahanu Garden in 1974. He might know which graves are still missing."

"Mahalo, Tutu, that's great information. I'll try to find Kaipo."

Their glasses were empty and they both stood up and hugged each other. Lani got into her car and made her way back to Koki Beach House. Half an hour later, she arrived at home and since it was still not later than mid afternoon, she decided to continue to Kahuna Garden and look for Kaipo. But first she called Max to ask whether he would be able to join her…

****

Chapter 25

"Hey, Max…"

"Oh, hey darling!"

"I just came back from Ana and she told me to look for the manager at Kahanu Garden regarding the graves. Since it's still early, I thought I'd drive over there right now. Can you join me? Since you started at seven today, I thought you might be able to get off work early…"

"Great idea! I have enough overtime that I think I can take some time off. Why don't you stop by and pick me up, that way you can meet my coworkers. We can get my truck on the way back."

"Sure. See you in a few minutes."

She drove through Hana and stopped at the fire station where Max worked as a fire fighter. Max was already waiting for her when Lani stepped inside.

He was shooting the breeze with a few coworkers, two of them were pretty female firefighters who seemed to be staring at him admiringly as he was telling a joke. Lani grinned to herself, admitting her own jealousy as she watched them and at the same time, she thought of Max's jealousy of William. He and William both had that same characteristic trait of being very flirtatious, drawing everyone to them.

Max spotted her, said "hang on a second," to his co-workers, walked toward Lani and gave her a kiss on the mouth while the coworkers all watched, waiting eagerly to be introduced.

"Here she is, guys," he said to the fire fighters, then to Lani: "I've already told my buddies so much about you that they just roll their eyes when they hear your name…" he grinned and continued: "this is Jennifer, Suzie, you know Billie, this is Sam and this is Tom…" They all shook her hand in a well-mannered way and Jennifer offered her coffee.

"Thanks, but I think we have to leave. We're going over to Kahanu Garden. They probably close pretty soon," replied Lani.

Max agreed. "Yeah, I think we have to leave. They close at four."

"Nice to meet you all," said Lani while they turned around to leave.

They walked over to Lani's car and drove a few miles up the Hana Highway until they turned into the driveway of Kahanu Garden.

After paying the entrance fee and asking for Kaipo, they were told that he was leading a group through the garden and they would probably find him at the heiau, the old Hawaiian temple.

They walked across a beautiful lawn surrounded by lush tropical plants, went through arched wooded trees that created a covered walkway and found a collection of all plants that were important to Hawaiians as a culture, as well as plants from Polynesia and the greater Pacific. There were various types of sugar cane, banana, even an ancient banana type that still had black seeds in it, various herbs and other plants.

Then they finally arrived at the remains of the largest stone temple in Polynesia, the Pi'ilanihale heiau. Lani read in her brochure: "Construction started in the 1200s, built in several stages, it was a massive five story archeological temple that was used by Chief Pilani in the 1500s, who was the first chief to unite the islands under one ruler (Pi'ilanihale means House of Pilani). Situated on a broad ridge and built from basalt rocks carried from hand as far away as Hana Bay, the heiau is 341 feet by 415 feet big, with a high front wall of 50 feet. The walls facing the ocean are made up of multiple stepped terraces.

Fifty years ago, the heilau was totally overgrown with pupui, hala and guava and all kinds of other bushes, until the Pacific Tropical Botanical Garden decided to restore and share the heiau with the public in 1974."

Finally, Max and Lani found Kaipo, an older gentleman with thick glasses and a panama hat, who was just finishing up his speech about the heiau, then answering the group's questions. He greeted Max and Lani in a friendly manner.

"Aloha, we are just finishing up the tour and the group is going to explore the grounds on their own. Can I help you with anything?"

"Hi, this is Lani Winters and I'm Max Palakiko, we live right by Hamoa Beach. Ana Kamealoha told us to contact you…"

Kaipo nodded. "How is she? She's an old friend of my dad's…"

Max continued: "She's doing well. We think we might have made an important discovery. Actually, it was Lani's dog. She found what looks like some really old abandoned graves right past Hamoa Beach where a builder has requested the zoning codes to be changed. I don't know if you've heard of it."

Kaipo nodded again. "Oh, yes, I was actually at the demonstration. I'm glad you came and found me. Whether you found graves of regular ancestors or former rulers, your discovery could provide important new information about the early Hawaiian culture and we might be able to stop any construction plans for now. In 1989 there was a similar case when 900 skeletons were discovered at an ancient burial ground which led to a temporary halt in building an $80 million beachfront hotel on the west side of Maui. Since then, some state laws have been changed and approval for new larger constructions has to be granted much more carefully. I will be glad to come and inspect the site and write up a statement that the application for construction has to be rejected. Too many ancient burial sites have been treated disrespectfully."

Lani and Max looked at each other and gave each other a high five, then they both shook Kaipo's hand. He was also excited about the news. It looked like Lilly had saved the day…

****

Chapter 26

On the way home, Lani's phone rang. It was Pike, Malani's lawyer in Kahului who Lani had met during the reading of Malani's last will and testament and who was now keeping an eye on the house renovations. Lani got nervous for a second and said "Uh oh," to Max, "I hope he's not calling because of the deadline for the house…"

She answered the call.

Kumu said: "Aloha, Lani. I hope all is going well with you and Max."

"Aloha. Yes, everything's fine…"

"I'm calling because I just received a call from Mrs. Bridgett Kent, Paul Kent's mother.

Lani's heart stopped beating for a split second.

"She asked me to let you know that she would like to invite you to come and visit her in the 1000 Islands whenever it's convenient for you. Just let me know a date and I will inform her. Indian summer would be a great time …"

Lani was speechless for a second.

"Ummm, sure. Thank you very much. That's very kind of her."

"Okay, just think about it and let me know."

"Mahalo, Kumu."

"Aloha."

Lani looked at Max and told him about the invitation.

"You should go," he said. "I can take care of the house."

"I'd love to meet her. I'll try to find a date after the gallery opening in Oahu… You know I have to leave again the day after tomorrow."

Max's expression became dark and gloomy. He didn't like the thought of Lani traveling to Oahu again and being around William all day.

"Are you okay?" asked Lani who noticed the drastic change in his mood.

"Yeah, everything's okay," he replied and pulled into the parking lot of the fire station and changed the subject. "I thought we could get some Huli Huli chicken tonight. What do you think?"

"Perfect. I actually had the same idea." Lani said and smiled as Max got out of the car to get his truck. "Shall we just meet there or eat at home?"

"Why don't we eat there? It's so nice to sit right at Koki Beach…"

"Okay, see you there." Lani got a head start while Max got into his truck and followed her.

At Koki Beach, they got two Huli Huli Chicken dinners from the food truck and sat down at one of the tables. "You can't have a better ocean view during dinner than here. The only thing I'm missing now is a frosty cold beer," said Max and stretched out his legs as he started his meal. "I guess we can have one for dessert," said Lani with a smile. They sat there quietly for a moment, looking out onto the ocean, enjoying their food and each other's company.

"Oh, I forgot to tell you about my visit to the vet's office this morning," said Lani. "Lilly had a really thin thorn in between her toes and even Kate had a hard time finding it. But listen to this: She told me that Joseph McAllen is her uncle and that she doesn't agree with his plans. I think she might be innocent. Do you think we should still go ahead and pretend we're leaving and have her watch the dogs?"

He thought for a moment. "Hmmm. I'm not sure. It really depends on whether we decide to trust her or not…"

"Well, I have to leave the day after tomorrow, and I guess we can see what happens when you're at work. Maybe we should get the cameras installed by then. And we can have Kate go over to the house during her lunch break to let the girls out. Has Billie gotten the cameras yet?"

"Yes, actually, he's installing them tomorrow. Also, someone is also coming to give us an estimate on a fence. That will be interesting – it won't be cheap considering the size of the yard…"

"We could consider just fencing a part of the yard. I wouldn't really want the dogs rooting around in the veggie gardens anyhow and you can't go all the way down to the water either because of the lava rock.

Let's maybe just do an area behind the porch or between the house and the guest house, just a place we can let them out to pee when we can't walk them immediately."

"Yeah, good idea, let's look at it when we get home."

Lani was staring out at the ocean and was unusually quiet; Max wondered what was wrong with her.

"I'm really worried about being so sure that the woman in Palalo Valley is my mother. What if it ends up not being her? And now I'm suddenly hearing from my father's mother. That's so strange. Maybe it's not such a good idea to go and see her. It might just tear old wounds open…"

"Maybe sometimes it's better not to expect anything. Then you'll be pleasantly surprised," said Max wisely. "Don't expect the woman to be your mother and, regarding Paul Kent's mother, just go and see a grandmother you've never met. It might be nice for her to suddenly have a granddaughter in her old age. Do it for her."

She looked at Max and gave him a hug. "You're so wise, Max." They looked into each other's eyes and their lips met for a tender kiss. Lani just wanted to sit there forever, holding Max and listening to the noise of the waves hitting the rough lava rocks.

It was slowly getting dark and the new moon was rising behind Alau Island as they got into their cars and slowly drove the last half-mile home…

****

Chapter 27

Two days later, Lani made her way to Kahului early in the morning. She had to catch a flight to Honolulu at 11am and this time she was going to have to drive all the way without taking a break. It was the first time she was actually commuting without stopping for the beautiful views and it was a whole different experience of white-knuckle driving doing this all by herself under time pressure. She got it done though, driving the 52 miles and 620 curves like a champ while still enjoying some of the beautiful views. She arrived at the Kahului airport at 9:30, allowing time to park her car in self-parking and take a shuttle to the departure terminal.

The flight was beautiful, but she already had a knot in her stomach about having to face William. She had avoided thinking of him the entire time in Maui and if she could, she would have cancelled this trip, but she had committed to being there and her name was mentioned in all of the announcements. It would be so much easier not to see him again and just forget what almost happened in Kona, how she had almost betrayed Max.

But the gallery opening wasn't until tomorrow, so first she was going to the Hawai'i Convention Center to go to the orchid show and see if she'd run into Luana. She took a taxi to the hotel to drop her carry-on suitcase off. It was too early to check in, so she simply freshened up in a bathroom in the lobby and grabbed another taxi to the Convention Center, which was on the other end of Kalakaua Avenue. The orchid show was gigantic and the Convention Center was hustling and bustling with orchid vendors and enthusiasts. It reminded Lani of the biggest show she had ever been to, the Tamiami International Orchid Festival in Homestead, Florida. She immediately regretted not having brought enough cash to go shopping, but hopefully there was an ATM somewhere.

There were vendors from all over the world and the selection was unbelievable. She walked from booth to booth, but – even though the variety of orchids was distracting – all she could think about was finding the *Blue Tropics Orchids* stand and possibly running into Luana.

"Hey, Lani!" Tom had discovered her and they were both so happy to see each other that they gave each other a hug like old friends. Tom was taking a break, just strolling up and down the aisles, chatting with the other orchid vendors who were all his friends.

"So, I brought your name up and the time she came to the nursery thirty years ago when we were alone the other day. She looked like a deer in the headlight and didn't want to talk about it," said Tom while they were walking through the crowds, heading toward the *Blue Tropics Orchids* stand. As Lani had already suspected, Luana (or Ana as she now called herself) wasn't there. Tom introduced her to Patrick Brinkmann, Ana's husband, who had obviously already been informed about Lani and was much friendlier to her this time. Max's friend Bianca was also working at the show today. She and Lani were excited to see each other again and gave each other a hug. Everyone was super busy, so all of the *Blue Tropics* staff was quickly distracted, taking care of customers who were now lining up around the stand. Lani looked at some orchids at the *Blue Tropics* stand and wandered away, from stand to stand, until she started feeling hungry and looked for the food court. She ordered a salad with an ice tea, sat down and ate slowly, watching the busy activity, lost in her thoughts.

Suddenly there she was. Luana! She was standing at the edge of the food court, staring at Lani. She was wearing a beautiful long mu'umu'u and had an orchid in her long dark hair with some natural grey highlights. She looked like she was drawn toward her, but on the other hand she looked like she was ready to turn around and run away. Lani stopped chewing, just staring back at her, with big eyes. She felt as if she were in a movie, staring at an image of herself in the future. She didn't know whether she should get up and walk toward her or wait. So she sat there, literally frozen. Finally, Luana seemed to pull herself together and walked toward Lani.

Lani arose from her chair and they just stood there, staring at each other. After all these long years, they were only 6 feet apart. They finally rushed toward each other and fell into each other's arms, both crying tears of joy and pain for all the years apart.

****

Chapter 28
Flashback (30 years ago – 1988) – Lanai and Honolulu

After sneaking out of the hospital, Luana walked out of Lanai City to the main road with just a duffle bag containing a few items that Elizabeth had brought her to the hospital along with a little purse and stuck her thumb out as the first car came driving up. The driver honked, not even slowing down, leaving Luana in a cloud of dust that made her cough.

The next two cars didn't even bother slowing down either. The next vehicle was a Jeep, inside was a young couple in their early twenties. They stopped and asked in a friendly casual manner:

"Aloha! Where to? We're going to Puu Pehe, wanna join us?"

Luana didn't exactly know where that was, but Lanai was small and she just wanted to get away from the hospital, so she just said "sure," and jumped onto the backseat of Jeep. The couple was on vacation, having a good time. Music was blaring out of the radio. The girl in the passenger seat wearing super short hot pants was smoking and chewing gum at the same time as she tapped her long red fingernails on the console to the music. It was bumpy in the back, windy and the smoke was wafting in Luana's face, but Luana didn't even care or notice. She was still in shock that she had just left that little human being behind in the hospital.

It was a spontaneous decision. The entire situation had overwhelmed her and she just couldn't stand being close to the sweet baby any longer that she was about to give away. She had the urge to run away. And she did.

The boyfriend parked the car. All three of them got out and walked toward the cliffs of Puu Pehe. Luana was in a daze as she looked down the beautiful red cliffs, out at the wild roaring ocean and Sweetheart Rock, which was not far out in the ocean and resembled a giant piece of chocolate sponge cake. There was a tragic story around Puu Pehe, Luana, with her own tragic story, felt somehow drawn closer and closer to the edge. She kept walking until the girl that was getting ready to go hiking with her boyfriend and tying her shoes, got scared and yelled: "Hey, listen, you should stop! You're going to fall!" The girl said to her boyfriend: "Don't you think we should talk to her? She looks like she's really upset and might jump."

The boyfriend pulled her along and replied: "She's fine. Let's mind our own business."

Luana didn't pay attention to the couple. She just sat down on the rocks extremely close to the edge.

Staring out at the waves crashing against the rugged rocks and at Sweetheart Rock, Luana sat there for a while. She thought about her own sweetheart she may never see again, as tears streamed down her cheeks. All she had to do was jump and it would all be over. She wouldn't have to feel bad about the baby for the rest of her life, she could forget about her parents and her body would probably never be found. But then she thought of Paul and how her heart was capable of loving someone so much. What if there was the slightest chance that she would see him again? And then, even though this entire area had very scarce vegetation and was all volcanic rock, a slight breeze came up blowing a little rugged plumeria directly to the ground in front of her. She picked up the pretty little flower that was already a bit tattered from being blown around in the wind. This was certainly a sign, she thought to herself. The world was full of such beautiful things that she still had to discover, plants and flowers were certainly some of these things.

She suddenly knew that she had to survive, maybe by going to Oahu and trying to find work somewhere in an orchid or plant nursery. She stuck the plumeria in her hair, took a deep breath, looked out at Sweetheart Rock one more time, then she turned around and hiked down toward the harbor. There were some loose rocks on both sides of the cliff path and she had to be careful to not sprain her ankle or fall.

After a 20-minute hike, Luana arrived at Manele harbor and was still on time for the first ferry to Lahaina. She walked over to the ticket booth to buy a ticket. Then she boarded the ferry in the midst of a larger group of tourists and locals.

She had no ears for the Captain's stories and eyes for the beauty of the sun rising higher and higher, making the calm ocean look like a sparkling carpet of diamonds. She was still upset, trying not to think of the baby that she had just left, its big dark eyes staring at her with the most serious expression. She still had its smell in her nose, a scent she would probably never forget. She tried to think of something uplifting and distracting, like Paul and being at Hamoa Beach with him or sitting to model for him while he gave her his riveted attention for hours and they just talked and talked. Then she imagined her future life in Honolulu, working in an orchid nursery.

People were doing double takes of this gorgeous young Hawaiian girl, her eyes swollen and red from crying, who appeared to be carrying the weight of the whole world on her shoulders. An older motherly lady walked up to her and asked: „Is everything okay, honey?"

Luana froze while she answered: „Yes, I'm okay, thanks" and quickly walked to the other side of the boat.

It was a breathtaking sight approaching the island of Maui in the sparkling morning sun with the West Maui Mountains in the distance. The ferry chugged into Lahaina harbor, and Luana spotted the pretty Colonial style buildings on Front Street and the big famous banyan tree, which looked like an entire little forest with all its aerial roots and took over an entire block. It had been planted almost a hundred and fifty years ago, in 1873.

Once the ferry had anchored and Luana and the other passengers had disembarked, she felt dizzy, realizing how hungry she was. After all, she had just given birth less than 48 hours ago. She sat down on the wall by the harbor and rested a while, but it was already hot in the sun. She remembered a really good Swiss breakfast cafe close to the banyan tree. She walked underneath the banyan tree past all the tourists and hippies sitting underneath in the dappled shade, crossed Front Street and walked right up to the Swiss café which was busy this time of day, but she was able to find a little corner table where she had some hot chocolate with a sandwich. She gulped both down quickly. She just wanted to get to the airport and take a flight to Honolulu. She asked the girl at the counter and found out quickly that there were regular shuttles to the airport in Kahului from most of the hotels.

It was easy to get a flight from Kahului to Honolulu because they departed every few hours. She looked into her wallet and counted the bills inside. Thankfully, Elizabeth and her husband had given Luana a more than generous allowance for working as their nanny and she had a little pad in her checking account, but it wouldn't last forever.

She walked up to a counter and requested a one-way ticket to Honolulu. The ticket agent looked at her a little suspiciously. This girl didn't look like she was over 18 and also looked quite pale and disheveled.

"Can I see your ID, please?" she asked.

"Sure," answered Luana, looked for her ID in her unorganized wallet and couldn't locate it. Her heart started pounding and she started breaking out in a sweat. But there it was. She handed it to the ticket agent.

The ticket agent looked at it and realized Luana was eighteen.

"No luggage?" she asked.

"No, just my carry-on," replied Luana.

She typed some more, then her printer spit out Luana's boarding pass.

"Here's your boarding pass. Gate two. Have a nice flight."

"Thank you," replied Luana, relieved. She took the boarding pass and walked down the hallway toward security.

When the young couple was getting onto a later ferry from Lanai back to Lahaina, Elizabeth stopped them and asked if they had seen Luana, showing them a photo. The girl, being a bit emotional, broke out in tears and said: "I think she jumped. She looked so upset and was so close to the edge…" That's how the rumor started that Luana might have jumped off of the cliffs of Puu Pehe…

Chapter 29
Cont'd Flashback - Honolulu

Once the plane landed in Honolulu, Luana took the first shuttle to the hotel district on Waikiki Beach that departed right from baggage claim. She didn't really have a plan or know where to go. The beach was the only place that came to her mind. She sat on the bus, looking out at the big city with its heavy traffic, the skyscrapers of Waikiki in the distance. After about ten minutes, the bus stopped at a red light, next to a beautiful old church.

"This is the famous Kawaiaha'o Church, one of the oldest churches in Hawaii," announced the bus driver. Luana's head spun around. She looked at the beautiful old church, surrounded by tall palm trees and a beautiful tropical garden in the back.

She remembered Malani mentioning the name. This must have been the church with the orphanage where a good friend of Elizabeth's worked and she was planning on taking the baby girl. Thinking of the tiny baby girl she had left behind made her eyes fill up with tears again. "I am a monster," she thought to herself. "How could I do that?"

The bus, full of chit chatting excited tourists and with distraught Luana, her eyes still red and swollen from crying, accelerated again. Ten minutes later, it arrived in Waikiki Beach. People started disembarking with their big suitcases and carry-on cases as the bus stopped in front of various hotels on Kalakaua Avenue. They all seemed to have a goal except for Luana. Looking out to the right, she caught glimpses of the ocean in between the buildings. They were about to reach Diamond Head in just three more stops and the bus was almost empty. The bus driver's and Luana's eyes met briefly. He was wondering what this lonely, sad looking Hawaiian girl was up to. She didn't seem to be a tourist like all of the other people. Sensing he might ask some uncomfortable questions, Luana quickly grabbed her dufflebag and got off at the next stop. She walked along Kalakaua Avenue past some expansive, elegant looking resorts. It was hot and muggy, so she decided to pass through one of the hotels and walk on the ocean side, where there she expected a cooler breeze. She walked past two bellboys who looked at her and then at each other with a quizzical look into a very nice, elegant lobby with high ceilings and big spinning fans. Luana just wanted to sit down on one of the big couches and take a nap but she didn't dare. She headed toward the back of the hotel which opened to the beach, snuck into a restroom where she used the facilities, let some cold water run over her wrists and patted her face with it. As she stepped back out into the lobby she felt like everyone was looking at her suspiciously. She stepped out onto a beautiful terrace with rattan furniture and tables covered with umbrellas where she was blinded for a moment by the bright sun reflecting off the sand and ocean. Just a few feet away from her was the strip of sand known as Waikiki Beach, and behind that the beautiful turquoise blue endless Pacific. Luaua walked past the terrace, onto the sands of Waikiki Beach.

She looked for her sunglasses in her purse, put them on, feeling a bit more like a tourist and less blinded by the bright sunlight. She took her sneakers off, put them in her dufflebag and walked down to the ocean. The sand felt soft and warm under her feet. She walked along the water until the beach ended and came up to a nice shady park with a sign that said: "Kapiolani Park". In the distance, she could see Diamond Head. She sat down on a bench, feeling dizzy again and realized that she hadn't had anything to drink since the plane. She looked around and saw a food truck toward the street, next to the sidewalk. It was already late in the afternoon, the middle-aged lady in the truck was closing up for the day. Luana walked up to the truck.

"Aloha! Can I still get something, at least something to drink? I'm dying of thirst," asked Luana.

The lady looked at her watch. She hesitated. It was late, but she had a lot of food left. So she unwrapped a few hamburger patties that were still warm, made six giant Hamburgers and handed them to Luana in a paper bag. Then she gave her another paper bag with a few cans of guava juice and some bottles of water.

"On the house," said the food truck lady. "I've already put my money in the car."

"Wow, I can never eat this much, but thanks," said Luana.

"Give the other ones to your friends. They're always hungry," replied the lady and pointed at a group of teenagers sitting in the grass under some trees. "Have a nice day."

"Mahalo!" answered Luana. The lady grabbed one of her big coolers and carried it over to her car that was in a little parking lot on the side of the park.

Luana didn't really know how to approach the group of young people sitting under a tree in the grass, spread out on towels and sheets. Some of them were sleeping, others were smoking what seemed to be a joint because they were passing it back and forth. She walked toward them and a wiry tanned girl with blonde dreadlocks in her early twenties, wearing shorts and a bikini top, jumped up and walked up to her.

"Hey, I'm Allison. Do you need help? Whatcha got? Looks like Mel gave you food for all of us?"

"Yes, she gave me a ton. I was wondering why. She must have thought I belong to you guys," replied Luana.

"I'm Allison," said the blonde girl, "and this is Mark, Tom and Glen," she continued introducing everyone while she passed out Hamburgers but made sure to set one aside for herself and give one to Luana.

"I'm... Ana," replied Luana, hesitating briefly but quickly dropping the L and U in her name, in case people in Maui and Lanai were looking for her. She unwrapped the foil and took a giant bite out of the delicious hamburger.

There was no awkward moment, it just seemed that Luana had known these guys forever.

"Yeah," continued Allison, "she is super nice and always gives us the food she wasn't able to sell. I guess it doesn't make sense taking the unused burgers home or throwing them away. Win-win," she added, while she took a big bite out of her burger and then a big swig out of a can of beer standing next to her. "Want a beer?" she asked.

"No, thanks," replied Luana, "I don't drink."

"Where are you from?" asked Allison. "Most of these guys are from California, just hanging out for a while. But I go to UH."

"I'm from Kona," Luana lied. It was probably better not to tell them that she was from Hana.

"Wow, must be beautiful," replied Allison. "Big Island's definitely on my bucket list."

"Where are you staying?" asked Luana.

"Most of these guys are sleeping right here," answered Allison with a grin. "They're all backpacking and just sleeping on the beach. Sometimes they get chased away by the police, but then they just go somewhere else. They've already slept here for 3 nights and no issues yet. Glen and I both live in dorms. We just like hanging out here..."

Luana and Allison had an immediate connection and talked and talked about this and that.

Suddenly, someone handed Luana a joint and just because she didn't want to say no to everything, she took a hit. She inhaled slightly and exhaled immediately.

"You have to inhale deeper," said Allison, grinning.

Luana took another toke and tried to exhale deeper, because Allison was watching her, but she immediately had a horrible cough attack and couldn't stop. Allison reached over and patted her back. "Uh oh, that might not be your thing either," she said, grinning. "I stay away from that stuff too. Doesn't do anything for me," she added.

Luana nodded thankfully. She had never been into experimenting with alcohol or drugs and didn't really think she was missing anything. Allison scooted off of the towels she had been sitting on and handed one of them to Luana who was sitting in the grass.

"Here, I have two towels. Feel free to hang out with us if you want."

"Mahalo," answered Luana. She used her duffle bag as a pillow, stretched out on the towel and was asleep in less than a minute.

Luana jerked awake, as one of the guys shook her, trying to wake her up. It was dark. She had slept all evening and through the entire night. The moon shining over the ocean illuminated the park with a surreal light. Allison had obviously left.

"Hurry, get up, we have to leave. The cops are clearing the park."

The entire group of young people had jumped up, was quickly gathering their belongings and rushing away, while in the background two police officers were shaking some homeless people, sleeping on benches, making them get up and leave. It was forbidden to sleep in the park. Luana took a second to gather her wits. She was the only one of the group left. She quickly grabbed her dufflebag and purse as well as Allison's towel that she had slept on. She didn't know where everyone else had gone, so she walked back toward Waikiki Beach and Kalakaua Avenue. She looked at her watch. It was 5am. She arrived in front of the nice hotel she had walked through yesterday and sat down on a bench near the valet stand. One of the bellboys, a young dark blonde Caucasian in his early twenties who had already noticed her yesterday, walked up to her.

"Do you need any help? I already noticed you here yesterday, but you don't look like a hotel guest."

"I'm looking for a place to stay, but I can't afford one of these hotels," Luana replied.
"A job would be nice too," she added and had to laugh while she looked at him.

"Hmmm… what kind of job? I know the hotel is always looking for people," he replied. "I'm Ben, by the way."

"I probably wouldn't mind working here, but my dream is to work in a nursery."

He looked straight at her and laughed. "Well, I guess you met the right guy. My parents own a nursery out in Palolo Valley." As she looked at him a bit clueless, he added: "That's kind of a suburb of Honolulu, in the north. There are lots of nurseries out there." He was a happy-go-lucky talkative guy and kept chatting. "I'm the black sheep of the family. Everybody works there except me. I hate plants. Guess because my parents always worked on weekends and made us help.

Sometimes they still rope me in for orchid shows. My brother Patrick is totally into orchids and wants to take over the nursery one day... Guess who they totally favor?"

Luana's eyes widened. "What, it's an orchid nursery? Orchids are my favorite plants in the world. I actually used to work in an orchid nursery in Hana... oops." She hit her mouth with her hand. She didn't want to tell people that she was from Hana in case her family was looking for her. But Ben had already moved on to the next subject. "My shift ends at 7:00. If you don't mind waiting that long, I can take you out there. I think we're looking for someone to help in the greenhouses and we also have a little cottage that some of the workers get to stay in sometimes."

Wow, she might have hit the jackpot. "Of course I don't mind waiting. That sounds perfect," she replied. "Thanks so much! Maybe I'll go and find something cheap to eat around here. Do you have any idea where I can find some breakfast that won't break the bank?"

"Yeah, Tilly's has really good egg sandwiches and coffee. But I don't think they open until six. It's right up that way, one block away," he said, pointing away from the beach, up a little alley between two hotel towers.

"Thank you, I'll be right back. Do you want me to bring you anything?"

"Sure, can you bring me a fried egg sandwich with spam and a coffee?"

"Sure! I'll see you in a bit."

Soon, Luana and Ben were leaving Waikiki Beach in an old beaten up sedan, driving toward the northern suburbs of Palolo Valley. It was becoming more and more rural with many gigantic greenhouses on both sides.

They drove through a wooden gate with a big sign hanging over it that said *"Blue Tropics Orchids"*. Luana looked at the sign and the giant greenhouses on both sides of the driveway and held her breath.

Even though she didn't even know whether Ben's parents would hire her, for the first time in a while Luana felt some perspective on her life...

Chapter 30
Back to present time

Luana and Lani had sat down at the table across from each other and were trying to have a conversation, but they both had a hard time expressing their feelings. They were very emotional and had teary eyes.

"I don't know how I can ever forgive myself for what I did. I can't even put myself in your shoes..." said Luana. "I don't know what to say. I'd understand if you could never forgive me."

"There is nothing to forgive. I don't know if I could have had a baby at 18 either, even if my parents had supported me. At least you and Malani made sure I was in good hands. I had very good adoptive parents, so please don't feel bad about that," replied Lani.

"I would really like to learn to know you more if you'll allow me to," continued Luana and carefully reached across the table to take Lani's hand.

"Me too. I'm so glad I found you and that you seem to be doing well," replied Lani, "do you know that I also owned a nursery in New York and I'm totally into orchids? Maybe it's not a coincidence, maybe it's hereditary..."

Luana was amazed about this news.

Mother and Daughter continued, not noticing anyone around them, as the years melted away. They were very happy and it showed on both their faces.

Lani and Luana's love for each other quickly blossomed. They had so much to talk about and so much in common that the time ran very quickly. Luana suddenly looked at her watch and realized she had been sitting there for over an hour and had to return to work. She got up. "Please come and and let me introduce you to my husband Patrick in a formal manner. He has not been able to stop talking about you. He and his family rescued me thirty years ago when I didn't know where to go after I had left Lanai."

Lani nodded, following her back to the *Blue Tropics Orchids* stand.

Patrick and Tom had been wondering where Luana was, but as soon as they saw her walk up with Lani, they both sighed a big sigh of relief and greeted Lani happily. They had both witnessed Luana's tortured soul for the past thirty years, of course never knowing why, and they hoped that now she would finally be able to forgive herself for what she had done. It looked like things were going well.

Lani jumped right in with the *Blue Tropics Orchids* team as a bigger group came up to the stand needing advice and they all felt like she had always worked with them. She had a great time working side by side with her mother, Bianca, Tom and Patrick. Several people made comments or asked whether Luana and Lani were mother and daughter or even sisters. This made them stop and grin at each other.

"Wow, that was great," said Patrick as the show had closed for the day. He smiled at Lani. "Can we keep you? We really needed the additional two hands."

"We want to pay you for helping us this afternoon," said Luana. She seemed as if a big weight had been taken off of her shoulders.

"No, I won't accept your money," replied Lani.

"Well, then, here…" Luana turned around and grabbed two beautiful Cattleyas out of the display, which she handed to Lani.

Patrick added: "Also, we usually go out for dinner together after the show, but we wonder if you two want to go by yourselves and it will be our treat, Lani?"

Luana was torn. She felt bad leaving her husband alone, but she really wanted to spend time alone with Lani, so she nodded.

"Thank you and sure, I'd love to go out for dinner with you," replied Lani, looking at Luana. "I don't have to meet my business associate until tomorrow."

The Brinkmanns, Tom and Bianca made long faces. "Oh, that's too bad," said Luana, "we were hoping you could come back tomorrow."

"I can come back for a little bit tomorrow morning, but I have a commitment in the late afternoon." Lani looked at them and hesitated. She should probably tell Luana about the Paul Kent exhibition. She wasn't sure how Luana would react to the Paul Kent subject, but then she remembered all of the Paul Kent hybrids in Luana's private orchid collection. Lani was sure her mother had not forgotten about her old love.

Tom, Patrick and Bianca went out for dinner while Luana and Lani went off on their own. They were close to Waikiki, but they wanted a quiet place, so they went to a little bistro they found within walking distance of the Convention Center.

It was funny for Luana and Lani to find out that they liked the same food and also had many other things in common. Both of them automatically wiped off their fork and knife with the napkin, looked up and laughed at each other.

"Well, I wanted to tell you why I'm in Honolulu…" started Lani.

"You have to tell me why you're in Hawaii at all," interrupted Luana with a smile. "I thought you told me earlier that your adoptive parents live in the Hudson Valley…"

"I suddenly got a letter from Malani's lawyer one day. Of course I had no idea who she was, but she had passed away and left her house, Koki Beach House, to me." Luana's eyes widened. She was shocked to find out that Malani had passed away. Lani told Luana the entire story about the house having to be fixed up within a certain time, meeting and falling in love with Max. Then she told her about how she had found the beautiful painting of Luana in the living-room that looked like her mirror image and how everyone in Hana and surroundings had told her how much she looked like Luana: how she had found more paintings and more information about Luana and Paul Kent everywhere she went and talked to people. She told Luana about how she and Max had gone to Lanai and talked to Elizabeth in the bed and breakfast, how she had found the collection of photos in the crawl space. She told Luana about the fire in Koki Beach House, how she had almost given up, how the people in Hana had all buried their feud and had come to show their support. Luana was happy to hear Lani explain how much Kumu regretted what he had done and what a kind old man he had become, how happy Leila was to have a granddaughter and how much she spoke about Luana. She told her about Kumu and Leila's beautiful courtyard with Luana's old orchids that they treasured so much.

Luana had tears in her eyes, thinking of her parents and the commotion she had caused in Hana and that it was basically her fault that Malani and her brother Kumu hadn't spoken for all those years. Now Malani was dead and nothing could be undone. She wondered about how both she and her parents would react when they saw each other again, a confrontation she had been avoiding for thirty years. She had tears in her eyes, thinking of Paul Kent, the love of her life, the man she had never called to tell him he had a daughter. She had thought he was married or had someone else he cared about, but she never really knew for sure. She had just run away like a coward and left her former life behind. And then she had heard about Paul's accident, thought he was dead and married Patrick…

"Well, what I wanted to tell you is that the collection of Paul Kent photos I found is quite the sensation. He was a famous painter and these photos are incredibly beautiful and valuable. Some friends of mine who own a gallery in Paia have organized a traveling exhibition and it's received a lot of press: the Waikiki part opens tomorrow with a big party. You should come with me… One of the guys is actually Aaron, your friend Glen's younger brother."

"I'm not sure if I can do that…" Luana replied. "I lead quite a secluded life. I'm not used to events like that, nor from what you're telling me, the commotion it will cause."

"Okay, but there's something else," Lani said. "Paul Kent's mother just contacted me and invited me to come and visit her in the 1000 Islands, in upstate New York. You should come with me!"

Lani could tell that she was going too fast. Luana withdrew a bit and looked down at her plate.

"I found the Paul Kent hybrids in your private collection…" said Lani a bit more carefully. "They're beautiful…"

Luana looked up, took a sip of wine and started talking slowly…

"Yes. I was never able to forget about him. Even though I'm married to Patrick, owe him so much and we've had a happy busy life together, Paul was the love of my life. I can still say that, even though I haven't seen him for thirty years. He and I were soul mates. What we had was special. Even though I'll never know if he was married and I was just his island fling. My father had found an article in the New York Times that showed him with this woman. They looked like a couple. But now it seems that he's dead. I'll never know." She stopped talking and had to wipe away the tears in her eyes. The memories overwhelmed her.

"Maybe it would be nice to go and meet his mom and see where he grew up and lived," said Lani. "Maybe it would give you closure... actually both of us..."

"Yeah, maybe... But what would I tell Patrick?"

"You'd just tell him that you're going for me!"

Luana put her hand on Lani's. "Give me some time and let me think about it. This is all quite a shock for me... everything is moving so fast. But I'm glad you found me. You are wonderful and your adoptive parents can be very proud of you."

They left the bistro together and slowly walked down Kalakaua Avenue together. It was already quite late, but Honolulu never slept and the streets were full of tourists, shoppers and street musicians. People turned their heads when Luana and Lani walked by. There was something about these two beautiful women with their resemblance that made strangers do a double take.

"Let's go down to the beach," said Lani as they reached Waikiki. They both removed their shoes and walked down to the beach, where the waves were gently washing ashore and the waxing crescent moon was shining bright in the evening sky. Lani pointed down the beach. "I'm staying right down there in the pink hotel, the Royal Hawaiian."

"Wow, that's really nice," replied Luana. "Why don't I walk you down there and then I can grab a taxi. It's getting late and we have to get up early."

"Sure." Lani was so happy to be with her mother and still had so many questions that she hated the fact of her leaving, but it was indeed getting late and she had to check in with William about tomorrow in addition to wanting to call Max to tell him the exciting news. "I wish we could spend more time together tonight," said Lani. "I have so many questions for you."

"Yeah," replied Luana, "Maybe it wouldn't be a bad thing to fly somewhere together. Life here is so busy that I can barely get away for a couple of hours."

Lani's heart skipped a little. It would be so exciting to go and see Paul Kent's mother with Luana. They had arrived at the hotel and walked in through the back entrance to the lobby and the front entrance where Luana grabbed a taxi after giving Lani a big hug.

"I'll see you tomorrow," said Luana and waved.

Lani turned around and walked toward the front desk to check in. Her heart was full.

As soon as Lani was up in her room, she called Max to tell him the news about Luana.

"I was sitting in the food court eating lunch and she was suddenly standing there. We had dinner together with amazing conversations! It's so funny, we have so many things in common and are so alike..."

"I'm so happy for you! That's great. Now you need to get her to travel to New York with you! That would be so awesome for both of you. By the way, I'm staying overnight at Billie and Alana's house. I thought we could still check out whether Kate is really telling the truth or not. And Billie installed the cameras."

"Wow, great idea," replied Lani. "

Next she called her parents who were as happy and excited for Lani as Max was and then finally, she spoke with William who was also happy for her.

"Do you want to meet for a drink?" he asked.

"No, I really can't, William. I am really tired after working the orchid show with my mother and her husband this afternoon, then having had a long dinner with her and walking all the way here from the Convention Center. What time do you need me tomorrow? I'd love to see my mother again for a bit in the morning."

"I totally understand. I don't really need you there until the first guests start arriving at five. Why don't you plan on being at the gallery at 4:45? Can you get her to come? That would be a sensation…"

"I asked her, but she seems overwhelmed, so I'm not sure if she'll come."

"Try to work on it, Lani!"

"Okay, I'll see you tomorrow."

"Good night."

Lani tried to read a bit, but she couldn't concentrate. She was much too excited about having met Luana and wondering how their relationship would develop. She walked out onto the balcony, sat down in a comfortable armchair and looked up at the moon with Saturn right underneath. She just sat there breathing deeply while she enjoyed the beautiful sparkling ocean, Diamond Head in the distance and the starry sky. Soon she was deep asleep.

****

Chapter 31

The big blown up photos of Paul Kent had been shipped to Honolulu and were now hanging in Manolo Wlaschek's beautiful oceanfront gallery. Lighting director J.R. and William had worked all day adjusting spotlights, making sure that the photos were presented in the most spectacular manner.

Lani worked with Brinkmanns at the orchid show all morning and had talked Luana into accompanying her to the exhibition opening. Their taxi stopped on Kalakaua Avenue in front of the gallery. They got out, walked across the sidewalk and stepped onto a red carpet leading into the gallery. Curious bystanders, who wanted to witness the glamorous event that was going on here, were standing on both sides of the roped off carpet watching Luana and Lani, the two Hawaiian beauties in colorful floral floor-length mu'umu'us with beautiful hakus made of orchids and leis around their necks, walk down the carpet and make their grand entrance into the building.

William had instructed Lani to arrive late, since he wanted the audience to be present when Lani and her mother Luana, the woman depicted in most of the photos, arrived. William had just begun his introduction speech when the two women walked in and a murmur went through the crowd. They walked up to the little stage area Manolo used for speeches. William stretched out his hand to help them up and introduced them:

"And now, ladies and gentlemen, meet Luana Brinkmann and her daughter Lani."

Everyone applauded and the two women bowed slightly, smiling at the audience.

William shook Luana's hand and gave Lani kisses on both cheeks. Lani was intimidated just by his presence but tried to be as natural as he was. The evening went great and Lani realized once again William was flirting with everyone. This time he didn't leave Luana's side all evening, flirting with her nonstop. Luana was extremely insecure because she wasn't used to being at such events, but at the same time she seemed to be enjoying the unusual attention.

Luana and Lani had more chances to bond and spent the entire evening looking at the beautiful photos, which Luana was in awe of. They had cocktails with William, Manolo and his wife Gloria. The press was there, taking picture after picture and Manolo Wlaschek had a great time hosting everyone.

When it was time for Luana to take a taxi and go home, Lani walked her to the taxi and begged one more time:

"Please think about going to upstate New York with me. It would probably be great for both of us to meet Mrs. Kent and I'd love to spend more time with you…"

"I'll think about it. Thank you for the exciting evening. Good night, Lani. I love you."

They hugged each other goodbye and then Luana got in the taxi, which blinked and merged heading into the slow, neverending traffic on Kalakaua Avenue.

A bit later, up in her room, Lani called Max and told him about the wonderful evening. "I'm so happy for you, Lani. Let's celebrate tomorrow evening when you're back."

The next morning, Lani met William at breakfast on the terrace overlooking the ocean. William had stayed in Waikiki due to the late event. She felt very shy and intimidated around him, but again she tried to act as if everything was okay.

"What a great evening, Lani, and the fact that you found your mom: spectacular! The place was packed and I'm sure it will stay that way for a while. Some of the photos and paintings have been spoken for already and you know our share is quite good. It is amazing how much you and your mom are alike, even the way you move and talk." He looked at her, full of admiration, but she looked down, avoiding too much eye contact. He put his hand on hers. She pulled it back as if she had been electrocuted. "Don't worry, Lani, I respect that you're in a relationship, but I do adore you and hope we can stay friends."

"Sure," she replied.

"By the way, I'm flying to Kahului with you. I have to meet Aaron to discuss some things and one of my best friends is on vacation in Maui this week, so I want to kill two birds with one stone."

This made Lani nervous all over again. She certainly wasn't going to drink champagne on the flight and become all light-headed… she took a deep breath to calm herself down. He was probably going to be in first class and she'd be in economy.

"I already got an upgrade for you and we can sit together and look at all the photos that some of the photographers have already sent me."

She hesitated but it sounded okay, at least they'd be busy. And she was curious about the photos herself. She nodded and excused herself to go upstairs and pack.

At the airport, they checked in and, indeed, William had upgraded Lani to first class.

The flight attendant automatically brought them a glass of champagne and Lani wanted to decline, but William said "Oh, come on, enjoy it, Lani. This is actually really good champagne…"

"Yeah, but I have to still drive all the way to Hana. I might fall asleep," she argued.

"Hmmm… good point. Take it, have a few sips and I'll finish it," he said grinning.

The plane took off and after a few sips of champagne Lani and William were laughing and joking about some funny things that had happened last night. They went through the photos that the journalists had sent him, which looked great. Some were of Lani and Luana in front of a piece of artwork. Some were of William and Lani, some of all three. Lani thought to herself, there's nothing wrong with being friends with William: he is quite a fun guy.

As soon as the plane had landed, they walked out of the terminal, still joking and laughing, William with his arm around Lani's shoulders, so that she could see a funny picture he was showing her.

They looked quite intimate and happy while they walked through the airport together.

Little did Lani know that Max had to run an errand in Kahului to get some construction supplies, had decided to surprise Lani and was standing at the exit to meet her. The blood in his veins began boiling as he saw Lani and William, walking together arm in arm through the airport, laughing and joking. He turned around and walked back to the parking garage before either of them could see him and drove the entire two-hour drive back to Hana without stopping once.

He walked into Koki Beach House, let the dogs out into the little area in the back the handymen had fenced in on a provisional basis, packed some things and threw them into the guesthouse. Then he walked outside, grabbed his surfboard, not without giving the pretty pink new surfboard that was standing next to it a dirty look, and walked down to Hamoa Beach to go surfing and let off some steam. He didn't pay attention to the dark clouds on the horizon and the nasty storm brewing in the distance.

****

Chapter 32

Lani stopped in Paia at Aaron and Mats' gallery to say hi and tell them about the successful opening last night. She always enjoyed being in Paia and she needed some coffee after drinking a glass of champagne on the plane, so she happily accepted their invitation to join them for lunch.

While the three of them walked down the street toward the Hana Highway, Lani tried calling Max, but he didn't answer his phone. He was probably working. They walked into a really packed flatbread restaurant, were lucky to get a table and ordered the lunch special, which was ½ salad and ½ flatbread of the day, grass-fed steak flatbread with arugula lettuce, dried tomatoes and mushrooms.

"So tell us about last night and Luana," said Aaron while they bit into their delicious pieces of flatbread. "Have you told Glen yet that you've been in touch with her? He'll be so excited."

"Hmmm…" she was still chewing and had to swallow. "I should have enough time to stop and tell him. Good idea. He'll be thrilled. I guess so many people bugged her about me that she finally became curious. But I went to the orchid show, she wasn't there again, and while I was eating lunch, she suddenly walked up to me… and now when we talk it's like we've known each other forever. And everyone else says she moves and talks exactly like me."

Aaron and Mats beamed. "We're so happy for you, Lani! Finally! You've waited so long. We can't wait to meet her!"

"Thanks. Yes, I'm very happy. It's much better than I ever thought it would be… we seem to have a real connection."

After lunch and a coffee, she felt much better than she had before. She tried calling Max again, but again, there was no answer. She left a voicemail. "Hey, Max, I made it okay and had lunch with Aaron and Mats in Paia. I'll be leaving Paia now, but I will make a short stop at Glen's to tell him about my mom. Hope all is well. Love you."

Aaron and Mats walked Lani to her car a block away from the gallery. "Drive really careful, darling," said Aaron looking up at the sky. "It looks like there's quite a storm brewing…"

"Do you know what, guys," added Mats, "maybe Lani should come back to the gallery with us and we'll check the weather forecast. It looks quite bad. I'd hate for you to drive on the Hana Highway by yourself in a storm."

Lani tried calling Max again. "I really wish he'd answer his phone."

"Text him. He might not be able to talk but might see the text message," said Aaron.

"Okay." She texted Max: "How's the weather over there? Might wait it out and check weather forecast. Looks pretty bad here."

Again there was no reply. She started worrying about him and wondered if she should call the fire department, but she felt a bit silly about that and didn't want to come across as The Clingy Girlfriend.

Aaron, Mats and Lani walked over to the gallery and checked the weather forecast on the computer there. It was definitely bad, so Lani decided to wait a few hours. She still had two to three hours until she had to leave to get to Hana before dark. After driving the route several times, she even felt confident enough to drive in the dark, but Aaron and Mats didn't want to hear anything about that. "You'll stay here for the night if it doesn't clear up on time," said Aaron.

Soon enough, the wind picked up outside and it started thundering and lightning, then pouring. They tuned in to the local weather channel on TV showing a severe storm warning for the Road to Hana and a flash flood watch, which meant it was likely to happen but not occurring yet. "I think you should stay," said Aaron. "It's actually almost worse after a strong rain in the hills around the Hana Highway." Lani thought of what had happened to Paul Kent who had the fatal accident after flash flooding on the Hana Highway and was never seen again. She decided to stay put and called Max's phone again. Again, there was no answer. Now she called the fire department. Jennifer, who Lani had just met the other day when she picked up Max, answered the phone. "No, Max isn't here today. He actually took the day off to drive to Kahului to run some errands."

That was strange. Lani didn't know about Max driving to Kahului. She replied, "I'm a bit worried since he hasn't been picking up his phone all day. If you hear from him, can you tell him I'm staying in Paia for the night? The weather looks really bad."

"Yes, that's a good decision," replied Jennifer. "I would do the same thing. I've heard about a flash flood watch on the Road to Hana. I'll let Max know if he calls. Maybe his phone is dead."

****

Chapter 33

In the meantime, Max on his surfboard was paddling like a machine further and further out into the ocean. He was so upset that he just wanted to be out there in the waves, fight them with all his strength and think about something other than Lani and William. All he could think about was them laughing arm in arm while walking through the airport. He was such a good swimmer that he didn't care about the dark clouds on the horizon. He'd be back by the time they got to Hamoa Beach.

He rode a few waves like the expert surfer he was. They were getting bigger and bigger, but he kept paddling out and didn't realize, nor care, that the situation was becoming dire. He didn't pay attention for just one second and a wave crashed over him. He hung onto his surfboard, gasping for air. He glanced up into the dark clouds that were already on top of him. I'll ride in on one last wave and then I should get out, he thought to himself. That next wave was coming up now. He could see it approaching fast. He started paddling toward the shore as fast as he could and got up on the board, but something was wrong. A shooting pain went through his ankle as he was getting up. He had somehow twisted it and couldn't put any weight on it now. With the big wave pushing him from behind, he fell off of the board and crashed into the water, which whirled up over him as he was tossed around in the big wave as if in a spinning washing machine with the tether of his surfboard pulling at his injured ankle. Suddenly, everything went black.

It was almost a miracle that Max didn't drown and he somehow washed ashore. He lay in the sand, unconscious until a vacationing couple came down to the beach after the storm and found him there. The water was extremely calm now, and the waves at the shore were lapping up around him.

"I think someone is lying down there," said the girl to her boyfriend. "Let's go and check what's going on."

They hurried down to Max and checked if he was breathing.

"We need to call an ambulance," said the young man, running up to get one of their cell phones. Of course, as usual on Hamoa Beach, they had no reception, so the young man ran up the stairs to the street and waved down a car that was just driving by.

"Please try to call an ambulance if you have reception or as soon as you do! There's an unconscious man down on the beach. It looks like he had a surfing accident."

The person in the car checked his phone but he had no reception either. He drove half a mile down the road and called 911.

A few minutes later, an ambulance sped down the Hana Highway toward Hamoa Beach with flashing lights. The paramedics knew that there was an access road past the stairs and drove down that steep access road as far as they could to get down to the beach.

They ran up the beach with their first aid kit and kneeled down next to Max.

"Oh my God, that's Max!" Of course, everyone in town knew him. In that instance, Max opened his eyes and looked at them.

"Hey, guys," he said weakly.

"Don't move, Max." said John, one of the paramedics, while he was checking him for injuries. "Do you know where you are?"

"Yeah, I was surfing and I think my surfboard hit me on the head… and everything went black." replied Max as he tried to sit up. "But I think I'm okay…"

"No, you're not okay, man! You have a giant bump on the back of your head," said John. "I'd rather get the stretcher and carry you, is that okay?"

"I think I can get up," said Max. "I can get to the ambulance and you can do your thing from there."

"Okay, but let us help you, you stubborn bastard!" said John, laughing. He was glad his friend seemed fine. He got on one side of Max and the other paramedic got on the other side.

But as soon as Max tried to put weight on his left leg, he grimaced in pain.

"It looks like you've hurt your leg or your ankle. Sam," he said to the other paramedic, "can you please go and get the stretcher?"

"Okay, boss," Sam ran down the beach and up to the ambulance to retrieve the stretcher.

They carried Max on the stretcher to the ambulance and took him to Hana Health where an urgent care doctor looked at his eyes, felt the bump on his head and did some other exams. "We are going to do an MRI on your head and also check out your ankle. I'm sure you have at least a concussion and an injured ligament in your ankle."

Everything was fine with Max's MRI, but he had sprained his ankle and had to wear a boot for a few weeks. He wanted to go home, but the doctor insisted on keeping him over night because of his head injury.

****

Chapter 34

Early next morning, Lani made her way back to Hana after a fun evening catching up with Aaron and Mats. But now she was really worried about Max. She stopped briefly at Coconut Glen's stand and told him about her mother and of course had an early delicious lilikoi ice cream, but she was anxious to get home, because Max still hadn't answered his phone.

She stepped into the house and shouted "Max!" The two Bassets jumped up on her full of excitement, almost knocking her over, they were so happy to see her. But Max wasn't there. Upstairs, Lani realized that most of Max's clothes and bathroom toiletries were gone. She was quite flabbergasted. Had Max gone somewhere? Or was he still pretending to be gone to see whether Kate was in kahoots with Joseph McAllen? But his truck was in the driveway.

Lani walked outside and checked whether Max's surfboard was there. It was. So he wasn't at the beach. She checked the door leading to the guesthouse, but it was locked. She saw a shadow limping around inside the kitchen and shouted again: "Max, is that you?" There was no answer and for a while everything was silent. But then, the door was unlocked from the inside and opened.

Max was pale, unshaven and was wearing a big boot. He looked quite gloomy and didn't greet Lani. She could tell that something was very wrong.

"Oh, my God! What happened, Max?"

"Nothing. I think it's better if we don't see each other for a while." And he slammed the door shut again.

Lani pounded at the door. "Max! You can't do that to me! Tell me what's wrong! Did you hurt yourself?"

No answer.

"But Max! What did I do?"

There was still no answer.

Lani walked back into the house. She had no idea what was wrong with Max and felt like her heart had just been torn out. While the

Bassets licked her and demanded attention, she sat down on the couch cluelessly, staring into thin air.

She called Alana to find out whether she or Billie knew what was going on with Max.

"Hi, Lani! How are you?"

"Hey, Alana, I just got back from Oahu. Max is actually not talking to me and I have no clue why. Do you know if anything happened to him?"

"Wow, you haven't heard? He almost drowned yesterday. Jennifer said she tried to call you, but you might have had no reception. He was out surfing in that storm and got hit in the head by his surfboard. But I don't know what that has to do with you. If you want to talk tonight, let me know. Billy has to work late."

"What? I had no idea. Thanks. I'll try to talk to him again. I'll keep you posted. Thanks."

"Call me later. I'd also love to hear everything about Luana. I'm so excited. Can't wait to see her."

"Okay." Lani ended the call and walked back over to the guesthouse.

She knocked at the door again.

"Max, please let me in. Can we talk about what happened? I heard you had an accident?"

Everything was silent for a while, but then Max finally opened the door, left it ajar, limped over to his old couch and sat down. Lani followed him and sat down across from him. He put his leg up on a footstool, crossed his arms and looked down, which was not exactly the most inviting body language.

"Max, what happened? You almost drowned? What's going on?"

"I went surfing, sprained my ankle and fell. Then my board hit me. That's all."

"That's horrible. Were you unconscious? You could have drowned. Who found you?"

"Some tourists…"

They were both silent for a moment.

"And why are you mad at me? What did I do to upset you like this?"

"I came to the airport in Kahului to surprise you…"

"And? Where were you?"

"Lani, do you really have to make it so hard for both of us? Do I really have to say it? Don't tell me there's nothing going on between you and William!"

Lani was absolutely speechless and flabbergasted. She had no recollection of anything happening at the airport that could have upset Max. Then she thought about the way William had put his arm around her shoulder to show her pictures on his phone and looked at Max…

"Max, William was showing me photos on his phone, if that's what you mean. That doesn't mean anything…"

"It sure looked like something to me," replied Max. "I think it's better if we take a break for a while."

"But Max…"

"Sorry, I don't feel good. I need to rest. You can find your way out?"

"Seriously, Max, there is nothing going on between William and me. You're the only one I love."

He had already picked up his phone and started typing a text message to someone. Lani got up and walked out, like in a daze.

She went back to the house, realized that someone had built a fenced enclosure for the dogs while she was in Honolulu and let them out. She got a glass of water, sat down on the porch and watched them for a while. Then she walked to the backyard down by the ocean and sat down on the swing, hanging from a tree. Staring out at the ocean, Lani wondered how she would be able to continue life in Hana without Max. How can I convince him that nothing happened between William and me? Tears were running down her cheeks as she sat there, staring out at the ocean and Alau Island. She loved this beautiful place, but she loved Max even more and didn't want to lose him…

****

Chapter 35

Later in the day, the follow up meeting regarding Joseph McAllen's application to alter the zoning laws for the area past Hamoa Beach took place. The mayor was going to announce the decision in the meeting.

People were walking into the Helene Hall Community Center to attend the meeting. Lani walked in by herself trying not to look too gloomy as she greeted all of her and Max's friends. It didn't seem like Max was attending and people seemed to assume that he wasn't feeling well enough, which was the truth.

Kaipo, the manager of Kahanu Garden and member of the Hawaiian Historical Society, was also present. He had written a statement with his opinion on the ancient graves Lilly had found and the impact a larger construction project would have on them. His statement was definitely against any type of construction.

Everyone in the hall was chit chatting until the mayor stepped into the room. They immediately became silent, full of anticipation.

The mayor acted a little like a judge and shouted. "Silence in the hall, please!"

He picked up a document and read. "I herewith announce that the application to alter the zoning laws in the twenty acres west of Hamoa Beach and plots 1005 – 1025 has been rejected due to the possibility of existing ancient graves. Their presence could provide important new information about the early Hawaiian culture. These might not be the only sites and therefore the entire area must be checked for evidence of further graves and/or a possibly existing heiau. The meeting is herewith closed. An appeal against this decision can be made within the next 30 days."

People were high-fiving and some of the locals high-fived Lani as well, but she felt lonely and forelorn in this crowd without Max. She got up quickly and walked out of the building, before the tears started rolling out of her eyes again. She got into the car and drove back home. A strange car was standing in the driveway. Max obviously had a visitor. Lani got the two hounds and walked toward Hamoa Beach with them. She followed the winding road along the coast and just walked and walked, crying and wondering how she could get Max to at least listen to her so that she could convince him that nothing between her and William had happened. She actually understood how he felt. The tables had turned after what had happened a few months ago between Max and his old flame Mandy. But she couldn't understand how bull-headed Max could be and not listen to her explanation.

Suddenly, Lani realized how far she had walked and that it might be too much for the girls to walk back home. She was almost at Waioka Pond and remembered how she and Max had come here the first time, searching for the cottage that Paul Kent used to rent over the summers. She started sobbing overwhelmed by her memories.

Suddenly, her phone rang. Lani was surprised that she even had reception here but she answered the call. It was Luana, who could tell that Lani had been crying.

"What's wrong, my dear? You sound upset..."

"Max and I had a falling out. He's not talking to me..."

"I'm sorry... Well, I have what I hope is some good news for you. I spoke with Patrick about going to upstate New York and he said the earlier we go, the better. He really seems to want me to go for whatever reason. Orchid show season is starting soon, but there's a two-week break right now in between the Honolulu show and the next one in Santa Barbara. After that I'll be busy all winter. And maybe it would be good for you and Max to have some space for a little while."

Besides not knowing what to do with the dogs, Lani thought that was a great idea. She could use a time out from all this commotion and maybe Luana was right. Maybe Max would calm down and realize how much he missed her when she was gone.

"It's always tough to organize someone for the dogs, but I guess I could ask the girl who has been watching them... or even Max... but he had an accident and sprained his ankle, so he can't really walk them... or I could ask my grandparents. Do you know what? The more I think about it, the more I like the idea. Let me check how much flights are if we go so spur of the moment."

She had been thinking about going back to Paul Kent's old cottage, but since she had the dogs and had to get back home somehow, she forgot about the idea. She started walking back and, as often happens in and around Hana, a friendly local pulled up beside her. It was Laura Cattleya, the artist.

"Wow, what a surprise! Lani! Do you need a ride with your two short-legged buddies here?"

"Oh, Laura! Yes, desperately! I didn't realize I had walked so far and now all three of us are exhausted. Thanks so much for stopping."

Now in a much better mood, Lani loaded the girls in and jumped into the car.

"How is everything going?" asked Laura. "I've been following the news about the exhibitions. It looks like you're having the time of your life."

"Yes, but it's putting a strain on the relationship between Max and I," Lani answered honestly. "I've been gone too much."

"Yeah, I can see that. Men think they can flirt as much as they want, but as soon as women are out having fun, the men go bananas with jealousy. That William looks quite sexy I've got to say. No wonder that Max is having a hard time."

Lani looked at her, bewildered. How did she know that was exactly what it was?

Lani and the dogs were pooped from the long outing, but Lani didn't have time for a break. There was too much to do. She immediately opened up her laptop to check on flights to Syracuse. Next, she called Pike to let him and Mrs. Kent know that she and Luana were going to come to upstate New York in three days. And after that she contacted Kate to ask if she could watch the dogs for a week.

In the midst of all this business, Lani's phone rang. It was Alana. Lani was glad she called, because she had almost forgotten.

"Hey, Alana, do you want to meet at the bar at the Hana Hotel in a bit, maybe for happy hour?"

"That's why I'm calling. I'd love to, I have cabin fever like you can only have it in Hana," Alana said and laughed.

Lani understood. Even though she had been traveling so much, she could imagine how lonely Hana became sometimes, but that's what friends were for.

She called the dogs inside, fed them, jumped in the shower and got ready to go out. The strange car was still in the driveway, which was a bit weird. Did someone else move in with Max already?

The bar in the Hana Hotel was busy. Unfortunately, not only pleasant people were there. As soon as Lani discovered Joseph McAllen at the bar yet again, she stepped out into the hotel's lobby and looked at the paintings while she waited for Alana. She remembered that some of Paul Kent's paintings were hanging in a corner, walked up and looked at them.

"Hey, sweetie," Alana walked up. "I want to teach you something," she said, trying to cheer Lani up. "This is called "Honi", the Hawaiian kiss. It's a Polynesian greeting in which two people greet each other by pressing noses and inhaling at the same time. This is very serious, as it represents the exchange of ha – the breath of life, and mana – spiritual power between two people."

She pressed her nose against Lani's and inhaled at the same time, while Lani tried to copy what she was doing. They both giggled.

"Thank you," said Lani. "I love learning Hawaiian traditions. So, guess who's at the bar? Joseph McAllen, the builder. Is there anywhere else we could go? I really don't feel like running into him tonight. He's probably in a really foul mood after getting his application turned down."

"We could go to the Henderson Ranch Restaurant. It's more down to earth than the bar here, but it's a nice place. They actually have a really good Mai Tai. Let's just walk there." She pulled Lani out of the hotel and they walked down the street past a beautiful church and a few stores. The bar area of the restaurant was quite empty as most people were still having dinner at this time, but it was nice and cozy and Lani discovered an impressive ukulele collection on one of the walls.

They had a great conversation and Lani told Alana all about Luana.

"Do you think you'll be able to get her to come to Hana?"

"I'm not sure how she feels about her dad. We haven't broached the subject yet, but she is very shy and lives very quietly. But then again, I couldn't believe that I got her to come to the exhibition opening with me... and even to New York..."

"I saw some of the exhibition photos in the news. Boy, that William is super hot. I hate to say it, but no wonder Max is jealous."

"But he should know that I love him! Sure, I might have flirted with William a little after a drink ... or two... but that doesn't that mean anything. And trust me, Max flirts with everyone himself!"

"Yeah, I agree. Max is quite fun loving himself."

"Here's another thing ... this strange car has been in our driveway the entire day. It's driving me crazy wondering who's visiting him!"

"Don't interpret too much into things, Lani. It could belong to one of the construction workers. Don't forget how busy your house has been."

"Hmmm. Good point," replied Lani. "Thanks for going out with me, Alana, I think I'd go nuts sitting at home by myself, thinking about Max right next door all evening."

"That's what friends are for."

As Lani drove home, she stopped briefly at Koki Beach and just sat in her car, staring at the bright moon that was becoming bigger again and was almost a first quarter.

The next morning, Lani knocked at Max's door with some pastries in a bag she handed to him. He thanked her, but didn't invite her in.

"I wanted to let you know that Luana and I are flying to Syracuse in two days to meet Paul Kent's mother. Kate will watch the dogs."

"I can watch them," he said.

"Yeah, but you can't walk them," Lani replied, pointing at his boot.

"Okay, anything else?"

"No. Except that I love you."

He just nodded and closed the door. She stood there for a moment and wanted to knock again, but she turned around and left...`

Chapter 36

Three days later, Luana and Lani got off of the plane and stepped into the brand new terminal of the Syracuse Hancock International Airport. They retrieved their luggage from baggage claim, walked over to the counters of the car rental agencies and picked up their rental car. It was about an hour and a half drive to the town of Clayton, where they were going to stay at the St. Lawrence Hotel and meet Bridgett Kent, Paul Kent's mother, at the Kent Museum & Gallery. It was a straight shot on Route 81, which basically led straight north and ended at the New York/Canadian border.

It was a beautiful Indian summer afternoon and the trees were ablaze in their variety of fall colors, the low sun shining through them. Lani was used to this spectacle of nature, but Luana, who had never been outside of the Hawaiian Islands, just stared speechlessly at the miles and miles of trees in their Indian summer glory. She had always thought that nothing could top Hawaii, which she loved dearly, but this was quite impressive.

"Wow, look at these colors, I think I love the autumn in New York now," she said, full of excitement.

"Yes, that might be one thing I'll miss while living in Maui," replied Lani. "I do love the four seasons. You need to come here in winter and spring too, it gets quite cold and miserable sometimes, but for a visit it's beautiful. You have never seen snow! And then when in spring everything starts growing and turning green again, it's really a wonder of nature."

In Watertown, they had to leave Route 81 and turn onto Route 12 to continue to Clayton. The road was very rural now as they drove through small towns and got stuck driving slow behind several narrow, black, old-fashioned looking horse carriages.

"Those are the Amish," explained Lani. "There are lots of them around here."

Luana got her phone out and wanted to take a picture. "Wait, you're not supposed to take photos of them," explained Lani. "It's against their beliefs."

Luana quickly put her phone back down. She was embarrassed. "Oh, I'm sorry. I didn't know that."

Lani explained: "They're not allowed to since personal photos can accentuate personal individuality and call attention to one's self. Also, they believe that photographs violate one of their commandments: "Thou shall not make unto thyself a graven image."

"Well, thanks for letting me know," replied Luana. "The last thing I want to be is a disrespectful tourist. Just as we don't appreciate disrespectful visitors in Hawaii."

The country road came to an end and they arrived in the little picturesque village of Clayton, with wooden houses on both sides and pretty yards, still full of fall flowers such as chrysanthemums, daisies, asters with white picket fences around them. Lani realized she had gone a bit too far and took a right down a small road with an arrow pointing toward "Downtown Clayton". They passed a boat museum on their left and then took another right leading down the main street, passing a few nice little shops, cafes and restaurants. There seemed to be lots of shops with River Rat signs: a River Rat cheese shop, a River Rat Café, a River Rat Gallery. I'll have to get to the bottom of why everything is called River Rat, thought Lani. There was even a small opera house, as well as plenty of other shops and boutiques. In back of the street on the left, they could make out the mighty St. Lawrence River, which was so wide, the shoreline on the other side looked very far away. Currently, a giant ocean freighter was passing by, upriver, probably on its way past Montreal to the Atlantic Ocean. Since they had their windows open, they could hear a loud humming coming from the ship. They continued straight ahead and arrived at the brand new St. Lawrence Hotel, a very nice, new hotel with a beautiful riverfront restaurant.

"Let's check in first and bring our luggage up to our room, then I think we can walk back to the museum and meet Mrs. Kent. It seems pretty close," said Lani.

Luana was nervous. She was about to meet the woman who almost became her mother-in-law thirty years ago. Due to fate, everything had turned out differently, but this still twisted her stomach in knots. Even though she shouldn't and had to think of Patrick, she still had feelings for Paul Kent.

They checked in quickly and went upstairs to drop off their luggage. They freshened up and walked back toward Main Street.

"Mrs. Kent said she's on the left, on Main Street as we walk away from the hotel," said Lani. And there it was, right before the little opera house: the *"Kent Gallery and Museum"*. Luana and Lani had only seen Paul Kent's tropical Hawaiian paintings so far, so they were quite amazed to see some of his older *"1000 Islands Collection"* in the window. He had obviously painted them before his "Maui" Period. There were paintings of boathouses, rows of colorful little cottages, beautiful sunsets behind tiny islands or people in old antique boats, beautiful paintings of flowers and other local plants and animals.

They stepped inside the museum and a little bell rang. Bridgett Kent, Paul Kent's mother, had been waiting for them. She was an elderly, slender lady, in her mid seventies, but she was in great health and looked and acted much younger. She was dressed casually, yet stylish in a dark green sweater, a pair of plaid slacks and dark green loafers. Her face lit up when she saw Lani and Luana, whom she recognized immediately. Polynesian women didn't come to Clayton very often. She walked toward them and shook their hands in a very cordial manner.

"Hi, ladies. Welcome to Clayton. I'm so excited that we finally made a contact and you could make it."

"Thank you very much, it's so nice to meet you too," they both said simultaneously.

Bridgett Kent was a bit nearsighted and took a closer look. "I'm sorry, my eyesight is not so good anymore. So, you must be Luana and you must be Lani. You look like you're sisters rather than mother and daughter…"

They both smiled and Lani asked: "May we take a look around?"

"Well, of course! Although I'd propose that we leave as early as possible. I'd like you to meet someone."

This was unexpected, but Lani took it in stride and said "Sure, let's do that first. Lead the way!"

Luana nodded.

****

Chapter 37

They walked back out into the street where Bridgett had her car, a little SUV, parked right in front of the gallery. "It's not far," she explained. "You ladies can drive with me."

They all got into the car and Bridgett drove out of the village, back onto a country road, and soon they arrived at a giant toll bridge, the 1000 Islands Bridge, connecting the U.S. mainland with Wellesley Island, over part of the St. Lawrence River.

"Make sure you take in the beautiful view," said Bridgett after she had paid the toll and started making her way across the tall bridge. Lani and Luana looked out of the window. The view was incredible. The bridge had to be high enough for the big oceangoing ships to fit underneath. Little islands were speckled all over the wide majestic river and little boats were zipping back and forth. There was also another big, red freighter approaching. The sun was shining onto the red metal and made it look spectacular. The view could have been one of Paul Kent's paintings. They reached the end of the bridge and exited onto a country road, once again leading through the beautiful Indian summer foliage. After about two miles, they took a right toward a little harbor and arrived in front of a beautiful, two story Victorian house. The sign read:

"Wellesley Island Inn".

Bridgett parked the car and they walked up to the steps made of the limestone that is common to upstate New York. She opened the door and made waving motions for the ladies to follow her.

The walked a few steps into the beautiful old house, furnished with antique furniture, until they came into a big sunroom with at least ten four tops, overlooking a big open field of grass, which looked like a golf course. It looked like the dining room of a bed & breakfast. The entire back wall was covered with bookshelves and there were some overstuffed armchairs and couches with little side tables in the corners.

A slender, tanned, tall man, in his mid to late fifties appeared. He had short, silver hair and was wearing a button up linen shirt with rolled up sleeves and baggy linen pants with bare feet. He was concentrating on setting the tables for what looked like the next meal, probably breakfast. He looked like he was totally lost in his thoughts. Bridgett called "Paul," and he finally looked up, startled. His dreamy blue eyes discovered Luana and Lani, quietly standing in his dining room, their eyes staring at him. The ladies' eyes were filling up with tears as they just stood there looking at him, in disbelief that he was still alive and wondering if it was really him.

His face lit up, possibly for the first time in thirty years. He walked toward them and said "Luana" and took her in his arms. They both stood there, holding each other for what seemed like an eternity. They both had tears rolling down their cheeks. Then he finally let go of Luana and looked at Lani. "And this is...? Our daughter?"

"Yes. This is Lani," replied Luana.

Now he took Lani in his arms and all of them, including Bridgett, started crying tears of joy.

Lani wanted to call Max so badly and tell him the news. She missed him terribly.

****

Chapter 38
Flashback (25 years ago – 1993) - Maui

After the year Luana disappeared, Paul Kent still came to Maui on a regular basis, but he was different than he used to be. He was depressed. He didn't come to paint anymore. Instead he came to spend his summers doing nothing but search for Luana.

He drove around the island, looking for her in all of the locations that they had visited together and questioning people they had met or who might have known her. From time to time, he'd stop and find an old sign pinned to a tree or a lamppost with a picture of Luana that her parents had hung up all over the island. He would just stand there, looking at the signs, forlorn and sometimes his eyes would fill up with tears.

He never contacted Luana's parents after that first unfriendly encounter with Kumu.

He even cancelled a painting workshop that was supposed to take place at the Hana Hotel the day before it started, because he heard that Luana was last seen on Lanai and he had to drop everything and go there. He never found her. He saw some of his paintings while in Lanai that a gallery there was displaying for sale… even one of the big paintings of Luana that he hated to part with, but he needed all the money he could get for his travels to Maui.

"Please call me anytime if you want to sell more artwork or if you just want to talk," said Lisa Holmquist, who had always had a crush on him, as he departed her gallery in Lanai City. "People love your paintings. They are going like hot cakes. I just sold the big painting to the Hotel Lanai, right down the road. I'll send you a check as soon as their payment hits my account."

"Thanks, I really appreciate it. And please let me know if you ever hear anything about Luana."

Lisa handed him a business card. "Here's my business card and I have your phone number. Call me anytime and I hope you get into the swing of things and feel like painting again soon."

Suddenly something either popped into Lisa's mind or she said it maliciously so that Paul would finally get over Luana. "I just remembered something. I've heard that the last time someone saw Luana was at the cliffs of Puu Pehe, also known as Sweatheart Rock. She was hitchhiking. A younger couple took her there and went for a hike. When they came back, the girl was pretty sure that she had jumped. Of course it was never proven, but maybe it will give you some peace of mind to go there. It's a magical place."

Paul, totally beside himself about this news, didn't even say goodbye to Lisa, got into his rental Jeep and drove up to Puu Pehe, which had a similar tragic story like his and Luana's. A warrior who was in love with a beautiful princess had hidden her from the other men in one of the sea caves and she drowned when the flood came in. Upset about what he had done, the warrior jumped off of the cliffs to his death.

It was a breezy day. Paul just stood there in the wind, looking at the big rock pointing out of the ocean a few hundred yards away from the cliffs he was standing on. The red rocks contrasted sharply against the deep blue ocean.

He imagined that Luana had been here years ago and shuddered as he looked down at the ocean. If she had jumped, she was certainly dead. This did not help his state of mind. He turned away quickly and went back to the harbor to catch the ferry to Lahaina.

He just wanted to leave Maui and never return. He changed his flight, cancelled his cottage and started packing. The next day while he was returning the easel that Aaron always loaned him, Coconut Glen happened to be there. Paul got out of the truck and shook Glen's hand.

"It's really nice to meet you, Paul, I've heard great things about you from Aaron. Thanks for teaching him. I can tell how his painting techniques have improved since he's been taking lessons from you. By the way, I was a good friend of Luana's in High School…"

Paul perked his ears. "Have you heard anything about her whereabouts?"

Glen replied, "No, but I don't think Luana would harm herself if she was pregnant. She was much too caring."

Aaron, standing behind Paul, made hand motions for Glen to stop talking.

Paul was in shock. "Wait … what do you mean? She was pregnant too?!"

Now it was Glen's turn to be shocked. Paul didn't know that Luana had been pregnant, the reason she had run away in the first place?

"Geesh, I'm really sorry. I wouldn't have said that if I had known that you didn't know she was pregnant… that was supposedly the reason she and her father had the big fight and she disappeared. That's the whole reason the entire town of Hana is in a feud…"

Paul was beside himself. Now Luana had not only possibly jumped off of the cliffs Puu Pehe, but she had also been pregnant. How could he have not known? That made things even worse. Now he had lost the love of his life AND his child. Also, as an outsider and visitor he hadn't heard about the feud that was going on in Hana due to the fight between Kumu Kalekilio and his sister Malani Kahele and people taking sides.

He needed to leave. Maui was cursed for him. The next day, Paul was done emptying his cottage, packing his suitcase and carry-on. His flight to Syracuse didn't depart Kahului until later in the evening and the only stop he had to make was at the gallery in the Hana Hotel to drop off some of his paintings that the gallery was going to put on display for him.

He met with the assistant gallery manager, Alana, as she stepped outside into the courtyard in front of the gallery with him. Their handshake turned into a hug because Alana felt sorry for broken-hearted Paul. She was Luana's best friend and she was as broken-hearted as Paul about Luana's disappearance.

"Don't forget to call me about shipping the paintings to you in New York when the exhibition in the hotel is over," she said. "We want to make sure you're home to receive them and that the shipping agency doesn't have to take them back to the warehouse like last time…"

"Okay, thanks again, Alana. And please let me know if you hear anything about Luana," Paul replied.

"Of course, you'd be the first to know," she said, emphatically. "Don't make too many stops on your way to Kahului, it's going to get dark soon…"

"Thanks, I'll be fine, I've driven the road so many times," he replied.

Paul got into his rental Jeep and Alana watched him take a left where the road parted a few hundred yards past Hana Hotel, the right side going down to Hana Bay and along the water and the left side leading straight to the Hana Highway, leading to Paia and Kahului.

Paul felt terrible and had a knot in his throat. He had no eyes for the beautiful scenery surrounding him. He just drove, dazed, not concentrating on the road. He had no sense for the beauty of the rainforest and the views that were presenting themselves to the travelers on this winding road, famous for its many twists and turns and also famous for the danger it presented, especially in rainy or slippery weather conditions. Even though Paul had plenty of time to catch his flight, he didn't bother stopping at any of the beautiful outlooks or stands that offered ice cream, banana bread and other typical Hawaiian delicacies.

He was going to stop for dinner in Paia and that was all he needed. As he was almost halfway to Paia, it started raining, thundering and getting dark. Instead of slowing down, Paul started cursing and kept going a bit too fast on the slippery road. As he sped around a curve, his car skidded and crashed into the side of a narrow one-lane bridge. He hit his head and passed out. His Jeep was now dangling half off of the road, with Paul unconscious and no other car in sight. He regained consciousness, just as the Jeep was starting to slide further down. He lifted his hand up to his head and felt a big bump, but he seemed fine. He opened the door, grabbed his little carry-on case in the passenger seat and jumped out of the Jeep, just as it was sliding down into an abyss of at least 50 feet below him. He just stood there for a while, wondering how he could be unharmed, almost wishing he had stayed in the car. At least he'd be reunited with Luana, if she, indeed, was dead. In that instance, an old banged up truck with two big Hawaiian guys stopped in front of him. They were listening to loud Hawaiian rock music and smoking a joint.

"Hey, man, waddya doin' out here, all by yourself? Need a ride?" the driver asked.

"Sure, thanks," replied Paul.

"Where ya goin', man?"

"To the airport."

"We goin' ta Kahului, we can take ya thea, man," said the passenger, who Paul could barely understand.

"Joey had a motorcycle accident a couple years ago," explained the driver. "Half of his tongue was chopped off."

Paul climbed into the truck, shuddered and nodded. "Wow, sorry to hear that."

"Want a hit?" asked Joey and stretched his arm out to hand him the joint.

"No, thanks, I'm good," replied Paul in the back.

They continued driving in the truck, quietly listening to the loud music, smoking their joint. Paul's Jeep was gone, with it some paintings that he had wrapped up in packaging paper and his suitcase. Paul had quite the headache from the bump, but never mentioned anything and nobody even asked about the giant lump on his forehead.

He had dinner at the airport in Kahului, changed planes in Los Angeles and made it to Syracuse, broken hearted and still wondering how he could be alive.

He never painted again, quit his teaching job at the university and bought a beautiful little bed & breakfast on Wellesley Island in the Thousand Islands with some checks that he received from galleries in Maui and Lanai along with some other savings. He ran the bed & breakfast, never owned a computer or a mobile phone and as soon as he started getting calls from galleries demanding more paintings, he told them he was someone else with the same name and had his former agent scrub his name and information off of the internet.

He was halfway satisfied with his simple life and didn't want to remember the past. There was something wrong, but he ignored it. His heart was broken and there was a void, but he didn't bother changing the situation. Several ladies in the Clayton and Thousand Islands area had crushes on the romantic, handsome bed & breakfast owner and pursued him, but he had no interest and ignored all of them. He never got over Luana.

****

Chapter 39
Back to present time – Thousand Islands

Bridgett had left, since she had an appointment in the gallery. Paul, Luana and Lani walked along a beautiful little harbor across the street from the bed and breakfast. They sat down at an empty table on a terrace belonging to a nice waterfront restaurant that was closed since the season was over.

"How come when I looked you up online, all entries said that you died in 2005?" asked Lani.

"Well, I kind of died and couldn't paint anymore. I was basically a different person. I told my publicist to put out official notices that I was dead, because I didn't want people hounding me and trying to force me to paint again. You can do anything for money. I started a new life and didn't want to keep thinking about the past."

Luana looked at Paul. She didn't quite know what she was going to do. She knew in her heart she still had strong feelings for Paul, her one true love. But what would she do about Patrick, her current husband who she loved, had been with her for almost 30 years, who had run the nursery businesses with her and who had even survived his battle with cancer five years ago? She loved Patrick too and couldn't just leave him.

Paul got up and walked down to the water's edge. He picked up a few flat little stones and threw them so they skipped over the water. Luana watched him adoringly. There was still something boyish about him that she had fallen in love with thirty years ago. She said, more to herself than to Lani: "He looks just like he did thirty years ago."

Luana and Lani weren't sure what was going on in his head, but he suddenly walked back up to the table and said: "I'll be right back. Are you ready to go? I can take you ladies back to Clayton."

He quickly walked over to the bed & breakfast as if on a mission. Luana and Lani just looked at each other quizzically and didn't know what he was up to, but he had already stormed through the house, into a storage room that hadn't been used in years, looking for canvasses and painting supplies behind some old boxes. Since he knew that most of his paints would be dried up, he wanted to drive to Clayton and buy some new supplies before the stores closed. After not touching a paintbrush for thirty years, he suddenly had this incredible urge to paint again and had to start immediately.

After a couple of days, Lani and Luana checked out of the St. Lawrence Hotel and moved into two guest rooms in Paul's bed & breakfast. The relationship between Luana and Paul was a bit awkward but they just seemed like old friends and Paul, who wasn't used to spending so much time with other people, would suddenly disappear from time to time. They quickly found out that they could find him behind his easel in the sunroom where he had cleared out a corner that now served as his studio.

They drove all over picturesque Wellesley Island and the 1000 Islands area with him in his old SUV and watched him paint. He was obsessed as if he had to make up for the thirty years he hadn't been able to express his creativity. In between, the ladies left him to do some sightseeing on their own. He painted down by the dock of Thousand Island Park, on the shore of St. Lawrence River, a beautiful little village made up of old little cottages that was founded in 1875 and used to be a Methodist summer camp. Luana and Lani walked up and down the roads with beautiful 100 year-old gingerbread-style Victorian cottages on both sides and took what felt like hundreds of photos. They went hiking in the hills around TI Park and rented kayaks. On a beautiful sunny day, they dipped their feet into the St. Lawrence River, but quickly pulled them out. In mid-October, the river was already too cold for swimming. The village currently seemed almost deserted, since summer was over and all the summer residents had left.

The next day, Paul took them out in one of his boats. He wanted them to see Boldt Castle from the water, take some photos and show them around.

"Oh, I remember Aaron telling me about your antique boats," Lani remembered, as they walked along the dock across from the bed & breakfast, looking for Paul's boat slip.

"I'll have to show them to you if you're interested," replied Paul, as he walked up to his little ski boat. He pointed at the small fast boat. "This is the only one I use in the fall. My other antique wooden boats are already in storage. I don't use them very much except for special occasions. I guess you'll have to come back next summer so I can take you for a ride in one of them. They're my pride and joy, especially my Chris Craft…" he looked at them and smiled.

"I'd love to see them," said Lani. "I also saw that there's a boat museum in Clayton, I'm sure it's interesting…"

"It's definitely worth visiting, but the Boldt Castle Yacht House also has quite an interesting variety of boats to see. We'll stop there after our visit to the castle."

They could already see Boldt Castle in the distance with its many towers and the impressive boathouse across the river from it, just a few hundred yards away from them, on the shoreline of small Tennis Island, just off the shores of Wellesley Island. Paul was the perfect tour guide. After all, it had been one of his summer jobs thirty years ago. "German millionaire hotel magnate George Boldt started building the castle in 1900 for his beloved wife Louise on a heart-shaped island called Heart Island. It was to be their summer home, but she died suddenly, before it was completed and, heartbroken, he stopped all construction. It was never completed. It was basically ignored and deteriorated for seventy years, until the Thousand Island Bridge Authority bought it in 1977 and started slowly completing it."

They passed some other little islands. Some of them were just big enough for a tiny house or just a tree. "Okay, the biggest question that people ask about the 1000 Islands is: How many islands are there actually? Does either of you want to guess?" he asked and grinned.

Luana shook her head and Lani said: "Well, it must be around a
thousand?"

"It's around one thousand eight hundred, and any piece of land in
the river that has a tree on it counts as an island."

Paul slowly drove the boat up to Heart Island.

"The docks you see here are for bigger tour boats. Many from
Canada, since it's just a stone's throw that way," as he pointed to the
other shore of the river. "We have to go around the island to the smaller
docks." They looked up at a beautiful stone building right on a shoal on
a corner of the island that looked like a little castle in itself, built in the
fashion of a medieval tower with a lovely pointed steeple. "This is the
Power House," Paul explained. "They were even planning on creating
their own power with two generators." They came to the next corner of
the island with another beautiful tower. "This is the Alster Tower,
similar to old defense towers on the Alster River in Germany. This
entire tower was only for entertainment, a dance hall and in the cellar a
bowling alley." Luana and Lani looked up at the beautiful old towers,
oohing and aahing. They came up to some smaller boat docks for
private boats and Paul jumped on land while Lani threw the rope to
him, then he tied the boat to two cleats. He helped Luana and Lani out
like the gentleman he was and they all walked up to the main entrance
of the castle. Paul's photography obsession was back as well and he
took pictures of everything, of course with Luana and Lani in most of
them. They toured the castle, walked through secret passageways,
threw some coins into the beautiful blue-tiled pool in the basement,
looked through beautiful gothic windows, were amazed to see the
renovated and completed rooms, compare them to parts of the castle
that hadn't been touched yet and had been sitting there for about 100
years.

After touring Boldt Castle, they drove over to the Yacht House on
the other side of the river, on Tennis Island. It was an imposing
structure with a steep roof, amazing towers and gables, 64 feet high,
with boat slips 128 feet long. Towering white bay doors on the

decorative façade could be opened to the outside and provided access to the river. Inside were the Boldt's family yachts and gigantic houseboat as well as various other antique boats, made out of fine timber. The Yacht House even had quarters for crew and staff.

They continued driving down the river past beautiful old mansions with even prettier boat houses, little Victorian cottages and some uninhabited islands with just one or a few trees on them. Sometimes their boat traveled into the wake of another faster boat passing them and they had to hold on tight as Paul maneuvered around the waves and the bumps making them go up and down. Lani rolled her eyes and she had a smile on her face. Paul's driving habits reminded her of Max. She missed him, yet her heart hurt as she thought about him. Would Max ever be able to forgive her? She got distracted quickly, since there was so much to see. They passed another beautiful mansion called Casa Blanca, which was built in 1892 by a Cuban sugar plantation owner.

"Wow," said Lani. "There must be some very wealthy people up here."

"Yes," answered Paul. "This area is known as Millionaire's Row. There were some very wealthy people who built most of these houses and came up here for the summers at the turn of the 20th century. A bit further down the river is another castle called Singer Castle, which was built by Frederick Bourne, one of the presidents of the Singer sewing machine company. That one has incredible hidden passageways and is known to be haunted. You'll definitely have to go and tour it one day."

They had to turn around soon, since the sun was going down and it was getting chilly. Paul surprised them with another incredible talent he had. He made dinner for them and turned out to be an amazing chef.

As they were sitting at the dinner table, Lani said: "In a couple of days it's time to head back to Hawaii… Why don't you come with us?"

"My season here doesn't end until the end of October. Even though I don't have many guests right now, some still might come to see the Indian summer."

"You'll have to come and visit afterwards then." insisted Lani.

He hesitated, but then he told them frankly: "I don't know if I can ever go back there. The last few times when I was looking for you were quite awful and I was quite depressed. I do have to think about my accident from time to time and am not sure if I purposely drove into the bridge pillar or not. I was really a bit out of it and didn't see any sense in living anymore."

Lani took him in her arms. "Now you have us. And I'd like to tell you guys a secret."

Luana and Paul looked at her, anxiously awaiting her next words.

"I haven't been feeling well and did a pregnancy test this morning. It was positive... So, you'll be a grandfather, Paul... and you'll be a grandmother, Luana."

Luana's face started beaming and she looked at Paul who was still processing the news and staring at Lani, but then also started smiling. "We'll be tutu and papa..." she said and rushed over to join Paul and Lani in the group hug.

As Luana and Paul were doing the dishes after dinner and happily chatting as if they had never been apart, Lani felt a little like the third wheel. She stepped out onto the back terrace and looked up at the full moon. She wondered what time it was in Hana, what Max was doing and how she would tell him about the baby. The cold October air made her shiver as she walked back inside. She missed Hana.

****

Chapter 40

Two days later, Lani and Luana left the magical 1000 Islands, returning to Oahu and Maui. This time it was Luana who was in tears.

"We'll stay in touch," said Paul Kent in a consoling manner as she hugged him goodbye and then got in the rental car to drive back to Syracuse airport. She still didn't know what she would tell Patrick, but she knew deep down in her heart that she belonged to Paul...

Lani and Luana had to say goodbye to each other in Oahu. Luana was home and Lani still had one more leg to Hana via Kahului. They hugged each other, but knew they would see each other again soon. As the little ten-passenger plane was descending down into Hana airport, Lani was fighting tears of joy, because she truly felt like she was coming home. She hadn't asked anyone to pick her up, so she called a taxi to take her home.

The strange car was still in the driveway. Lilly and Lucy went crazy when Lani walked into the house. She kneeled down and they knocked her over, jumping and trying to lick her face, full of excitement. Lani let them out into the little fenced in area, but she knew that Kate had just walked them, so they were fine.

She didn't care if Max wouldn't let her in again and she just walked over to the guesthouse and knocked. She had to see him. There was no answer. Lani walked to the front and to her surprise she saw that his surfboard was gone, even though he probably couldn't surf with his ankle. She walked back inside, changed into her bathing suit, grabbed her surfboard and almost ran down to Hamoa Beach. She didn't care about her pride. She wanted to see Max.

Max was out in the ocean, just hanging out on his surfboard. He seemed to be resting or just daydreaming. Lani pushed her board into the calm ocean, layed down flat on it and slowly paddled out toward him. He looked up, surprised, but his gloomy face lit up as he saw her.

"Max Palakiko," she said, "I don't care if you're still mad at me for just flirting with some other guy who doesn't mean anything to me, but I want to let you know that I can't stand being without you and that I love you. Will you please marry me?"

He just looked at her, paddled closer and sat up on his surfboard.

"Yes, I will, Lani Winters. Yes, I will," he said with a broad smile as he pulled her closer and started passionately kissing her over and over again. Their surfboards banged against each other in the surf, but they didn't care.

As the sun was setting, they slowly paddled back to shore, because Max couldn't surf with his ankle. The waves pushed the surfboards gently into the sand. They were the only people on the beach.

"And by the way, you're going to be a dad…" said Lani quietly.

Max wasn't sure if he had heard correctly, but he was beside himself with happiness if she had just said what he thought. "What did you just say?" He had to hear it again.

"You're going to be a dad, Max."

He took her in his arms and kissed her again. He said: "Aloha wau iā 'oe. That means: I love you."

A little while later, Max and Lani walked up to Koki Beach House. It was almost dark. One of the handymen that had been helping with the house on an irregular basis was loading some wood onto a trailer that was standing behind an old truck in the driveway. It was Jacob Mahoe, an older guy who had no regular income and lived out in a small ramshackle house past Charles Lindbergh's grave with his single daughter and six grandchildren.

Max walked up to him. "Jacob, what are you doing here?"

Jacob covered his face with his hands and sat down on the edge of the trailer.

"I'm sorry, man, I'm totally broke. My roof has been leaking, my house really needs some repairs, but I don't know where to find the money… with all those grandkids…" He started crying.

Max put his hand on Jacob's shoulder. "It's okay, man. Take the wood. And tomorrow I'll come out with Billy and we'll check what needs to be done. I'm sure everyone can pitch in a little. Maybe you can work here and in return we can give you some supplies."

Jacob started smiling. "Thanks, man, you're awesome. That's true aloha spirit."

"You should have told us in the first place, Jacob. Don't do it again. Lani needs her stuff too, but I'm sure she'll share some of it with you. We were actually accusing someone else, which is not very nice."

He looked at Lani who nodded.

After Jacob had left, Max pointed at the strange little station wagon that was still standing there and said: "By the way, that's yours." Again, she fell into his arms and kissed him.

****

Chapter 41
Two months later – Hamoa Beach

It was the morning of Max and Lani's wedding. Everyone had flown in and was getting ready or still arriving, either at Koki Beach House that looked bright and shiny with its new roof and a fresh coat of paint, the Hana Hotel or some other private accomodations. The whole town was abuzz with activity.

Paul Kent was sitting alone on Hamoa Beach in the same spot he used to paint and where he had first met Luana, just looking out at the ocean, watching the waves crashing ashore. He had never realized how much he missed this beautiful peaceful piece of paradise inbetween the lush green hills. It still took away his breath after all these years.

Suddenly, Patrick came walking down the stairs. He walked quite slowly and Paul noticed that he looked quite feeble for only being in his late fifties or early sixties. It seemed as if he was looking for someone. Paul shouted: "Hey, Patrick!" Patrick looked up and waved. Paul was the one he had been looking for. Slowly, he walked down the beach and stopped in front of Paul.
"May I?" he asked and as Paul made an inviting motion, he sat down on the boulder next to him. The two men just sat there for a while, watching the rough waves. Neither one was a man of many words. Finally, Patrick cleared his throat.
"I'm glad Luana found you. I can see the way she looks at you. She doesn't know it yet, but my cancer has returned. I only have a few more months to live." He got up and, while his voice broke, he said: "Please take care of her."
Paul jumped up and put his arm on Patrick's while he shook his hand with the other. He didn't have to say a single word.

The waves were crashing onto the shore and the sun was standing low but illuminating the beautiful crescent shaped beach in a beautiful light. Half of the town had gathered in the sand, including William, Aaron, Mats, Lani's parents Lynn and Mark, her two girlfriends Theresa and Sarah, Anna and Bill, Pike Kahananui from Kahului, Lani's grandparents Kumu and Leila Kalekilio, the artist Laura Cattleya, Max's handyman friends Keanu and Billy, Billy's wife and Luana's old friend Alana, Glen, Phillip Bancroft who had provided tons and tons of fresh flowers, Luana and her husband Patrick, Max's friends from Honolulu, Allison from Kihei, Ana Kamealoha and her granddaughter Pekelo, Lenny and Tammy.

Max, who looked extremely handsome in a white linen suit and a lei around his neck, and a Hawaiian priest were standing in front of the group closest to the ocean. They were all waiting for Lani. The entire group suddenly became quiet and looked up at the stairs.

Lani was now walking down the steps leading down to Hamoa Beach, wearing a beautiful simple white long dress, which couldn't hide her baby belly anymore. She was wearing a white haku with fresh flowers on her head and her father Mark Winters was beaming with pride as he led her down toward Max and the priest.
Lani's heart was full as she first looked at her father Mark, then at the group that had gathered in front of the priest close to the water. She spotted Luana, Patrick, her adoptive mother Lynn and Paul Kent. She now suddenly had five parents.

Mark handed Lani's hand to Max and stepped back. The priest performed the ceremony and the two Bassets came waddling up with one ring each strapped to their backs on a fancy little pillow, quite risky, but they seemed to know that it was important and did well. Paul Kent, back to being an artist, was in the background, taking pictures of the wedding.

As soon as they had exchanged leis and Max had kissed the bride, everyone cheered and congratulated the bride and groom. Then the entire group walked the few hundred yards over to Koki Beach House where Pekelo, who was catering the event with her Thai specialties, had set up enough food to feed an army. They ate and drank and danced on the back porch as the sparkling full moon slowly rose over Koki Beach House...

Hawaiian Wedding Blessing:

Max and Lani, may your love for one another be blessed
with endless moon phases, countless sunrises and as many
happy days as sparkling stars in the sky.
May Koki Beach House remain the happy home for you
and your family and the Aloha spirit always live inside.
May the roaring waves of the Pacific that you surf on
carry peace into your hearts.
May your lush garden and your love for plants and growing
things bring you endless flowers for leis of happiness.
May the kindness that already lives in your hearts give
you strength and forgiveness as you walk this tropical
path together and forever united.

****

CPSIA information can be obtained
at www.ICGtesting.com
Printed in the USA
LVHW081055031219
639279LV00008B/528/P